CASH RULES EVERYTHING

ROXANNE TAYLOR

The story, including all names, characters, and incidents portrayed in this production, is fictitious. No identification with actual persons (living or deceased), places, buildings, or products is intended or should be inferred.

Edited by: Sheryll Donerson

Cover Design: Talena Tillman

ISBN (EBook): 979-8-9938238-0-5

ISBN (Paperback): 979-8-9938238-1-2

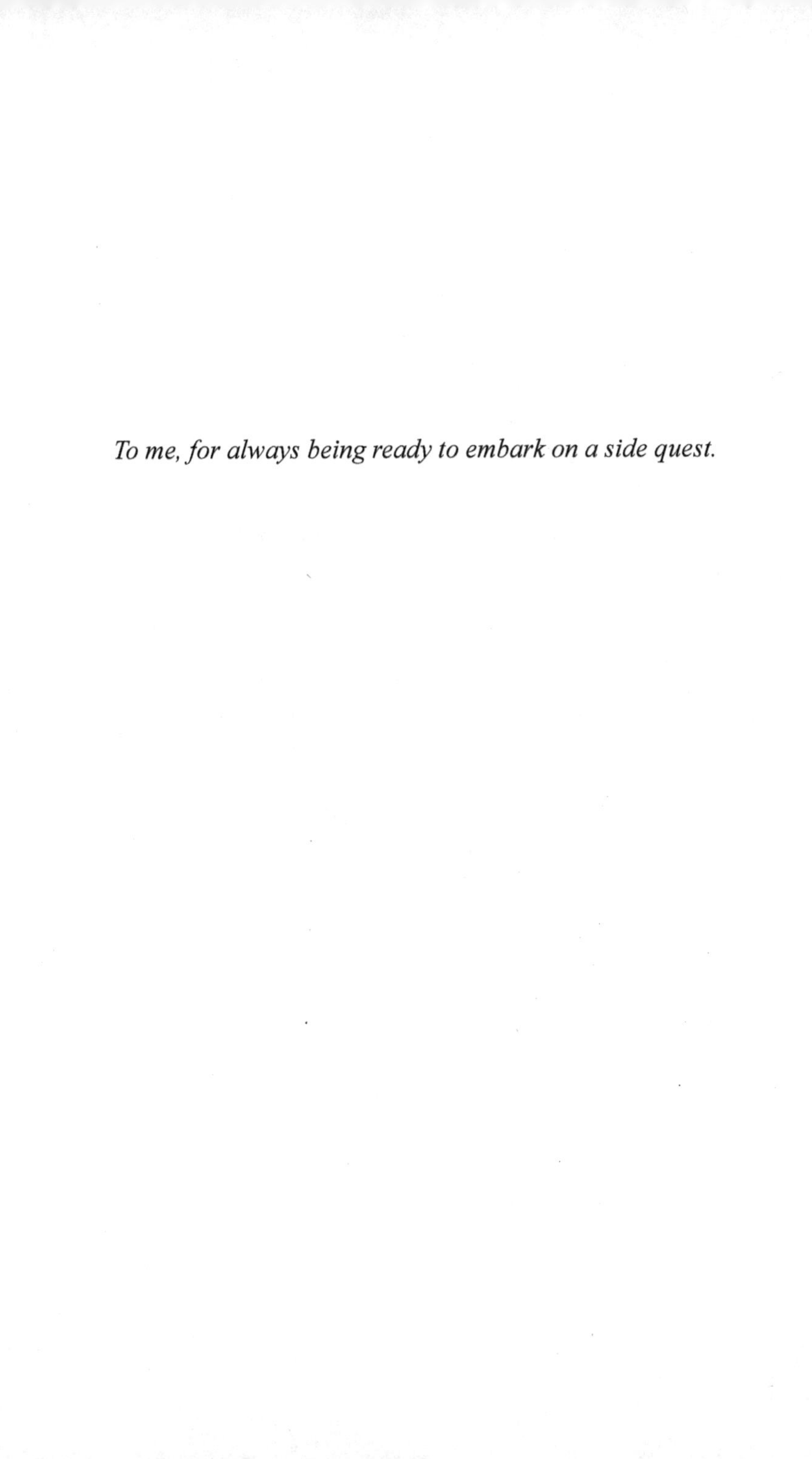

To me, for always being ready to embark on a side quest.

AUTHOR'S NOTE

Hi, hello, welcome!

Quick content warning:

- On-page description of violence (these niggas be shootin')
- Assault (not sexual)
- Profanity (these niggas be cussin')
- Sexually explicit (these niggas be hunchin')

Welcome to the world of the Banks Crew. Hope you enjoy the ride!

Scan to listen to the Cash Rules Everything Spotify Playlist

Cash + Jas's Playlist

CHAPTER 1
CASH "MONEY" BANKS

"CAN WE JUST KILL THIS NIGGA AND GO? I'M TRYNA GET MY dick wet tonight." My younger brother Jelani grumbled, looking up from his phone.

It was muggy as fuck in the old farmhouse. The industrial ceiling fans weren't doing shit but circulating hot, stale air. It felt like the Georgia heat was pressing in from every direction. It was the last place either of us wanted to be tonight, but when we got the heads up that Rahmel was strolling through the hood like there wasn't a price on his head, I knew we had to move fast before he disappeared again.

Rahmel's bloodshot eyes darted frantically between us as he thrashed against the metal chair bolted to the floor. His screams were muffled by the duct tape over his mouth, and his wrists were raw from the cuffs digging into them as he struggled.

"Nah," I said, pushing off the support beam I was leaning on. "I wanna hear what this nigga gotta say first."

When we pulled up on the Eastside, this goofy motherfucker was chilling on his aunt's porch, drinking with his cousins like he hadn't stolen twenty grand from me. Jelani and I ran up, snatched that nigga, and shoved his ass in the trunk—all while his cousins watched. They knew better than to intervene, and nobody on the block was about to call the police.

For the past hour, we'd taken turns beating the shit out of him. By the time he finally passed out, my knuckles were raw and stinging. Jelani had woken him up with smelling salts a few minutes ago so we could wrap this shit up.

"Money, my nigga, please don't make this shit more dramatic than it needs to be," Jelani sighed as he walked over to our former lieutenant. Rahmel winced as Jelani roughly ripped off the tape covering his mouth. "Tell him what he wants to know so we can send your ass to hell. I'm not trying to be here all fucking night," Jelani said, slapping him hard across the face.

"I didn't do shit!" Rahmel screamed. Spit flew from his busted lips as he twisted in the chair. "I swear—"

I started whistling, cutting him off. Shaking my head, I rolled up the sleeves of my white button-down and reached into my pocket for the brass knuckles. The cold metal bit into my torn skin as I slipped them on.

"Rahmel, Rahmel, Rahmel," I muttered, flexing my fingers. Excitement surged through me as I stepped closer. I bent down to lift his chin with two fingers and forced him to look at me. "You think I'm stupid?" I asked calmly.

"Money, I swear, bruh! It wasn't me!" Rahmel pleaded desperately. "I wasn't shorting y'all! On everything—"

"Shut the fuck up!" Jelani cut in. "You think we don't know about the shit you've been pushing down here?"

Rahmel stiffened, his eyes widening as he looked at Jelani, then back at me. Panic rolled off him in waves. He tried to shake his head, but I tightened my grip on his jaw to hold him still.

"Them ODs not on me," he croaked.

I raised an eyebrow, standing slowly. "Who said anything about ODs?" I asked. "Did you say anything about ODs, Lani?"

Jelani shook his head, feigning confusion. "Ain't say shit about that."

Rahmel's mouth opened, but no sound came out.

"The fuck?" Jelani exclaimed, screwing up his face. "Did this nigga just piss himself?"

I looked down and saw a dark, wet spot spreading on Rahmel's gray sweatpants.

"Ol' pissy-ass nigga," Jelani spat, looking at him with disgust.

I tilted my head, studying Rahmel. "I'm confused, Rahmel," I said calmly. "Why would an innocent man run?" He opened his mouth to respond, but I cocked back and drove my fist into his face. The sickening crunch of his nose breaking made Jelani flinch.

Rahmel let out a garbled scream, coughing as blood poured from his mouth and onto the floor. He spat out a mouthful of it, his chest heaving as he strained to breathe. This time, when he looked up at me, his eyes weren't filled with fear.

It was hate.

Ah, there it was.

"Fuck y'all, niggas!" he yelled. His voice was hoarse, but there was no mistaking the defiance in it. "Y'all run everything—I want my own shit!"

I couldn't help the laugh that spilled out from me. "So, wait. You decided to rob *my* shit? That was your big play?" I shook my head. "This how you do the niggas who held you down and put money on your books when you were locked up? The ones who made sure your girl had more than enough to take care of your son?"

"Unbelievable," Jelani muttered.

"We don't pay you enough, Rahmel?" I asked.

Silence.

I turned to Jelani. "This nigga ever mention being in a bind?"

Jelani crossed his arms and glared at Rahmel. "Never. And I know his son goes to that nice ass private school in Alpharetta. That shit ain't cheap," he sneered.

I nodded, stepping closer. "So, you can afford to put your youngin' in the best school, and I know you just bought your girl a new whip..." My voice trailed off as I punched him in the ribs.

Rahmel let out another guttural cry; the chair rattled as he jerked against the restraints.

"By all accounts, you living real good off *my* money, my nigga," I said, pulling off the brass knuckles and tossing them onto the ground.

"The issue I'm having is not that you got greedy. That's to be expected." I reached for the 9mm Beretta in my waistband. "My problem is that you think my brother and I are soft. And I really can't have that." I tapped his forehead with the barrel of the gun.

"Two questions before you die," I continued, lifting his chin with the edge of the gun. His left eye was swollen shut, and his breathing had become ragged. "One, where's my money? And two, who's been helping you?"

"I ain't—" Rahmel wheezed, blood dribbling from his mouth. "I ain't no fucking snitch," he choked out, coughing wetly.

"Tsk," I sighed. "That's unfortunate. Guess I'll have to

pull Toya out of that nice house you built. She and your son are gonna end up back in the hood with your cousins by the time I'm through with them."

Rahmel's head snapped up at the mention of his family. "They ain't got shit to do with this!" he gritted.

"Oh, but they do." I crouched again to meet his gaze. "'Cause one way or another, I'm getting my lick back. So you can tell me where my shit is and who's helping you, or I'll make your baby mother regret ever fucking with your bitch ass. And you know I'm a man of my word, Rahmel."

"Say, man, tell this long-winded motherfucker what he wants to know so we can kill you. I got shit to do." Jelani interjected, grabbing Rahmel's broken nose.

"FUCK!" Rahmel roared. "Fine, I'll tell you." He groaned and proceeded to rattle off the number of a storage locker at the airport and where to find the key. As for who helped him?

"Kyree."

I glanced at Jelani, who was already walking off, phone in hand.

"Much appreciated. I'll make sure to send Toya some bread for the funeral," I said, taking the safety off the gun. "Unfortunately, it won't be an open casket. When you see the devil, tell him I said 'what's up'."

I let off two rounds in his head before he could utter any last words.

"Slim's gonna get the money from the locker and take it to the safe house tonight. What you wanna do about Kyree?" Jelani asked, ending his call.

I exhaled slowly, my pulse still racing from the adrenaline coursing through me. It was tempting to handle Kyree tonight, but I knew better. There was something bigger happening, and Kyree would help me uncover it.

"I'll have Nairobi deal with him," I said, unbuttoning my

shirt and tossing it on the floor. The clean-up crew would get rid of it for me. "Have one of the young boys dump this nigga's body on his cousin's porch."

Jelani's eyes lifted in surprise. "That's fucked up."

"Yeah, well," I said, rolling my shoulders. "It's time niggas remember who the fuck we are."

CHAPTER 2
JASMINE MILLER

I swear I'm blocking this nigga's number as soon as he leaves tomorrow

Amber: Oh lord, it's that bad?

He just asked for a strawberry Hennessy? What the fuck is that even?

"SO, WHAT ARE WE GETTING INTO AFTER THIS?" GAVIN asked, pushing his barely touched plate away. "I'm trying to experience Atlanta nightlife before I leave tomorrow."

"*We* aren't getting into anything," I said. "I told you I have three back-to-back twelve-hour shifts; I need to rest. Don't you have frat brothers out here? Call one of them."

Gavin handed the server his platinum American Express before they could place the check on the table.

"Yeah," he said, leaning back in his chair. "But I came down here to see you."

I rolled my eyes. "Boy, bye. You came down here to fuck, and to try convince me that a long-distance relationship could work."

He cringed. "You have a nasty mouth, you know that?"

"Oh brother," I scoffed, downing the rest of my drink. "Like you ain't have your tongue in my ass last night."

Gavin's head snapped around, checking if anyone heard, but the restaurant was too loud with everyone wrapped up in their own conversations to notice.

I adjusted my shorts as we stepped out into the humid Atlanta night. I hadn't even wanted him to come down this weekend. I was sure taking this contract in Atlanta would be enough to break things off with him, but I'd barely made it through my probationary period at the hospital before he texted me to say he'd booked a flight. At least he'd had the sense to get a hotel, but the entire time he'd been here, he kept trying to convince me we could make long-distance work.

This entire date was a flop. He barely touched his food, and when I asked him why, he claimed he didn't like tacos like that—like I didn't send him the restaurant's menu before he came out. The man told me it was cool and he was excited to see me. *Niggas*.

For someone so smart, Gavin Humphries was a simple-ass man. I loved eating out and trying new foods. He humored me most of the time, but if there wasn't a steak or burger on the menu, he defaulted to chicken tenders and fries.

We'd met a few years ago at his firm's holiday party. I'd been invited by my best friend Amber, who worked as a paralegal. He was handsome and charming—5'11, chestnut-colored skin, a Cesar that he got trimmed weekly, and the nicest set of lips. We hit it off immediately. He'd just made partner and was eager to show off the hefty bump in his pay.

What he lacked in culinary sophistication, he made up for with lavish gifts and good dick. He was my best eater, but that's where it ended. After a year of hooking up, I realized he was just a pretty face and nothing more.

Our server returned, setting our drinks in front of us.

"Can we also get the check when you get a chance?" I asked them.

"Sure, do you want any of this boxed up?" they asked, looking at Gavin. He wasn't paying attention, sipping his beer and scrolling through his phone.

I sighed, shaking my head.

"How about we just kick it at your place?" he suggested, unlocking the doors to his rental car. I turned to face him, making sure he saw the seriousness in my eyes. "Look, Gavin. This weekend was fun, and it was nice seeing a familiar face, but if you're coming over, understand this changes nothing. I'm not doing a long-distance relationship with you. We can be friends, but that's it."

He nodded. "I feel you, baby."

"No, but do you really?" I pressed. "Because I'm not tryna have this conversation again."

Gavin let out a humorless chuckle as he rounded the car to the driver's side. I exhaled as I slipped into the passenger seat, bracing myself for another round of his whining.

"I just don't get you," he said, starting the car. "We've been good for a year. It's not like there's no chemistry—the sex is fire. And aren't you coming back home in six months?"

I closed my eyes, holding back the scream threatening to come out. "I don't know! I've never lived outside of New York, and I'm trying to have a fresh start—one that doesn't include a man."

His jaw ticked as he gripped the wheel. "It's like that?"

"Yes, Gavin. It's like that," I huffed, slumping back against the seat. "You're handsome and successful, you'll forget about me soon enough with some new chick."

An awkward silence settled between us. I could sense the weight of my words settling with him.

"You really think I'm that shallow?"

I turned to face him, giving him a small smile. "No, I just know how these things go."

He opened his mouth like he wanted to argue, but closed it instead.

"Aight, Jas. You got it," he grumbled, backing out of the parking space.

♡$♡

"You said all that to him and let him up to your apartment?" Monica asked, arching a brow.

It was a rare, slow day in the ER, a few days after Gavin left. We were catching up on charting between patients.

"Sure did," I said as I entered my notes into the computer. "I told you—he's corny, but the man can put it down."

Monica shook her head, laughing. "You're a menace."

"I'm saying though! He had the nerve to side-eye me for being crass at the restaurant, but when we got back to my place? He was on that freaky shit *all* night," I smirked. "I think he was still trying to change my mind, but it wasn't happening. Definitely blocked him as soon as he texted that he made it back to New York."

"Cold-blooded." Monica cackled.

I shrugged. "Protecting my peace." I wasn't about to deal with another surprise pop-up in a few months.

"So if he shows up again with another Van Cleef bracelet and dick, you're gonna turn him away?" she asked, giving me a knowing look.

I hummed, but didn't answer, and she burst out laughing, shaking her head at me as she tapped away on the computer.

Monica had been the one to show me the ropes when I started at Peachtree Memorial, and we immediately clicked. She was younger than me, but a seasoned ER nurse with an amazing bedside manner. With patients, she had the patience of a saint. With men? She, like me, had zero tolerance for the bullshit.

I needed her friendship—not just because I came here not knowing a soul, but because this hospital wasn't for the weak. A surge of fentanyl overdoses had been stretching the understaffed ER thin, and in just a month, my nursing skills had been pushed to the limit.

At least working most shifts with Monica kept me sane.

"Speaking of men—" I said, logging out of the computer. "What's up with fine-ass Dr. Matthews? Don't think I haven't peeped how he's been hovering over you."

Monica groaned. "Jas, please."

"What? He's a doctor, so you know he got money. And he's not-so-subtly been dropping hints that he's feeling you."

She snorted. "He's not my type. Plus, I told you, the women here are catty as fuck. I don't need them in my business."

"Not even a cute lunch date?"

"We need staff ready to receive EMS inbound from a three-car pile-up!" Dr. Crawford, the attending physician on duty, called out before she could answer.

Monica and I exchanged a look.

"So much for a quiet day," I sighed, heading toward Dr. Crawford.

CHAPTER 3
CASH "MONEY" BANKS

TWO WEEKS LATER

OUR BANKS ENTERPRISE FOURTH OF JULY BLOCK PARTY WAS in full swing, taking over Underground Atlanta like it did every year. Hundreds of people were milling about in the Atlanta heat—the excited screams of kids in the bouncy house mixed with the 2010s hip-hop blasting from the DJ's speakers. Food trucks lined the street, serving up free food, and the mobile bars kept the liquor flowing.

Heads turned as Nairobi cut through the crowd. Her dark, oversized sunglasses hid her gaze, but I could feel her dark brown eyes locked on me. She sucked lazily on a lollipop, ignoring the lingering stares. I leaned back against the hood of my Range, waiting.

"Cash Money," she greeted me, wrapping her arms around my neck. Her voice was sweet enough to mask the ruthlessness beneath.

Nairobi Montgomery was more than a pretty face. She was deadly. That's why I fucked with her. She was the perfect honey trap: tall, slim-thick, with smooth cocoa-brown skin, and legs that seemed to go on forever. Her beauty made it easy to get close to men, and whether the price was high enough or her mark had outlived their usefulness—sometimes both—she knew how to get rid of them efficiently.

"Why you come to my shit dressed to cause a fuss?" I asked, giving her a once-over. Her legs were on display in tiny frayed denim shorts and a white crocheted bikini top. Her short pixie cut was now a silvery blonde, a switch-up from the bright pink she had last time I saw her.

Nairobi stepped back, pushing her frames onto her head with a frown. "The fuck are you talking about?" she asked, looking down at herself. "This is a casual fit. I wore this to the market."

"Oh shit! What up, Nai!" Jelani yelled, weaving through the crowd with Slim and Fontaine.

Slim hit me with a nod, grinning as he took a swig of beer. Me and him had been tight since Pop Warner—when we lived on the Westside and before Pops moved us out the hood. Pops always looked out for him, and he was the first of my friends that he recruited in the business. Slim was a solid, lowkey dude, which meant people often slept on him, until they saw him get busy with his hands.

Fontaine hung back, eyes lingering on Nairobi like he was debating whether to shoot his shot. He'd been my roommate freshman year at Duke, and we clicked right away. Bro was a literal genius—coding laps around the professors before the semester ended. He could've easily gone the corporate route, but he loved the fast money and hacking into systems he had no business touching.

The four of us helped me grow my father's legacy into something bigger. Something that was truly ours.

"Lani, your brother says my outfit is too much," she said, twirling around with a smirk. "Is it bad?"

Jelani was damn near drooling, his eyes sweeping over her shamelessly. Her ass cheeks peeked out from the bottoms of her shorts, and I shook my head. She knew exactly what she was doing.

"Hell nah. You look good as fuck," he replied, cheesing at her.

"Thank you, Lani. That's why you're my favorite Banks brother," she beamed, rewarding him with a kiss on the cheek. I rolled my eyes.

"Whatever, man. Get in and let me holla at you." I unlocked the doors, and Nai strolled around to the passenger side.

"What's the play, boss man?" she asked, biting down on her lollipop.

"We had a mishap," I said, retrieving a pre-rolled blunt from the center console. "And I think it's tied to some bigger shit."

"Mishap how?"

I lit the blunt and took a long pull before answering. "You heard about the ODs we've been dealing with?"

She nodded.

"One of my lieutenants stole twenty G's from us. Nigga was using it to start his own shit with a plug he found in New York, but whatever he's selling is laced with fentanyl," I explained, passing her the blunt.

"Well, fuck," Nai muttered, taking a hit.

"Yeah. That shit isn't a good look for us. If people keep OD'ing, the police are gonna start sniffing around my shit, and we don't need that kind of smoke."

We had a good amount of cops on our payroll, including the commissioner, but even he couldn't stop the mayor and city council from cracking down if bodies kept dropping.

"So where do I come in?" she asked, exhaling a cloud of smoke.

"He told us who he was working with. I wanna know what else that nigga got going on and who the fuck his New York plug is."

"Send me the details, and I'll handle it. Give me three weeks, but I can probably do it in less time," she said, reaching for the door handle. "You know the drill, half up front and the rest when I'm done."

"Nai, you already know half the money was wired to your account this morning," I replied, unlocking the door. She paused and looked back at me with mischief in her eyes.

"I'm staying at my condo in Buckhead if you want to come by when this is done," she said, licking her lips. There was no mistaking the heat in her gaze.

Nairobi was playing with fire. We'd hooked up a few times, but us being a thing was bad for business. Not to mention, I appreciated her too much as a friend to burn bridges.

"I'm good, mama. Just let me know when the shit is done. Fontaine will send you the info," I replied, exiting the car. Nai sucked her teeth, as if we didn't do this song and dance every time she was home.

She said her goodbyes to Jelani and the rest of the guys before disappearing into the sea of people.

"I'm gonna make shorty my wife one day," Fontaine declared once she was out of sight. I whipped my head to look at him and saw he was dead serious. Nigga practically had hearts in his eyes.

"You got a crush on Nai for real?" Jelani asked, staring at him like he'd lost his mind. Fontaine knew Nairobi was one of the best contract killers in the country. She never stayed in one place too long, and in the decade I'd known her, she never had a serious relationship. She was the queen of casual flings, and with the type of motion she was working with, even at thirty-six, I doubted she was settling down anytime soon.

"Not a crush. That's my wife," Fontaine asserted confidently.

"You do know she's a man-eater," I said, scanning the crowd.

"She can eat this di—"

POP! POP! POP!

The happy screams of children were replaced with cries of panic as gunshots rang out. Chaos erupted, and the crowd scattered in every direction. I pulled the Glock from my waistband and pushed through the frenzy, not waiting for Jelani. At the edge of the barricade, I spotted a beat-up Honda with a masked shooter hanging out the back window, spraying bullets into the crowd.

There was no way for me to get a clean shot from where I was, so I dropped low and moved closer.

"Money, get back!" Lani yelled from somewhere behind me.

I ignored him and kept moving, stepping over an older man groaning and clutching his arm. My nostrils flared as I stood, locking eyes with the shooter. He lowered his gun and lifted the bottom of his mask just enough to reveal a twisted grin. I raised my piece and fired twice. One round hit his shoulder, jerking him back. He faltered for a moment, but didn't duck into the car. The nigga had heart, I'd give him that.

Before I could get off another shot, hot, searing pain tore through my abdomen. I looked down, confused, as red bloomed across my white tee.

"Rahmel sends his regards from the grave, bitch!" the

shooter shouted, his voice dripping with hatred. The tires of the Honda screeched against the pavement as he raised his gun again. I clenched my teeth, trying to ignore the pain, and squeezed the trigger. Another sharp pain tore through my chest. My body jerked back as the world around me blurred. I stumbled, fighting to stay upright, but I couldn't. It was getting hard to breathe.

"Money!" Someone yelled my name — Lani? Slim? I couldn't tell. Everything was a blur of noise and chaos. A hard bump against my shoulder brought me to my knees as someone ran past.

I clutched my stomach in a desperate attempt to stop the blood pouring through my fingers. Darkness pressed at the edges of my vision.

"Cash!" The voice was faint now. I gasped, my lungs burning as they struggled to get air.

This wasn't how it was supposed to end.

I exhaled and let the darkness swallow me whole.

CHAPTER 4
JASMINE MILLER

THE FOLKS IN THE TRAVELING NURSING FACEBOOK GROUP HAD warned Peachtree Memorial was no joke, but no—I thought I was hot shit and got greedy. It was the highest paying contract I'd ever been offered, and how bad could it really be? Even when Monica warned me when I started that most travel nurses didn't last more than a month, I brushed her off. I'd survived some of the toughest hospitals in the five boroughs—I could handle whatever Peachtree Memorial threw at me.

Now? After every shift, I seriously considered packing up my Altima and heading back to Queens. The money was good, but lately, it felt like I was trading my mental health for a paycheck, and I was beginning to wonder if it was really worth it.

Tonight was shaping up to be one of those shifts that tap-danced all over my nerves. The ER was always chaotic, but we were short-staffed, and it was packed like everybody in the damn city had an emergency. Everyone was on one. One patient got so fed up with waiting that he threw literal shit at Monica when she finally got to him.

"They don't pay me enough for this shit!" she screamed, ripping off her badge. "Fuck this job!"

"Monica, wait!" I called, chasing after her to the nurses' locker room.

"I'm done, Jas," she snapped, yanking her locker open. "On everything I love, I'm out this bitch." She started shoving her stuff into her bag and slammed it shut.

"Woo-sa," I said, gently touching her arm. Monica's meltdowns were legendary. After eavesdropping on a few of the older nurses, I'd learned this happened at least once a quarter. Administration would give her a verbal warning, threaten a write-up or suspension, but they'd never let her go. She'd been here too long. And truth be told, she was a damn good nurse.

Brodie stuck his head through the door.

"Miller, we need you back on the floor. Mass casualty incident at the Underground—got a shit ton of victims coming in."

Monica rolled her eyes and dug her keys out of her purse. "Girl, quit this bitch with me right now, and we can go get a drink."

Technically, she had a few hours left in her rotation; I only had twenty minutes. But we were slammed and critical patients on the way, it didn't matter how tired I was—I couldn't walk out in good conscience.

"I'll be out there in a minute," I told him.

He nodded, glancing at Monica. "See you next week, Mo," he snickered before ducking out the door.

"I bet you won't," she grumbled, flipping him off as it swung shut behind him.

I sighed dramatically, poking out my bottom lip. "Alright, sis, let me get back in the trenches. I guess I'll see you around."

"Don't be like that, New York,"she teased, using the nickname she'd given me. "This place is too fucking much. I'm a nurse. These niggas need me more than I need them," she huffed, tucking a braid behind her ear.

She wasn't wrong.

"Text me, though," she added. "We can go to that new hookah lounge Honcho opened."

"Bitch, I'm not going to no damn hookah lounge," I scowled.

"Miller!" someone yelled impatiently from the hallway.

"I said I'm coming! Damn!" I shouted back.

Monica chuckled, slinging her bag over her shoulder. "Sis, go help them. If they yell one more time, I'm liable to burn this motherfucker down."

I gave her a quick hug and rushed out.

My jaw dropped when I got back to the floor. In the five minutes I'd been gone, the ER had become a complete shit show. Doctors shouted over one another while nurses scrambled behind them like worker bees. Gurneys lined the hallways, and patients spilled into every corner—it was packed like sardines in a can. For a moment, I froze, my brain struggling to process the scene in front of me.

"We've got a trample victim here!" a paramedic's shout snapped me back to reality. They pushed past with an older man on the gurney, his face twisted in pain, and his right arm was bent at an angle that made my stomach drop. I shoved down the nausea, yanked a pair of gloves on, and scanned the floor for where I was needed most.

"I need a doctor right now!"

A man's panicked voice cut through the frenzy. I turned to see a tall Black man, covered in blood, looking around wildly. He stormed toward me the moment our eyes locked.

“Are you a doctor?” he demanded, grabbing my wrist with a death grip.

“N-nurse.” I stammered, trying to pull free. “If you let go, I can find one.”

“No!” he shook his head, voice breaking. “My brother’s been shot! He’s losing too much blood—he’s dying! I need a fucking doctor!”

“Sir, is he in one of the ambulances?” I asked, doing my best to stay calm even though my heart was racing.

He dropped my wrist and started pacing in frantic circles. “Fuck, fuck, FUCK!” he yelled, slamming his hand against the wall. I couldn’t let this man lose his shit and make things worse.

I opened my mouth to tell him to breathe, and I’d help him find a doctor, but froze when I saw him reach for the gun in his waistband. My hand darted out before I realized it. “No.” I shook my head, keeping my voice even. “Take me to him. I’ll help you find a doctor.”

My eyes darted around until I spotted an abandoned gurney. I sprinted over and grabbed it before anyone else could. “Come on,” I said, pushing it toward the doors.

He grabbed the other end without hesitation and started moving like a man possessed.

“Slow down!” I hollered, nearly tripping as I tried to keep up. This guy had to be at least 6’3—my short legs weren’t built for this.

“My bad, ma!” he yelled back, but he didn’t slow down.

We burst through the lobby doors, where a blacked-out Range Rover was idling at the curb. As soon as we got close, the passenger door flew open. He abandoned the gurney and rushed to help another man pull out the body of his brother from the car.

"Grab his feet, Slim!" he barked. Together, they pulled a limp, blood-soaked body from the back seat.

My breath caught at the sight of how bad it was—his brother was shirtless, barely conscious, and wrapped in half-assed bandages that were already soaked through. I rushed to secure the straps as they laid him on the gurney.

"We don't have time for that shit!" the man snapped, grabbing the gurney like it weighed nothing and charging back inside. I pushed through as my feet screamed in protest, and hustled to keep up.

"I got a gunshot victim!" I shouted as we made it back to the ER floor. I shoved him aside to do a more thorough assessment. His brother was fading fast—his breathing was labored, and his lips were turning blue.

"Shit," Dr. Crawford muttered, stepping up beside me. "Call upstairs and have them prep an OR, stat!" she ordered the nearest resident. "Miller, you're with me."

She grabbed the gurney and wheeled it toward the elevator. The man tried to follow behind us.

"I'm sorry, you have to wait down here," I told him, blocking his path.

"The fuck I will! That's my brother!" he growled, as he tried to push past me.

"Lani, chill! Chill!" his friend grabbed his arm and yanked him back.

"What's your name?" I asked. I was trying my best to remain calm, but I was close to losing my mind right along with him.

"Jelani," he gritted, eyes locked on the elevator like he could will Dr. Crawford to defy protocol.

"Okay, Jelani. Please just trust us to do our job. I'll come back with updates as soon as I can."

I turned and caught up with Dr. Crawford. Another nurse,

Regina, held the elevator doors open as she pushed the gurney inside.

"Dr. Crawford," I said. "I'm not an OR nurse. I really should stay and help out down here."

"No, you brought him in," she said, checking his vitals without looking up. "I need you to be the family liaison."

The man groaned, his head rolling weakly to one side.

"I don't understand," I said, looking between her and Regina as the elevator doors closed.

Regina looked at me like I missed the obvious. "Don't you know who this is?"

I cut my eyes at her. "I've only been here a month, Regina. No, I don't know who he is," I snapped, not bothering to take the edge out of my voice. This was the kind of petty shit that had Monica cussing folks out regularly.

Dr. Crawford let out a deep sigh. "This is Cash Banks. If he dies, heads will roll—starting with us."

$

It was after midnight, and I was still stuck outside the OR, waiting on updates about a man everyone seemed to know except me. I got tired of sitting around, so I snuck downstairs and slipped past Jelani, who was pacing the floor like a caged animal. I grabbed my phone from my locker to do some digging.

Turns out, Mr. Banks was a hood legend.

He grew up in one of Atlanta's roughest neighborhoods with his parents and younger brother. The hood blogs said his dad was a big-time drug dealer in the '90s and early 2000s, and managed to move the family to the suburbs by the time

Cash was in high school. He'd gotten a football scholarship to Duke, but had to drop out when his father was killed during his junior year.

It gets a little murky after that. Everyone assumed Cash took over for his dad, but he also managed to start Banks Enterprises and Commercial Realty before he turned thirty. They rehabbed run-down buildings and leased them out to small business owners at fair prices. The city loved him for it.

But it was clear he was still into some shady shit. Why else would Dr. Crawford make it a priority for us to keep him alive? I sighed and rubbed my temples. My head was throbbing, and the harsh fluorescent lights weren't helping. I grabbed my phone and opened the text thread with Monica.

Friend, why am I still stuck at the hospital? Shit's been wild all evening.

Monica: For real? I picked up some lemon pepper wet and on my fourth glass of wine. Told you to leave with me, bestie. 😌

This bitch. The hard plastic chair creaked as I shifted into a more comfortable position.

Anyway. 🙄 You know some dude named Cash Banks? He came in shot up. Crawford is forcing me to be the family liaison.

Monica: Big Money Banks got shot??

Big Money who?

Monica: Bitch, that nigga runs Atlanta. That's that old-school drug money right there.

"Jasmine."

Dr. Crawford's voice pulled me from my phone. I looked

up to see her standing over me, clearly as drained as I was. I shoved my phone into my pocket and stood.

"How is he?" I asked.

"He's stable," she said, taking off her glasses to rub her eyes. "We removed the bullets and stopped the internal bleeding. He lost a lot of blood, so we put him in a medically induced coma."

"Thank God," I murmured, remembering what she said in the elevator. The last thing I wanted was to be the one to tell Jelani his brother didn't make it—he'd probably shoot me on sight.

"You can give his brother the update and head out," Dr. Crawford said, offering me a tired smile before turning back to the OR.

"Wait—" I called after her. She paused, turning to me.

"I – uh… where are they taking him?" I asked. Something tugged at me to go put eyes on him. "So I can let Jelani know."

"ICU. He'll be there for observation before they move him."

I moved to the elevators. My finger hovered over the button for the lobby. I could go home and follow Monica's lead—grab some wings and make myself a nightcap. Lord knows I needed one. But curiosity got the better of me. Biting my lip, I hit the button for the ICU floor instead.

The ICU was eerily quiet, a stark contrast to the chaos in the ER. The security guard on duty barely looked up from his phone as I walked past.

What was I doing? I should be clocking out right now. But my feet kept moving, like they had a mind of their own. Halfway down the hall, I spotted a nurse flipping through charts outside a patient's room.

"Excuse me," I said softly. She looked up.

"Do you know which room Cash Banks is in?"

"Two doors down on the left," she replied, going back to her work.

My pulse quickened as I approached his door. I paused and took a deep breath before pushing it open.

The room was dimly lit, with the only sounds coming from the soft beeps of the monitors that said he was still here. Cash lay motionless, with tubes attached to his arm and chest.

I moved closer, stopping at the side of his bed.

Even banged and bruised up, he had this… presence.

His deep mahogany skin was dull from the blood loss, and a few cuts marked his face, but none of that took away from how fine he was. His sharp jaw, his full lips—Cash Banks had the kind of face that would make you do a double-take. The kind that had you doing silly shit like staring at him while he was comatose at 1 a.m.

My gaze drifted to the bandages across his chest. I reached out, fingertips grazing the edge of the dressing, feeling solid muscle underneath. The minutes stretched as I stood lost in thought, my exhaustion blurring the lines between sense and reason. Maybe it was the delirium of being in the hospital for over eighteen hours, but I couldn't pull myself away.

And then, for reasons I still can't explain, I leaned down and pressed a soft kiss to his cheek.

"Aye yo, the fuck you doing?"

I jumped, spinning around to find Jelani standing in the doorway, his eyes blazing with rage.

"I—I—" I stammered, caught completely off guard.

He stormed across the room and shoved me so hard that I slammed into the side of Cash's bed.

"You trying to kill my brother?" he growled, pressing something cold and heavy against my head.

It took a second for my exhaustion-laden brain to register what it was.

"No!" I yelped, panic rising when I realized it was a gun. "Oh my God, no! I was just checking on him. I was about to come downstairs to get you."

"Then why the fuck were you in his face for?" he barked, jamming the muzzle harder against my temple.

"Nigga, I'm *tired*!" I snapped, tears finally spilling. The stress of the entire night—mass casualties in the ER, working six hours past my shift, and now this nigga holding a gun to my head—all broke through at once. "I'm so fucking tired," I sobbed, falling to my knees.

Jelani's face shifted, the anger leaving it a little as he lowered the gun. He stepped back, looking around uncomfortably. "Come on, ma. Don't cry," he muttered, scratching the back of his head with the gun.

"Don't cry?!" I let out a hysterical laugh. "I was supposed to clock out *six hours* ago! And then you run up in this bitch, damn near shot the hospital up—while I'm the one who got the nigga in surgery! *Me*!" I slapped my chest, standing up. "I did that! Why the fuck would I try to kill him?"

I shoved Jelani hard in the chest.

He blinked at me, stunned. After a moment, he reached into his back pocket and pulled out a wad of cash, holding it out.

"For your troubles," he said stiffly.

"*Fuck you*," I slapped the money out of his hand and stormed out of the room with my mind made up. Cash Banks and Peachtree Memorial could both kiss my whole ass.

CHAPTER 5
CASH "MONEY" BANKS

THREE MONTHS LATER...

My body jerked, and I let out a low grunt as I came in her mouth. Princess didn't flinch, looking up at me through her thick lashes as she swallowed like a champ.

"Mmm… still taste good, Money," she purred, licking her lips.

I rolled my neck and blew out a hard breath as I fixed my boxers and headed for the bathroom. I wiped myself down with a warm washcloth before pulling on my pants and checked myself in the mirror.

Despite everything, I was still him. I ran a hand over my freshly trimmed beard, adjusted my collar, and slid on the new AP watch I'd treated myself to.

When I stepped back out, Princess was perched on the edge of the bed, legs crossed, smiling like she hadn't just been choking on my dick.

"You look good, Daddy," she said.

"Mm," I hummed in response. I could've had on a cruddy outfit, smelling like outside, and she still would've gotten on her knees for me. That's just how Princess moved. Always playing a long game, thinking she was three moves ahead.

We had an on-again, mostly off-again thing—but ever since the shooting, she'd been trying to play nurse wifey. Cooking for me like I ain't have a private chef. Fussing over me when I was still on pain meds, acting like we were in some kind of relationship.

She was definitely trying to get permanently chose this go-round, but that was never happening.

She'd been ran through by damn near every heavy hitter in the city—rappers, hustlers, Tubi actors, whoever had a little paper. That wasn't the issue. I'd never been pressed about her body count. The problem was, Princess wasn't as slick as she thought she was. She swore she was playing chess, but she moved like a groupie—chasing men to fund her lifestyle in the hopes that one of them would eventually wife her.

And no matter how many times we fell out, she always circled back, 'cause none of them other niggas had motion like me.

"Come on, P," I said, walking out of the room without acknowledging her compliment.

We were heading to the big-ass party Jelani insisted on throwing for me, calling it my "return to the streets."

Like I ever really left.

I tried to get discharged a few days after I came out of the coma, but my body was too fucked up. I ended up hiring a private medical team to handle my recovery at my condo close to the hospital, because there was no way in hell I was eating that nasty-ass food for another month. It took a minute, but aside from the occasional phantom pains, I was still breathing.

That's all that mattered.

And I was ready to smoke out the bitch-ass niggas who tried to take me out.

"I'm so excited!" Princess squealed, sliding into the back seat of the Maybach.

Hassan, my driver, gave me a nod in the rearview mirror. "You lookin' like your old self, Money."

"Appreciate that, bruh," I smiled, climbing in beside her.

She was already pouring herself a glass of champagne from the center console.

"Damn, you couldn't put your seatbelt on first?" I asked, raising an eyebrow.

She giggled, passing me the glass. "This was for you."

I side-eyed her, taking it knowing damn well she wasn't thinking about me. Honestly, this was probably the last night I fucked with her. I know she thought this invite meant we were taking things to the next level, but I just needed arm candy… and maybe a little pussy later.

Princess poured herself a glass and slid her hand between my thighs, rubbing on my crotch.

"Whatchu doing?" I asked, moving her hand away, even though I was starting to get hard.

"I thought we could have some fun before we got there," she whispered, leaning over to kiss on my neck.

"P, chill with all that," I said, shrugging her off. "I'm not trying to have your makeup all over my clothes and get there smelling like sex."

She sucked her teeth and poked her bottom lip out. "Thought you liked the way my pussy smelled," she mumbled.

"Don't start this shit," I sighed, already regretting that I brought her.

"Start what, Money? I'm just trying to love on my man before his party."

"Your what?" I almost choked on my drink. I set the glass down and turned to face her. "Princess, we've never been anything more than fuck buddies—please be so fucking for real right now."

Her face dropped, and her bottom lip started to quiver. "But—"

I held up my hand, cutting her off. "Nah. Don't do that. I appreciate you being around during my recovery—but I never asked you to do that. And if you're gonna be on some goofy shit tonight, I'll have Hassan turn around and take your ass home."

She glared at me, her mouth drawn in a thin line, clearly debating whether to crash out or not. But she didn't say shit, and we didn't say another word for the rest of the ride. Hassan turned the music up to fill the silence while we busied ourselves with our phones.

"Fix your face," I muttered as we pulled up to Palladium.

Outside was jumping. Cars were double-parked, folks were arguing with security, and the line stretched down the block. Cameras started flashing the second I stepped out. Hassan had to hold the photographers back while I helped Princess out of the car.

The woman was irksome, but I had to admit she had that shit on tonight. Her white mesh dress looked painted on, and her hair was slicked into a high ponytail that brushed her ass.

Three glasses of champagne and half an edible in, I was halfway rethinking about cutting her off after tonight.

Halfway.

"Bout time you got here, bitch nigga!" Jelani hollered from the club entrance, grinning. "Bring your bougie ass on!"

I laughed, shaking my head as we bypassed the line and walked up.

Inside was packed. The DJ had the crowd going crazy

spinning Lil Baby's *Never Finished.* The whole place smelled like weed, sweat, and bad decisions about to be made.

I threw my arm around Princess's waist, rapping bar for bar with Lani as we pushed through the dance floor. Cheers erupted the second we hit the stop of the VIP stairs. Slim, Fontaine, and the rest of the crew were already posted up with bottles, blunts, and beautiful women. Bottles were popping, and the drinks were flowing.

The vibe was immaculate.

"This is love," I said, clapping my brother on the back. "Thank you, bruh."

"Don't get soft on me now, pussy," he laughed, pulling me in for a hug before I could brush him off.

"Whatever, dickhead," I smirked.

"What's up, Jelani?" Princess cut in, handing me a shot.

"P," he said flatly, not even bothering to look at her. He hated Princess, but he had promised me he would be cordial with her tonight.

I tossed back the shot, the burn settling in my chest as I scanned the crowd below.

"Security is tight tonight," Jelani said, leaning against the railing.

"I wish a nigga would try and fuck up my party," I scoffed, getting heated at the thought.

"They won't," he said, tapping the piece tucked into his waistband. "But if they do… you already know—"

"We on go," I finished our old line.

"Ay! We turnin' up, or y'all finna talk all night?" Slim yelled, waving a bottle of Hennessy and a blunt in the air.

Shit got hazy after that. The shots kept coming, and I lost track of how many blunts were in rotation. My head was buzzing, but I felt invincible. Standing on the couch with my Gucci shirt hanging open, I rapped along to Jeezy's *Who Dat.*

The whole section was lit, feeding off my energy. Even Princess was swaying, drink in hand, like we weren't just beefing a few hours ago.

I hopped down and headed to the railing—I needed a minute to breathe.

That's when I saw her.

Might've been the weed. Could've been the liquor. But it was like everything in the club fell away. The music faded, the lights blurred, and all I could see was *her*, moving through the crowd with her friend in tow.

Shorty was thicker than a bowl of grits—little waist, thick thighs, and an ass that had me ready to risk it all. Her black lace black bodysuit clung to her like second skin. Her smooth, toffee-colored skin seemed to glow under the club lights, and her long, wavy hair fell down her back.

Her glossy lips curved into a smile as she leaned in to whisper in her friend's ear.

She moved like she knew she was that girl.

She didn't belong down there with the regulars. She belonged in VIP. Next to me.

Her friend tugged her arm, trying to guide her through the crowd, but she moved at her own pace—unbothered by all the bodies brushing past her.

I leaned over the balcony, tracking her every move. I didn't just want her name—I needed to know everything about her. Needed to know where she was from and what I needed to do to make her smile like that.

I tore my eyes away from her just long enough to find the stairs and started moving.

I didn't know who she was yet, but one thing was for sure: I wasn't leaving this club without talking to my future wife.

CHAPTER 6
JASMINE MILLER

I SWEAR I WAS TOO OLD TO BE AT THE CLUB, BUT MONICA said she was tired of me being grumpy all the time, and if I wasn't getting laid, then we needed to go out, shake some ass, and let fine men buy us drinks all night.

That's exactly how I ended up in a bodysuit with my goodies out, pregaming at her condo like we were in our twenties.

"Exactly, friend!" she said, nodding approvingly at my outfit when I showed up. "You were starting to look like thoughts and prayers. We had to wake up your inner bad bitch."

I rolled my eyes and threw back another shot of tequila.

It'd been rough in the two months since *the incident*—what I'd been calling that wild-ass night at Peachtree. People said I was being dramatic for taking two weeks off after that mess, but I'm sorry—how was I supposed to work after having a gun pressed to my head? I'd seen a lot of shit in my ten years of nursing, but never that. I didn't even tell my parents. If my daddy found out, he'd be on the next flight down, dragging me back to Queens like a wayward child.

Monica did actually quit for real this time—kind of. She cut her hours down to per diem and got a sweet gig at Southside General. Meanwhile, I was still stuck at that fuck-ass hospital. I had a few coworkers I was cool with, but it wasn't the same without my girl on the floor with me regularly. I was keeping my fingers crossed for a travel nurse position to open up, but until then I was stuck.

The only upside in all this was the five-figure deposit that hit my account a few days after everything went down. I had a strong suspicion Jelani was behind it, but I wasn't trying to do any mental gymnastics to figure out how he got my info. I had no desire to run into him ever again.

Wouldn't mind seeing Cash, though.

When our Uber dropped us to the club an hour later, I was tipsy and already forgetting about the bullshit from work. The DJ had everybody going up for a Gucci Mane track and the bass thumped so hard that I could feel it in my chest. For the first time in a long time, I felt good.

"Let's dance!" Monica shouted over the music, grabbing my hand and pulling me towards the dance floor.

We pushed through a tangle of sweaty bodies, laughing until we found a spot in the middle. On cue, the DJ switched it up and played the opening of Travis Porter's *Bring it Back* —the whole club lost it.

"This my shit!" I screamed, throwing my ass back as the beat dropped.

"Whatchu know about this, New York?" Monica teased, as she danced right along with me.

It felt like the whole club was caught up in the same wave. My hair stuck to my forehead from the sweat, but I didn't care. The liquor had me loose and I leaned into the feeling—remembering when nights like this were a regular thing for me.

I tensed when I felt a warm body press up behind me. Big hands found my hips—not rough, but firm enough to get my attention. He started moving with me, matching my rhythm a little too well. I usually didn't dance with random dudes in the club, but fuck it.

"Okay, Jas! I see you!" Monica hyped me up, still doing her own thing.

I grinned, silently praying that this dude didn't look like a gremlin. His grip stayed steady as I bent over and popped my ass like I had Megan Thee Stallion's knees and not thirty-six-year-old ones.

He pulled me closer, and the hardness pressing against me let me know exactly what time it was. A slow smirk spread across my face, and I rolled my hips a little harder—just to see if he could handle it.

He slid his hand up my back, guiding me upright until I was flush against his chest.

"Damn, girl," he murmured in my ear.

I bit my lip. *Please God, if you love me, let him be fine.* 'Cause that voice alone made my stomach flutter.

The DJ transitioned into a slower, more mellow track, breaking me out of my trance. Breathless, I moved his hand off me and started to step away—but he caught my arm.

"Hol'up," he said, gently pulling me back toward him.

I spun around, ready to tell him to fall back, but my mouth fell open instead.

Cash Banks was standing front of me.

The same man partially responsible for the worst shift of my life.

Very much alive. Very much awake. Shirt open, sweat glistening on his tattooed chest.

"You," I breathed, yanking my arm free as heat rose up my neck.

His head tilted slightly, curiosity lighting up his eyes. "I know you?"

The man was fine as frog hair, but that cocky look made me want to swing on him.

"Ay, can I get everyone's attention?" the DJ's voice boomed over the speakers, cutting the music with a record scratch. A spotlight beamed down on me and Cash like we were the main event.

"We're here to celebrate the big homie, Money Banks!"

The crowd went up—the way everyone was screaming and cheering, you would've thought the DJ said Beyoncé just walked in. Cash smiled, tossing up a lazy wave like he was in a pageant.

"Good to see you back on your feet, my boy! And much love for covering the medical bills for everybody that got caught up at the block party!"

More cheers.

So I guess the blogs weren't lying about everybody loving him.

"BC in the building tonight! Let's go!"

When the DJ dropped another track, I slipped out of Cash's grip, snatched Monica's drunk ass, and hauled us off the dance floor before he could follow.

"What the hell, Jas?" she slurred when I finally stopped near a dark corner by the VIP stairs.

My heart was pounding, and it felt like something was squeezing my chest as I took in short, shallow breaths. Seeing him brought me right back to that night—the screams, the blood, his stupid brother…

"Jasmine!" Monica waved a hand in front of my face.

"Sorry," I muttered. "I think I just had a mini panic attack."

"Because of *Money*?" She looked at me like I had two

heads. "Girl! This is perfect! You need to go back over there and let him trick off on you. Tell him it's PTSD compensation."

"Yo, nurse!"

Our heads whipped around to see a very drunk Jelani stumbling down the stairs.

Of course. Because this night couldn't get any worse.

"Oh, hell no," I muttered, grabbing Monica's hand, ready to make another quick exit—only to slam into a wall of muscle.

Cash.

"Why'd you run off, lil mama?" he grinned, showing off his gold fangs.

And Lord help me—if I thought he was cute laid up in a hospital bed, the man was a walking vision of sin right now. The shape-up was crisp, his beard was moisturized, and his dark brown skin was practically glowing—a complete 180 from the comatose version I'd seen a few months ago.

"Nurse! What you doin' here?" Jelani slurred, cheesing at me like we were old friends. He looked like a baby-faced version of his older brother. They were built the same, but Cash had a few inches on him. And while Cash kept his hair in a fade, Jelani had locs with tapered sides.

"It's still fuck you," I snapped, mushing him in his forehead when he got too close. Monica gasped as he stumbled back onto the steps, barely catching himself on the railing.

"Aw, come on, you still mad about that? I said I was sorry," he whined, slumping against the wall.

"You pressed a gun to my head!"

"Yeah, yeah… but I sent your mean ass fifteen bands," he shrugged.

"That's not a fucking apology."

"Fifteen thousand?" Monica echoed, eyes wide. She was probably kicking herself for walking off the unit that night.

Cash looked between us. "Yo, how you know my brother?"

"Yeah, *Lani*," I said sweetly, dragging out the nickname. "How *do* I know you?"

Cash's expression darkened instantly. "*Lani*? The fuck she calling you nicknames for?" He hemmed up Jelani by his shirt and slammed him against the wall.

Jelani blinked slowly and shoved Cash back with one hand. These two were *drunk,* drunk.

"This the nurse that got you into surgery," Jelani nodded toward me like he was giving me a Yelp review. "You owe her. Probably the only reason your dumb ass is still breathing."

I rolled my eyes, but my face was burning.

Cash turned to me, licking his lips slowly. "Word?"

The simple gesture was enough to make my pussy throb.

"I just did my job," I said quickly. "Monica, let's *go*."

I reached for her hand, but she didn't move.

"She don't look like she tryna leave," Jelani chuckled.

"Bitch, you're a traitor," I hissed at her, narrowing my eyes.

"Jas, come on!" Monica whined. "We can just chill for a little bit and have a few drinks. I need to sit down—my feet hurt."

I felt Cash's eyes burning into me, waiting for me to decide.

"Ain't no harm in having a little fun," he said, sliding his arm around my waist. "I don't bite…unless you ask me to."

Jelani nodded beside him, rubbing his hands, gaze zeroed in on Monica. "We just two rich niggas trying to show y'all a good time."

Cash leaned in, lips brushing my ear. "I'm tryna get to know the woman who saved my life."

My brain was screaming at me to run, but my body was a traitor—like Monica. His cologne wrapped around me like a spell, and I felt myself slipping.

"Jasmine," I blurted.

"Huh?"

"My name's Jasmine," I said, pushing him off harder than necessary. "Fine. But we're not staying all night."

Monica squealed and let Jelani lead her up the stairs. I followed behind, ignoring the smug ass grin spreading across Cash's face.

Their section was on a whole other level—literally. An armed security guard was posted by the roped-off section, stepping aside when the Banks brothers approached.

It was like a private lounge, plush couches wrapped around low glass tables covered in bottles and hookahs, and a thick haze of weed and fruit-flavored smoke hung in the air.

"This is *nice*," Monica whispered as we followed them deeper in.

The energy shifted when they walked in—they radiated power. Both brothers had big dick energy, but Cash was different.

Women eyed him hungrily as he moved past, their eyes flicking between me and Monica, then back to Cash and Jelani. They were sick. I'm sure they were wondering how the two of us managed to pull the biggest ballers in here.

I flipped my hair over my shoulder, trying to ignore the voice in the back of my mind screaming that this was a bad idea. I had no business getting mixed up with a man who allegedly moved in illegal circles. Old school drug money? I'd watched *Power*—none of this would end well for me.

But knowing better didn't mean I was leaving.

Monica dipped off with Jelani to a private bar in the back. Cash dropped down onto one of the couches and pulled me straight onto his lap. I tried to get up, but his arm locked around my waist.

"Nah, you good right here," he murmured, his nose grazing the back of my neck.

I squirmed, trying to shift out of his hold. "I can sit next to you."

The drinks I'd had tonight were catching up, and with the blunts going around, I was definitely about to catch a contact high.

"You could," he chuckled. "But I promise—you right where you need to be."

His hand slid up my thigh, fingers lingering high enough to make my pulse jump.

"Money, you good?" a familiar voice asked.

I glanced up and saw the dude who'd helped Jelani bring Cash into the ER that night.

"Oh shit, it's the nurse!" he grinned.

I groaned. "Can y'all not call me that?"

"I'm straight, Slim. Just grab me another drink," Cash said, waving him off before turning back to me. "You want something?"

I shook my head. One more drink and I'd be waking up in this man's bed butt-ass naked.

"So how come all my boys met you at the hospital, but I didn't?"

"Because I called out for, like, two weeks after that," I said. "Did you miss the part where your brother pressed a gun to my head? That shit was traumatizing. I wasn't exactly pressed to see either of y'all again."

"What the fuck, Money?!" a woman screeched, interrupting our conversation. A tall, brown-skinned woman was glaring down at us with fire in her eyes.

I started to get up, but Cash's arm tightened around me.

"Princess, what's the problem?" he asked, sounding bored.

"Are you serious? You brought me here—now you got some cheap-looking bitch sitting on your lap?"

I scoffed. "I could never give cheap, sweetheart."

I wasn't trying to start shit, but she wasn't about to talk sideways to me.

"Chill with all that, P. You're drunk. Go sit down," Cash said, stifling a yawn.

"You know what?" I said, untangling myself from him. "Maybe I should just go."

Princess folded her arms, lips curling into a nasty sneer. "Yeah, maybe you should, wack bitch."

I stood up so fast her face dropped.

"You really tryna start shit over a nigga that clearly doesn't respect you?" I said, getting in her face.

She blinked, clearly not expecting me to say anything.

"If it was like that between y'all, he wouldn't have brought me up here and had me on his lap in front of you. You not embarrassed?"

"Oh shit," someone nearby muttered.

"Ain't nobody worried about you bi—"

She wasn't about to call me a bitch again.

Pop!

My fist met with her mouth. She screamed, stumbling into the table behind her and sending a hookah crashing to the floor.

"I'ma fuck you up!" she screamed, scrambling to her feet.

Her friends rushed over to help her up at the same time I heard the click of a gun cocking.

My stomach nearly fell out my ass seeing Cash's Glock pointed at Princess and her girls.

What was with these niggas and pulling out guns?

"I *told* your ass to sit down," he laughed like this was a big joke. "Now look at you. And y'all not about to try and jump her."

My jaw dropped. This nigga was insane.

"Monica!" I yelled, spinning around looking for my friend.

She was in a corner with her tongue halfway down Jelani's throat. I stormed over and yanked her off of him.

"We're leaving," I snapped, dragging her towards the stairs.

"Call me!" she giggled, waving at Jelani over her shoulder.

Cash stepped in front of us, blocking the way like he didn't just threaten to knock Princess's head off five seconds ago.

"Where you going?" he asked with that arrogant smile still plastered on his face.

"Move, Cash!" I shoved at his chest, but he didn't budge. He was enjoying this a little too much.

"Why you in such a rush?"

"Because I'm going home, nigga!" I shouted. "This is too much—got me in here about to fight your funky ass girlfriend! I don't do shit like this!"

His smile faltered. "You serious?" He genuinely looked confused, like he really couldn't understand why I was mad.

"Do I look like I'm playing? Fuck out my way!"

I pushed past him, dragging Monica behind me. My chest tightened as we hurried down the stairs.

I should've listened to that little voice earlier, because it was obvious nothing but drama came with Cash Banks.

"You good?" Monica asked once we were outside, pulling out her phone to order an Uber.

"I just want my bed," I muttered, rubbing my forearms. I was still trying to figure out how the night spun out of control so fast.

"Me too," she sighed, glancing back at the club like she was debating running back in.

"You can go back in if you want," I told her, feeling a twinge of guilt.

"What? No! It's fine, Jas. Really." She slipped her phone back in her purse. "But don't front…you know you had fun."

I exhaled, shaking my head. "It was aight… 'til it wasn't."

"Girl, bye! You were definitely getting cozy on Money's lap."

I was too tired to answer her—my ears were ringing, and I felt a dull headache forming at the base of my skull. All I wanted to do was shower and scrub the memory of Cash off my skin.

His hands.

His voice.

That damn cologne.

My curiosity had been satisfied.

I never needed to see him again.

CHAPTER 7
CASH "MONEY" BANKS

"YOU'VE GOT A BIG PROBLEM, BOSS MAN," NAIROBI SAID AS she skimmed the menu.

We were meeting up in Midtown so she could update me on Kyree. Getting shot had thrown everything off. A situation that should've taken a few weeks to wrap up was pushing on almost three months.

Nairobi had agreed to stay on a little longer and started working at Stilettos—the strip club where Kyree spent most of his free time flexing his BC affiliation. He had a weakness for long legs, and Nai played right into it, giving him enough extra attention to hook him. A few private dances quickly escalated into backroom meetings with his makeshift crew, with him parading her around like she was his girl.

"What could be bigger than niggas trying to kill me?" I asked, sipping my water.

My mind drifted back to Jasmine. It'd been a week since the party, and I still couldn't get her pretty ass out of my head. She was sexy, and that slick mouth made my dick hard. I wanted her real bad.

"Cash!" Nairobi snapped her fingers in front of my face.

I blinked, snapping out of it. "My bad, Nai. Say that again?"

She gave me a sharp look and opened her mouth to speak, but clamped it shut as the waiter approached the table.

"You guys ready to order?" he asked.

"Yes," she said, handing him her menu. "I'll have the cod and a glass of white sangria."

"And let me get the ribeye—medium rare—with mashed potatoes and broccoli. Oh, and a lavender lemonade." I said.

"Lavender lemonade?" she asked, raising an eyebrow.

"That shit's good," I shrugged.

"You're distracted."

"I'm not."

"You're lying, but whatever." She leaned back. "Rahmel was poaching from y'all to fund his own operation."

I burst out laughing. "That dumbass thought he could go to my suppliers behind my back? They've been working with us since before my daddy died."

My pops solidified those connections decades ago. When he got killed, a few tried to take the crew from me, but I put foot to ass and made it clear this empire was staying in the Banks family.

"That's why he went and found a plug in New York," she said, pausing as the waiter dropped off our drinks.

I rubbed my jaw. "I still don't get how they thought this could work without running into problems."

"You were supposed to be dead," she said plainly. "They figured BC would eat itself from the inside out."

I snorted. "And they thought Lani would sit back and let that happen? These niggas don't know my brother for real. He got a few screws loose."

Jelani might joke, but he didn't fuck around when it came

to me or the business. If I hadn't made it that day, the city would've burned.

"I wonder where he gets it from," Nairobi smirked as she sipped her drink.

"Haha, smart ass," I said, sipping my lemonade. "Can you get the names of these snake-ass niggas? And who the fuck shot me?"

"Still working on the first part. They're pretty tight-lipped about the shooting when I'm around. But if I had to guess? Rahmel's people."

Rahmel's cousins were small-time hustlers from the Eastside, barely scraping by on the shit they moved. They were fucking bums. Rahmel came to me because he knew I was his only shot out of the projects; if he'd stayed with them, he'd be working out of dirty trap houses into his fifties.

I was getting too old for this shit. I knew I couldn't fully leave the game, but I was ready to fall back. At thirty-eight, I wanted something real—a wife, a couple of kids. I'd been laying the foundation for my exit over the past few years. Jelani could have the streets. He loved this life more than I ever did.

Growing up, he was Pops' shadow, trying to learn everything. I had to force him to finish college, just so one of us could. The minute he graduated, he came home ready to be my right hand.

I dragged a hand down my face. "Alright, let me run this by Lani and figure out how we finna deal with these Eastland niggas."

$

After lunch, I swung by my mother's house. I wasn't surprised to see Jelani's BMW parked in the driveway.

"Hey, baby," she called from the kitchen as I walked in. Jelani was at the island, inhaling a plate of food. He nodded at me mid-bite.

"Hey, Ma." I leaned in, kissing her forehead. "What up, Lani?"

"What you doing here?" Ma asked, eyeing me like she knew I didn't just stop by for a casual visit. "You hungry?"

"Nah, I just ate."

She nodded. "Alright, I'll fix you a plate to take home."

Sydney Banks never co-signed what our daddy did, but she loved Ricardo Banks— and the lifestyle his money bought. It was easy to look the other way when your man moved you and your kids out the hood and into a mini-mansion. She made me promise I wouldn't follow in his foot-steps. That promise went out the window after he got killed. I didn't have a choice.

Pops was a genius at moving product. The issue was he had no long-term vision—there were no legit investments, no properties in Ma's name. Not even a life insurance policy. Just stacks of cash that couldn't stretch forever. She'd become a stay-at-home mother since Jelani was born, and by the time he died, she hadn't worked in twenty years. So, I stepped up and made sure she and my brother were straight—no matter what it cost me.

"Lani, let me rap with you real quick," I said, catching his eye while Ma packed my to-go plate.

"Ma, make me a plate, too," Jelani added, rinsing his plate in the sink. "That cabbage was good as hell."

We went into the back room, out of earshot from Ma—we never talked business in front of her.

"Rahmel and Kyree were recruiting niggas from inside

the crew to help them set up their own operation," I said, dropping into an armchair.

Jelani let out a low whistle and leaned against a bookshelf. "So we got some disloyal ass niggas in the circle?"

"Looks like it," I said, stretching out and kicking my feet onto the ottoman. "Nai's still digging and trying to get names. Shouldn't be much longer."

"What about who shot you?"

"She thinks it's them Eastland niggas. But I want to be sure before we move on to them."

Jelani frowned and then snapped his fingers as something clicked. "I used to talk to a chick out that way. Let me holla at her and see if she knows something."

I gave him a look. "Why the hell you messing with a bitch from over there?"

"She's pretty, got a fat ass, and sucks a mean dick," he said, ticking off each point on his fingers. "What can I say?"

I shook my head as my phone buzzed in my pocket.

Fontaine: Jerome said he just seen your nurse walk into Blue Sky with some square looking nigga.

Bet.

"You talk to that nurse?" Jelani asked, switching the subject. I frowned.

"How I'm supposed to talk to her without her number?"

He held up both hands, laughing. "You mad, bruh? Why you actin' like Fontaine can't hack the damn planet and get you her info?"

"She'll give it to me," I muttered, slipping my phone back in my pocket.

Jasmine seemed stubborn, but the way she was squirming in my lap at the party? She was definitely feeling me.

"So you *are* stalking her!" Jelani teased.

"Whatever, nigga. You all in my shit—what about you? I saw you sucking on her friend's face at the club."

"Monica? She cool. I might hit her up tonight," he said. "Oh—and you know Jasmine's just here on a contract, right? She's a travel nurse."

"Damn, why you know so much about her?" I asked, feeling a weird twinge in my chest that I chalked up to my wound acting up.

"Women talk. Monica and I been texting."

"Yeah, well, worry about your own shit," I muttered.

All this meant was that I had to apply some pressure. And lucky for me, that was my speciality.

CHAPTER 8
JASMINE MILLER

"I'm really glad you texted me," Amir said as we walked to his car.

"Me too. Dinner was really good," I smiled at him.

Amir was a dude I'd met on a dating app before I moved to Atlanta, and he was quickly becoming a favorite. Tall, brown-skinned, clean-cut, with shoulder-length locs. He was smaller than what I usually liked, but claimed he did CrossFit—so I figured there was some hidden strength under there somewhere.

He wasn't flashy and I liked that. Tonight, he had on khaki shorts and a navy blue polo—very laid-back and neat. It suited him. I think he was some kind of software engineer… or maybe he worked for the CDC. Either way, he had a little bit of money and liked taking me out.

He had been on his best behavior all night, and I was pretty sure I was gonna invite him up for a nightcap when he dropped me off.

Amir drove for a few minutes before he pulled into a strip mall parking lot.

"What are we doing out here?" I asked, looking around,

confused. The lot was packed, which wasn't unusual. I quickly learned that in Atlanta, even a Juicy Crab could turn into a club.

He laughed. "I know this looks sketchy, but there's a lounge here."

I bunched up my face. "Amir, just so you know, my homegirl has my location—and I got a switchblade that I know how to use. No funny shit."

"Damn, that's violent," he said, trying to laugh it off, but he looked a little nervous.

We crossed the lot and entered a dimly lit lounge with a DJ tucked in the corner. A few tables and booths were filled with folks drinking and puffing on hookah.

"Is this… a hookah lounge?" I hissed as we found an empty booth.

"Yeah," he grinned. "This is my cousin Honcho's spot. It's a cool lil' joint to vibe and chill."

Honcho. That name sounded familiar. Monica used to mess with him and had been begging me to come here for months.

"Oh." My shoulders slumped. I knew he saw the disappointment on my face.

"Oh?" he echoed, picking up my mood shift. "You don't like hookah?"

"No, I don't. And you would've known that had you asked me," I rolled my eyes and grabbed the drink menu. "Let me guess—you got a hookah at your place too?"

He looked away, embarrassed. And he should've been. The nerve of him thinking I was the type to be impressed by mango shisha and a grass wall.

"My bad, Jas. It won't happen again," he said, resting a hand on my thigh.

"It's fine," I replied as I moved his hand. "Enjoy your lil hookah. I'm gonna drink on your dime."

After a few espresso martinis, I was feeling a little less annoyed. Amir wasn't a terrible conversationalist, but this spot still wasn't my scene. I pulled out my phone to text Monica, hoping she could come save me.

Girl, Amir got me at Honcho's hookah spot. You wanna come through?

Monica: Oh, now you're at a hookah lounge?

Not by choice. I didn't know he was bringing me here. Come spend his money with me.

Monica: Sorry, boo. No can do. Jelani's coming over tonight 😈

Ew, Cash's brother? Y'all been talking?

Monica: Uh, yeah. That nigga is fine and paid. I'm tryna have some fun with him. I'm telling you, you should talk to Cash. Y'all looked real cute together.

Hell no. You forgot I got in a fight that night? I'm good off him.

I sighed and slid my phone back into my purse.

"I'm gonna run to the restroom, then we can head out," Amir said, kissing me on the cheek. I forced a weak smile and nodded. As soon as he was out of sight, I let out a deep breath. That nightcap was off the table, and I was debating on blocking him after he dropped me off.

I threw back the last of my martini as the doorbell over the entrance chimed. I looked up and nearly choked on my drink when I saw Cash stroll in, that cocky-ass smile spreading across his face the moment our eyes met.

"What did I do in a past life to deserve this?" I muttered under my breath as he walked over.

"Sup, sweetheart?" he said, sliding next to me.

I groaned, trying to shift away from him. "Are you stalking me?"

I hated the way he looked sexy without even trying. He had on camo cargo shorts, a white Rhude Wear tee, fresh retro Jordans, and a big-face Rolex—the complete opposite of Amir.

"You not happy to see me?" he asked, draping an arm over my shoulder and pulling me in close.

"Um, Jasmine?"

Amir was standing at the edge of the table. His face twisted in confusion as his eyes bounced between me and Cash.

Heat rushed to my cheeks. This was beyond messy.

"Amir, we can go. He's nobody," I said quickly, trying to stand.

But Cash's hand clamped down on my thigh possessively.

Goosebumps prickled across my skin as I sank back into the booth, folding my arms over my chest.

"We just talking, baby," Cash said smoothly, his drawl thick and syrupy.

I bit the inside of my cheek, feeling heat spread between my legs. *Why the hell did he have to sound like that?*

Amir's eyes dropped to Cash's hand still gripping my leg. The confusion on his face flipped to irritation, real fast.

"Jasmine, you got me taking your ass out when you got a whole nigga already?" he gritted.

I peeled Cash's off, shaking my head. "He's not my man."

"All you bitches are the same," Amir laughed bitterly to himself.

"Excuse me?" I barked, jumping to my feet. "First of all, I told you I was dating other people. And this nigga?"—I pointed a finger at Cash—"He's not even one of them!"

"I'm supposed to believe that?" Amir scoffed. "Man, you was just using me for a free meal."

"A free—"

THUD.

My stomach dropped, hearing something heavy hit the table.

Here we fucking go.

Cash rested his hand on his gun.

"Choose your next words carefully, my nigga," he said, eyes locked on Amir like he was just waiting for an excuse to shoot him.

"What is your problem?" I hissed, sinking back down beside him. I looked around. A few people were now blatantly watching us. I tried pushing his hand onto his lap, but he had a death grip on that thing.

He didn't even flinch. His gaze stayed on Amir, who suddenly didn't seem so tough. That big dog act disappeared the moment he saw what Cash was holding.

"Man, fuck this," Amir spat, puffing up his chest, trying to sound hard. "Your pussy ain't worth all this shit."

Cash was out of the booth, moving faster than I could process.

CRACK.

The sound of metal meeting flesh made me gasp as he pistol-whipped Amir across the face.

Amir hit the floor, howling as he clutched his forehead, blood gushing from the wound.

"Bron, get this bitch ass nigga out my face before I really fuck him up," Cash called out.

The bouncer, Bron, was on it. He scooped Amir off the floor and dragged him to the door. Amir didn't even try to fight back—just held his face and let himself get tossed out like garbage.

Cash rolled his shoulders, sitting down like he hadn't just pistol-whipped a man in public.

"You didn't have to do that," I snapped, still trying to catch my breath. "What if he presses charges?"

Cash let out a deep-bellied laugh, showing off his perfect smile.

"That nigga not stupid enough to press charges," he said, putting his gun back into the waistband of his pants. "He think just 'cause his people own this spot that he got pull, but I own the building. So, it's whatever."

"Uh huh." I grabbed my phone, already pulling up the Uber app.

"Who you calling?" he asked, leaning over to peek at my screen.

"Damn, nigga, you not my daddy!" I fussed, elbowing him.

"But I could be," he whispered in my ear, kissing my neck.

My mouth fell open—the audacity.

He snatched the phone from my hand and stood, striding toward the exit.

"Hey!" I yelled as I grabbed my purse and chased after him.

He was leaning against a blacked-out Range Rover, smirking and holding my phone hostage between his fingers.

"What'd you do?" I demanded, snatching it back.

It immediately lit up, and **Big Daddy Cash** flashed across the screen.

I gave him the nastiest look I could muster. “I’m gonna block you.”

“Go ‘head,” he said, completely unfazed, nodding toward the open passenger door. “Get in the car, sweetheart.”

“No.” I planted my hands on my hips. “You can’t just show up—”

“Jasmine.” His voice dropped low, and he stepped into my space. “Get in the car before I pick your thick ass up and put you in.”

“I don’t need you to take me anywhere.” I held my chin up. “For all you know, I got another date lined up for tonight.”

“Oh yeah?” he laughed dryly. “Are your other dudes corny like that nigga Amir? ‘Cause I’ll follow you to the next spot and press you there too. And I wish they’d try to stop me.”

My heart thudded so hard I could feel it in my ears. He was doing too much, and it had no business turning me on the way it did.

I blew out a frustrated breath, bumping his shoulder as I climbed into the truck and slammed the door.

“I know you in your feelings, but don’t be slamming my shit like that,” he said, starting the engine.

I cut my eyes at him but kept quiet. I was already embarrassed and irritated on multiple levels.

“So, you not gonna tell me where you live so I can drop you off?”

“I’m surprised you don’t already know,” I said. “Since you clearly stalked me here.”

He didn’t say anything, turning up the music as he pulled out of the lot.

I closed my eyes and tried to steady my breathing. My heart was still racing from what happened in the lounge. I wasn't sure it was from seeing Amir getting his face smashed or from how Cash had managed to hijack another evening from me.

"How'd you know where I was?" I finally asked, breaking the silence.

He shrugged, keeping his eyes fixed on the road as he turned on 85.

"Fucking Monica," I muttered. She was with Jelani—it made sense. I was gonna curse her ass out next time I saw her.

"So, you make it a habit of dealing with corny-ass niggas?" he asked as if we were casually catching up.

"Why do you care about who I'm dealing with?" I shot back. "And Amir was nice."

"Nice?" he scoffed. "Baby, that dweeb was dressed like he was headed to the golf course and took you to a hookah lounge. Be serious."

That pulled a reluctant laugh out of me. "I told him that too," I admitted. "He just… assumed. But I had a few drinks and made the most of it."

He shook his head. "Nah. You too fine to be 'making the best of it.'"

"Thanks," I said softly.

He glanced over, tongue sliding across his bottom lip as his eyes dropped to my thighs. I squeezed them together and turned back to the window.

We fell quiet again, and every now and then I could feel him watching me. And truthfully, I couldn't stop myself from looking at him either.

It was something about the way Cash carried himself—like he was God's gift—that pissed me off and turned me on at the same time.

When we finally pulled up to my building, I looked over at him and narrowed my eyes. "So you really did know where I lived."

A smile tugged at his lips. "Let me walk you to the door."

I should've told his ass no and shut this whole thing down. But I didn't. I opened the door, stepped out, and felt him close behind me. I made sure to switch my hips a little harder, knowing he was watching my every move.

I fumbled with my keys at the door—my hands shaking partly from the nerves and the heat of his stare.

"I want to take you out on a date," he said, tilting my chin up so I had to look at him.

"I'm not sure that's a good idea, Cash." My voice came out quieter than I wanted.

He pulled me in, and my body melted against his like it was the most natural thing in the world.

"Yeah, aight," he murmured, dipping his head to nuzzle the side of my neck. His hand slid down my back, caressing the bare skin. I let out a soft moan when he pressed into me, the thick bulge in his shorts brushing up against my thigh. I clutched the hem of his shirt to steady myself, feeling my knees threatening to buckle.

"Why you fighting me, Jas?" he whispered. I felt my panties dampen as his lips traced the shell of my ear.

I didn't have a good answer. At this point, I was ready to let him fuck me on the hood of his car.

But he stepped back before I could say anything, leaving me panting and flushed.

"I'ma holla at you," he said, flashing that same grin and turning back to the street like he hadn't just gotten me all worked up.

"I hate you!" I yelled after him, voice shaky.

He didn't look back—just threw up the deuces, got in his truck, and drove off.

Dickhead.

CHAPTER 9
CASH "MONEY" BANKS

"You know you ain't have to come," Slim said from the backseat.

Jelani's little jumpoff came through and confirmed what we already suspected—Rahmel's people were the ones that shot up the block party.

"Nah. Niggas wanna try and kill me? They gon' have to see my face before they die," I gritted. I hadn't moved like this since Pops got killed. What they didn't get was he made sure we were built for this life long before he died. It didn't matter that I was on a football scholarship or that Jelani was in private school.

"How many did she say usually be in there?" I asked Jelani.

"Five on a good day. But she said they're lazy as fuck—just be in there bullshittin' and playing XBOX," he said, pulling his ski mask down and checking the safety on his gun. "We robbin' these niggas too. I'm tight I had to leave my shorty's house early for this."

"Oh, you and Monica a thing now?" I asked, tugging my own mask into place.

"Not officially. But she knows what it is."

Fontaine nodded toward the house. "Ayo, look."

A pretty dark-skinned woman stepped onto the porch with a baby balanced on her hip and headed straight for the Audi truck parked out front.

"This nigga got his girl coming in and out the trap?" Slim shook his head.

We all watched as she buckled the baby into the car seat and pulled off. Ain't no way in hell I'd bring my girl—let alone a baby—into a spot that could get hit any second. That's sloppy as fuck. But at least she left before we went in. No need to traumatize her more than she will be once I killed her bitch ass baby daddy.

We waited an extra ten minutes to make sure she didn't double back. Thankfully, the block was dead. A few junkies were hanging around the bandos, but the Eastland Crew didn't sell on this street, so we weren't worried about lookouts.

"Aight, let's move," I said, popping the car door. The others slid out behind me—Slim and Jelani circled around to the back while Fontaine and I crept up the sagging porch.

Fontaine looked over at me as we took our positions on either side of the door.

Go time.

I stepped up and kicked the door off its flimsy hinges with my black Air Forces.

The music was blasting, so it took them a second to realize what was happening.

"What the—"

I popped the one sitting closest to the door in the leg. He screamed, clutching his knee as blood soaked through his jeans. That got the attention of the other four, who were glued to the Madden game on the TV.

Daemon, the nigga I came for, reached for his strap just as Slim and Jelani stormed through the back of the house. Slim hit him over the head with his gun, knocking him out cold.

"Turn this shit down!" I barked.

Fontaine shot the Bluetooth speaker, which cut the noise instantly, minus the dude crying on the floor and the game still running on the TV.

Hands went up fast. They didn't even try to put up a fight. Fucking pathetic.

"This y'all stash house?" I bunched up my face, scanning the room. The shit was trifling—it smelled like stale sweat and weed. Empty takeout containers and bottles of Olde English were scattered all over the carpet, which was crusted up with God knows what. It was trash like the niggas who ran it. "How the fuck y'all get anything done in here?"

Jelani clapped his hands and stepped into the middle of the room. "Here's what's finna happen. Y'all getting robbed today. Wasn't the plan, but my girl's mad I left early—and now I gotta buy her something nice to make up for it."

"And your boss is dying," I deadpanned.

I looked around. "Which one of y'all drove the day of the block party?"

They all turned to the dude I shot.

"Bet." I raised my gun and put one in his head. Blood splattered on the wall behind him.

"Now, show him where the stash at," I ordered, nodding at Jelani. "And starting today, we're taking forty percent off everything y'all make."

Two of them stood, visibly trembling. Jelani followed close behind with his gun trained on their backs.

Daemon groaned on the floor, starting to come to.

I nudged him with my foot. "Wakey, wakey, bitch."

He blinked up at me, dazed. "The fuck is this?"

"A stick up," I replied, nodding at Slim to grab him. He yanked Daemon off the floor and dumped him onto one of the filthy couches.

I pulled off my ski mask and leaned in. "Let me ask you something, Daemon. How the fuck did you think this was gonna go?"

His eyes went wide when he saw my face.

"You had to have known that, whether I lived or died, someone was coming for you."

"You dumped Rahmel's body on my mama's porch!" he spat.

"Yeah, well, your cousin was a thief. Did you know that?" I asked, watching his face tighten. "I see. Let me guess—he told you he'd put the family onto whatever bullshit he was building on the side?"

"Fuck you."

Jelani and Fontaine came back upstairs, lugging two heavy duffle bags each.

I sucked my teeth. "Look at you. About to go join that nigga in hell."

Jelani stood over him. "Yo, how you got your baby mom and your kid in this shit?"

"Don't touch my girl!" Daemon yelled, his eyes welling up.

Why was it that these niggas only seemed to remember their families at the end? Not when they were stealing shit from me. Not when they were lighting up a block party full of kids.

"Ain't no one touching her, bruh. I'm not that heartless," I said. "You see, Toya got a nice life insurance payout. The least I can do is make sure your girl is straight for a year. But from now on, the Eastland Crew works for BC. And when you see Rahmel? Tell him I said 'fuck you'."

I fired two shots to his head and watched his lifeless body slump back, eyes still open.

"The rest of you niggas get the fuck out!" I roared.

Slim was already dumping gasoline everywhere, soaking the couch and curtains. The others damn near tripped over each other scrambling to the door.

I grabbed a lighter off the coffee table and sparked it, setting one of the cheap curtains on fire. Flames licked up the fabric, smoke quickly filling up the room.

"Money, we out," Slim called, tossing the empty can on the ground. The house was basically a tinderbox, and the flames spread fast. Fontaine slammed the trunk shut, loading the last bag, just as the windows exploded—glass raining onto the pavement.

A sick sense of satisfaction filled me, reigniting that old hunger I'd buried for years.

"That shit's gonna blow any second," Jelani said, getting in the car. The house groaned as flames and black smoke filled the sky. In the distance, the wail of sirens grew louder.

My phone buzzed.

Future Wife: Did you delete the dating apps off my phone??

Why would you need apps when you have me?

Future Wife: Something is really wrong with you, Cash.

Jelani shoved me. "Fuck you cheesing about? Twelve 'bout to be on our ass."

I laughed, tossing the phone on the console. Slim climbed in last, slamming the door as I peeled off. Red and blue lights flashed past us, racing in the opposite direction towards the fire.

This was just the beginning. Nairobi was still working Kyree. It was time to dig out the rot threatening my crew next. No way in hell I was letting these niggas ruin the legacy my pops built.

CHAPTER 10
JASMINE MILLER

"Do you think you'll come home after your contract ends?" my mother asked hopefully.

Her phone was propped up on the kitchen counter, giving me a full view of her washing dishes. This was our weekly FaceTime date—our way of putting physical eyes on each other, even though we talked almost daily.

"Mommy, you asked me that yesterday," I said, walking into my closet.

She smiled, eyes crinkling. "I know. I just miss you, that's all."

I sighed softly. The four months I'd been in Atlanta were the longest I'd ever been away from home. I was a diehard New Yorker, through and through. When I initially decided to try out travel nursing, I kept it local to the tri-state area. It was great for a while, but after the pandemic, I decided I wanted a real change of scenery that wasn't another borough. I went back and forth for months before applying to Peachtree Memorial. I broke my lease, put most of my stuff in storage, and came down here.

Atlanta was a completely different world from what I was

used to, and working at Peachtree felt like I was in the trenches most days, but Monica had quickly folded me into her friend group. Shit, I even had a cute little dating life— at least before Cash pulled that stunt with Amir. I was having fun, but I really needed to get a new contract. I wasn't sure how much longer I could last.

"Maybe I'll come up in a few weeks to see you and daddy," I said, making a mental note to check flights this week.

"Yes! We'd love that," she beamed.

"Where's daddy anyway?" I asked, rifling through my closet for something to wear to brunch.

"Chile, he's with Leonard down at the athletic club, playing pickleball," she shook her head. "All I need is for him to come home limping 'cause he set off his arthritis again."

We chatted a little longer before hanging up.

As I settled on my outfit, my phone buzzed with a text.

Big Daddy Cash: When you gon' let me take you out, Jas?

I couldn't stop the smile creeping across my face. It'd been over a week, but I was still thinking about how he had me damn near drooling outside my building the last time I saw him.

Never

Big Daddy Cash: I thought you blocked me?

Getting ready for a date, ttyl!

Big Daddy Cash: Stop fucking playing with me, Jasmine.

I snickered, tossing the phone on the bed as I headed for the shower.

The chemistry between us was off the charts—but what did I look like getting caught up with a street dude at thirty-six?

It didn't matter that Monica swore up and down that Cash's hands were more clean than dirty these days. I wasn't naive. He and his brother were too quick to pull out their guns like they were invincible. That was a young girl's game, and I loved my career too much to risk it.

But that sexy ass southern drawl? The way my whole body reacted when he brushed against me?

I chewed on my bottom lip, feeling a tingle between my thighs at the memory of his lips skimming my neck, and that bulge in his pants that let me know he had something heavy between his legs. Yeah… if we ever slept together, it'd be a wrap.

I threw on a white tank-top bodysuit and a pair of high-waisted shorts to keep it simple but cute. After doing a quick makeup look, throwing on a few gold bangles and some gold hoops, I was good to go.

I stepped outside and slid my sunglasses on as the heat of the midday sun hit me. I was halfway across the sidewalk when the passenger window of a white Porsche Cayenne rolled down.

I nearly tripped when I spotted Cash in the driver's seat, scowling.

I rolled my eyes and kept walking. I didn't have time to entertain his antics today.

"Word, Jasmine?" he called out, the irritation clear in his voice.

I adjusted my purse strap on my shoulder without breaking my stride.

"Now you pissing me off. Come here," he said.

I paused. He was the type to cause a scene, and I didn't need drama outside my building. Sucking my teeth, I turned and walked over to his car.

"What do you want? I got a reservation to make," I said, leaning into the passenger window.

"Let me give you a ride so me, you, and your new nigga can get acquainted," he said, mugging me.

"I was just fucking with you!" I rolled my eyes. "You really came all the way here 'cause of that text?"

"What I tell you the last time I saw you?" he asked, raising an eyebrow.

I waved him off. "And *I* told *you*—you don't run shit. I'm meeting Monica for brunch. I'm only telling you so you don't cut up outside my building."

He gave me a hard look before tapping something on the car's display—a call rang out on speaker.

"Yo," Jelani answered groggily.

"Monica with you?" Cash asked him, his eyes never leaving mine.

"Nah," Jelani yawned. "She's said she's getting brunch with her cousin and your nurse."

Cash hung up, looking smug.

"See? I told you, you psycho." I threw my hands up.

"I'm taking you out tonight."

"Huh?"

"You can't hear now? We're going on a date, Jasmine. Have your pretty ass ready by eight."

"You can't just tell me we're going on a date," I protested.

"Clearly, I can. You seem to respond better to orders than when I'm tryna be nice. See you at eight, sweetheart." He winked and rolled the window up.

$

"I got a bone to pick with you," I said, jabbing a finger at Monica.

She frowned, her hands twisting her faux locs into a messy bun. "What'd I do now?"

"Did you tell Jelani I was at the hookah lounge with Amir?"

"Um, why would I do that?" she replied, scrunching her face up.

"'Cause I hit you up to come through, and magically Jelani just happened to be going to your place that same night."

She burst out laughing so loudly that a few people turned to look at us. "Girl, that nigga was blowing my back out all night. Trust me, nobody was trying to get intel for Cash."

"Cash who?" Rochelle cut in.

Rochelle and Monica were cousins who moved like twins with how in sync they were. They shared the same sienna-brown skin, wide doe eyes, and heart-shaped face, but Rochelle carried an extra thirty pounds. We instantly clicked over our love of good food, reality TV, and shit talking.

"Big Money Banks," Monica grinned at her knowingly.

Rochelle's eyebrows shot up. "Oh, he's *fine,* fine."

"He's a fucking pain in my ass," I huffed. "Tell me why he showed up at the hookah lounge and pistol-whipped Amir?"

Monica's eyes went wide. "Wait—was he mad you were out with another guy?"

"Not even," I sighed. "Amir came out the restroom and

saw Cash sitting with me. I told him Cash was nobody, but then Amir started talking to me all kinds of crazy. I didn't even know he had it in him to be honest."

Monica and Rochelle exchanged a look, then busted out laughing.

"What's so funny?"

"Sorry," Rochelle said, still laughing. "It just sounds like Money was sticking up for you."

"I could've handled Amir on my own!"

"Jas, Amir should've gotten slapped for taking you to a hookah lounge," Monica said, pouring our drinks. "I been asking you to go since I met you, and you always tell me no. You should be grateful—Money saved you from a wack night and probably some wack dick."

"The date was fine *until* the hookah lounge. But that brings me back to the question—how the hell did he find me?"

"Maybe it was a coincidence?" Rochelle offered with a half-shrug.

I shook my head. "No way. That man walked in like he knew exactly where I'd be."

"Maybe he's having you followed," Monica joked.

Sadly, that wasn't even far-fetched—Cash already knew where I lived without me telling him.

"Ugh. He's so annoying. I told him I had a date today just to fuck with him, and when I walked out, this fool was parked out front waiting for me."

"Did you tell him it was a joke?" Monica asked.

"You know I did! Then he called Jelani to see if you were with him." I downed my mimosa and immediately refilled my glass. "And speaking of Jelani…"

"Oh, yes!" Rochelle exclaimed, turning to Monica. "What's going on with y'all?"

Monica's cheeks flushed as she tried to hide her smile behind her glass.

"Aww, shit. Mo', this man got you blushing?" I teased. "I thought you were going to let him trick off on you and keep it light."

"I swear I was," Monica sighed dreamily. "But we've been spending a lot of time together. He stays over a lot... been on a few really nice dates. He wants to take me to Miami next month." She traced the rim of her glass with her finger, staring off into space with stars in her eyes.

"Girl, you are gone," Rochelle laughed. "Jas, if you don't want Money, let me know. I'm trying to see if big bro got that same kind of energy."

She was clearly joking, but it still rubbed me the wrong way.

"He says we're going on a date tonight," I admitted, rolling my eyes.

"But I thought you *hated* him," Monica said, throwing my words back at me.

"Ever since that man got shot and rolled into the ER, it's been nothing but chaos every time I see him. Plus, he's into illegal shit—I'm too grown for all that."

"Jasmine, that man's money is long," Rochelle said, leaning back in her chair. "You're not from here, so you don't really know how deep this shit goes. But this ain't no local street king type shit. Cash took whatever his pops left him and quadrupled it. The cops don't bother him because he keeps the other crews in check. He's got politicians on his payroll—"

"Allegedly," Monica cut in, smirking.

"Allegedly, allegedly," Rochelle echoed with a wave. "But real talk? He invests in the community without shaking people down too hard. The Banks family is easily worth a few hundred million."

"I bet he's gonna take you somewhere fancy," Monica added with a nudge.

"You gotta do it for the plot," Rochelle said, raising her glass. It's drier than the Sahara Desert over here, so I'm living vicariously through you. I want a full report."

♡$♡

I walked through my building's lobby later that afternoon, thankful to escape the heat and into some AC.

"Ms. Miller!" Rayna, the concierge on duty, called out.

"Hey, what's up?" I asked, heading toward her desk.

"This came for you." She lifted a long, rectangular gift box tied with a sleek black bow and set a matching black gift bag beside it.

I frowned. "That's weird, I didn't order anything."

"A real fine man dropped it off at the start of my shift and told me to make sure I handed it to you personally."

My heart skipped. *Cash.*

"Oh, okay—thanks," I said, trying to play it cool as I scooped up the boxes.

Curiosity and anticipation grew as the elevator climbed to my floor, and by the time I got inside my apartment, I was practically buzzing.

I kicked off my shoes and dropped the packages onto the couch before slipping into yoga shorts and an old T-shirt. Settling cross-legged on the rug, I reached for the gift box first. Tucked in the bow was a small handwritten card:

BE A GOOD GIRL AND WEAR THIS FOR ME. – MONEY

I bit my lip, untied the ribbon, and lifted the lid. My breath hitched as I peeled back the tissue paper to reveal a black leather dress.

"Shit," I whispered, running my fingers over the buttery material. I loved fashion, but I'd never bought anything this expensive. My eyes nearly popped out of my head when I saw the Versace tag—this was easily a few thousand dollars. The corset-style top and gold hardware screamed high fashion and sex.

"I didn't even know they made stuff like this in my size," I muttered, reaching for the gift bag next. My mouth dropped as I pulled out a sleek pair of Tom Ford stilettos.

"Cash, you aren't playing fair," I whined, scrambling for my phone.

I FaceTimed the only person who'd understand.

"*¡Que lo que!*" Amber chirped, her grin lighting up the screen.

"Sis, you busy?" My stomach flipped as I glanced at the time. It was 5:00 p.m.—if I was going to be ready in time, I needed to start now.

"Never too busy for you, bestie."

Amber and I had been best friends since middle school. She was one of the few people who encouraged me to take the contract in Atlanta. She reminded me that if it sucked, there was no shame in coming back home.

I sighed dramatically, staring at the open box. "Remember that fine ass dude I told you about—the one who got shot a few months ago? Then I ran into him at the club recently?"

"Mmhm."

"Well, I saw him again today before brunch. He told me

we're going on a date… and I just came home to a leather Versace dress and Tom Ford heels."

"Bitch?!" Amber shrieked, jumping off her couch.

"I know, girl. Apparently, he's a real big deal here, but he's… outside," I whisper-yelled like I didn't live alone.

"How outside we talking?"

"Like Marcus."

She sucked in a breath. "Damn, I haven't thought about him in a minute. Isn't he still locked up?"

I threw up my hand. "Who cares?!" I said. "Point is, I'm too old for this right? I already punched a bitch over him, and he crashed a date. Tell me this is a bad idea."

"Friend, I don't think it's that deep," she chuckled. "You're not marrying him, Jas. Let him spread his bread on you—clearly, he got it."

"Everything about him is so intense. He gets under my skin."

"Have you met you?" she teased. "Y'all sound like a match made in heaven."

I rolled my eyes because she wasn't wrong. It'd been a while since I met a man who wasn't intimidated by my smart mouth.

"This shit goes left, we're fighting next time I'm home," I warned.

She laughed. "Yeah, alright. Just make sure you send some pics so I can see the full 'fit."

We ended the call, and I stared at the dress in its box.

This date was beginning to feel like the point of no return.

By 7:55, I was ready to turn heads. I was pleased with my decision to slick my hair back into a high ponytail. The Versace dress hugged my curves without feeling restrictive. The stilettos made my legs look longer, which I loved. I kept the accessories simple—diamond studs, my gold J initial necklace, and the Van Cleef bracelet my parents got me for my thirty-fifth birthday.

I snapped a few selfies in front of my full-length mirror to send to Amber. I had to admit—Cash had impeccable taste.

My phone buzzed. *Speak of the devil.*

"You ready for me?"

The deep timbre of Cash's voice sliding through the phone made my pussy thump.

"Do I have a choice?" I asked, trying to sound unbothered even though my palms felt clammy.

"Nah, you don't," he laughed. "Come downstairs so I can see how good you look."

"Here I come."

I grabbed my clutch off the dining room table. Running my hands over my hair, I took one last look in the mirror and headed out.

My heels clicked against the marble floor of the quiet lobby. Outside, Cash's Cayenne sat at the curb like it had been earlier—but this time, he was leaning against the passenger side. A few women walking past gave him double takes, but he paid them no mind. His eyes were locked on me, smile widening as I approached.

"Okay, okay—" he nodded, holding his hand out. "—you got that shit on, sweetheart."

My cheeks warmed as I placed my hand into his.

He spun me around slowly, his eyes drinking in every inch of me. "I don't know if I want anyone else seeing you in this," he murmured, wrapping his arms around my waist. His hands drifted lower to cup my ass.

"Behave," I said, swatting his chest playfully.

He licked his lips. "I don't know how behaved I can be when you look like this," he chuckled, before opening the door for me.

"So where we going that you got me all gussied up?" I asked once he got in and started the car.

"You don't like surprises?"

"After all this?" I looked down at the leather dress and heels.

"The limit does not exist," he said with a grin.

I blinked. "Nigga, did you just quote *Mean Girls*?"

"What? It's a classic," he said, completely serious.

I lost it, doubling over with laughter. "I'm sorry—but picturing your gangsta ass watching a Lindsey Lohan movie is hilarious."

"I contain multitudes, baby."

We laughed and kept the conversation light until he pulled up in front of *Le Flambeau*. I'd seen the French steakhouse all over social media but never had a reason to go. And I definitely couldn't afford it on a nurse's salary.

Cash handed the keys to the valet and came around to open my door.

"Let me find out you got home training," I smirked, taking his hand.

He laughed and kept a hold on me as we walked inside.

Le Flambeau wasn't your basic steakhouse like Ruth's Chris—it exuded an old-money vibe. Dim lighting cast a warm glow over the polished marble floors. Warm wood paneling wrapped around the room, and faint notes of jazz music floated in the background.

"Ah, Mr. Banks," the host greeted us warmly. He was an older white man with thin brown hair slicked back into a ponytail. "So happy to have you back. Your usual table is ready." He clapped his hands together, turning to lead the way.

Cash placed a hand on the small of my back as we followed. Looking around, I noticed the restaurant was completely empty. There were no other guests and no servers moving between tables. Just us.

"Cash, why is no one here?" I whispered.

"Because I rented it out for a private dinner," he said with a sly grin. "Surprise."

The host led us to a secluded booth in the back.

"Carlton will be serving you tonight. Enjoy," he said with a slight bow before leaving.

I turned to Cash. "You booked out the entire restaurant? Why?"

"One because, I knew how good you'd look in that dress —and I'd hate to shoot a motherfucker on our first date," he said, his gaze lingering on me. "Two, because I can."

I took a moment to really look at him. It should've been illegal for someone to look this good. His black ribbed silk shirt hugged his chest, showing off the tattoos snaking down his arm like art. And his cream slacks were too perfect to be off the rack. The combination of the Patek on his wrist and the thin gold chain around his neck screamed money and power.

"You showing out tonight, huh?" I teased, picking up the menu.

"Yeah, 'cause I'm tryna show you I'm serious," Cash said, sliding his hand onto my thigh.

"Serious about what? You don't even know me for real," I replied, trying to ignore the heat blooming through me from his touch.

"So, tell me about you then."

"There's nothing really to tell," I chuckled, setting the menu down. "I'm a travel nurse. Been here a few months. This contract ends soon and I haven't decided if I'm staying or going home."

"Where's home? You from up north?" he asked.

I frowned. "Up north?"

"New York," he clarified.

"Queens, born and raised."

"I knew I wasn't trippin' when I heard that accent."

Carlton smiled. "Good evening, Mr. Banks. Always a pleasure," he turned to me. "What can I get you to drink?"

"I'll have a glass of the rosé," I said.

"And your usual, Mr. Banks?" Carlton asked. Cash nodded.

As soon as he stepped away, I couldn't help myself.

"*Your usual, Mr. Banks?*" I mimicked in a faux-posh accent. "Damn, how often do you come here? And why does everyone know you? You the unofficial mayor of Atlanta or something?"

Cash smirked. "When shit isn't hectic, maybe once a month. But yeah—my name rings bells out here."

"Hm," I hummed, pretending to look over the menu again.

"Hm, what?" He watched me closely. "Why you acting shy when we both know you got a slick mouth?"

"How freely can I speak?" I raised an eyebrow.

"Say what's on your mind, shawty."

"I know what you do," I said.

He cocked his head. "You know, or you heard?"

"What's the difference?"

He grinned. "Depends who you heard it from. If it wasn't from me, it's probably bullshit."

"You want me to speak or nah?" I narrowed my eyes.

"My bad. Go 'head." He motioned for me to continue.

"The first time I met you, you were bleeding out and on death's door. So I know you're into some questionable shit," I said, watching his face. He stayed neutral, so I kept going. "Obviously, there's something between us—annoying as that is—but you come with a lot, Cash. And I'm not sure I'm willing to gamble my peace or my nursing license for it."

I exhaled, brushing my fingers through my ponytail.

"My ex lived this kind of life, and he's doing twenty years off a RICO. I stopped dealing with niggas like that in my twenties."

I left out the part about how Marcus hounded me for years after he got locked up. I had to intercept the mail, not wanting my parents to ask why I was getting letters from a federal prison. Or how he'd have people call me on three-way just to talk, even when I'd told him to stop.

"I'm not them, Jasmine," Cash said, shaking his head. Carlton showed up with our drinks and took our dinner orders. Once he left, Cash pulled me closer, his voice dropping low.

"I'm not gonna sit here and pretend I'm a saint—we both know I'm not. But don't lump me in with those other niggas. I worked my ass off for everything I have. I'm not some low-level hustler asking to stash shit in your apartment."

I traced a finger down the stem of my wine glass and let his words sink in.

"So that's it? I'm just supposed to accept that you're a big-time dealer and move like life is normal?"

Cash cupped my chin, his thumb brushed my jaw as his deep brown eyes bore into mine.

"You don't have to accept anything but me. But don't assume you know what I do. If you want to know, ask me. I'll tell you. What I won't do is drag you into anything. If we ever get to that point, it'll be on your terms. Until then, let's just enjoy the night."

Something in his tone shifted the energy between us, and conversation flowed easier than expected. We talked about what brought me to Atlanta, his childhood, his scholarship to

Duke, and even a little bit about his father's death. He didn't go into too much detail about his work, but it was clear he'd been in some shit. And there was no regret in his voice, just an acceptance that everything he'd done was all part of the game.

By the time our entrees arrived, I was floating off my third glass of rosé. The restaurant definitely lived up to the hype.

"So…" Cash said, cutting into his porterhouse. "You still hate me?"

I paused, my fork hovering over my plate. I thought back to how he'd gotten me so worked up last week.

I cleared my throat. "I hate you less."

"Here you go," he chuckled, shaking his head.

"You're a bit of a menace."

"You fuck with it, though. Don't lie."

I set my fork down. "I'm stuffed. This was so good."

"You want them to wrap this up for you?"

I nodded, and he signaled for Carlton.

"I'm tryna slide past my people's spot real quick," Cash said, as our plates were cleared.

"I thought you didn't want anyone to see me in this dress?"

"Tuh. Niggas know how I get down in there."

I rolled my eyes because I knew he meant it.

Carlton returned with our leftovers. "I hope you enjoyed your evening," he said, turning to me with a warm smile. "Miss, I hope we'll see you again soon."

"What about the bill?" I asked.

"Jasmine, don't insult me," Cash replied, looking at me like I'd lost my mind.

I laughed under my breath. *Was this what dating a real baller feels like?* Because I could get used to it.

His car was already waiting when we exited the restaurant. We drove a short distance before stopping in front of a small cocktail bar called The Emerald Lounge. Early 2000s hip-hop played as we walked in.

"What up, Mike?" Cash greeted the security guard at the door.

"Cash Money, my nigga!" Mike dapped him up, then gave me a once-over and nodded."This you?"

Cash pulled me into his side. "All me."

"I see you, bruh." Mike grinned as he pulled back the velvet curtain.

The lounge was small and intimate, lit in a soft green glow. Chocolate velvet booths lined the walls. The music was at the perfect level—it was loud enough to vibe to, but low enough for conversation.

Cash led me to a private corner with plush couches.

"What you drinking, baby?" he asked.

"Surprise me."

I watched him walk away, wondering if he knew how easily he commanded a room. Several people came over to shake his hand or dap him up as he waited for our drinks. Another couple walked in and sat at the bar. The man spotted Cash and went over to greet him, but the way Cash's jaw tightened told me he wasn't too thrilled to see him.

The woman with him was stunning. She was tall, with mocha skin, in a black mini dress. Her pin-straight hair fell down her back, and she tossed it over her shoulder like she didn't realize she was the baddest bitch in here. On anyone else, the deep plunge in her dress would've been tacky, but on her it looked like haute couture. She was way too beautiful for the plain-looking dude she was with.

Her eyes met Cash's, and a flash of something passed between them, but she didn't speak.

What was that?

Cash came back with our drinks and placed mine in front of me.

"You know them?" I asked, trying to keep my tone light.

"Who?"

"That couple." I tipped my head toward the bar. "You know them?"

"The dude works for me. Don't know his girl."

"She looked like she knew you," I muttered. She'd been stealing glances at us since Cash sat beside me.

"Come here," he said, pulling me into his lap. "Why you look like you in your head?" He shifted me so my legs were draped over his. I stole one last glimpse at the bar—the couple was gone.

I sipped my drink."Mm. This is good."

"Are you good, though?" His voice dipped lower as his lips brushed my shoulder. His fingers began tracing a slow path up my calf, sending heat surging through me. He moved deliberately slow, teasing, until he reached the hem of my dress.

I adjusted myself in his lap, suddenly aware of how shallow my breathing had become.

"I asked you a question, Jasmine." The rasp in his voice sent a jolt through me as his fingers toyed with the edge of my dress.

I grabbed his wrist. "Cash—" I hissed.

He sank his teeth into my shoulder, just enough to make me arch back against him.

"You not gonna answer me?"

"I'm good, baby," I panted. "But what if someone sees us?"

"I'll shoot a nigga for looking over here," he growled.

This was crazy, I should've stopped him. But my legs

seemed to widen on their own volition as his hand continued its journey under the hem of my dress, his fingers brushing the lace of my thong.

"She wet for me?"

I swear his accent made me even wetter.

Cash took my drink and set it aside. Then, with one slow, deliberate pull, he slid my thong down. I lifted my hips to help him.

"I'm keeping these," he said, shoving them into his pocket.

His hand found its way back up my thighs, teasing over my skin. My nails dug into his arm as he brushed against my clit. My body tightened as he circled it before dipping his between my slick folds.

"Shit. All this for me, Jas?" he muttered, kissing the base of my neck.

I didn't answer. The thrill of possibly being caught made everything more intense. *Better*. My mouth parted with a silent moan, and I bit down on my lip hard.

"Should I let you come?" he asked, voice gritty.

I rocked against him as he pumped his fingers in me.

"Mm…" I nodded, the growing pressure made it hard to think straight.

"Use your words, baby girl."

"Cash, please—" I managed to choke out as he pinched my clit.

Stars exploded behind my eyes. My whole body trembled in his lap as I braced myself against him, riding the wave crashing through me.

"You're doing so good, my baby," he praised, low in my ear. "Nobody knows how nasty you're being for me right now."

"I'm c—" The words died on my lips. I buried my face in

his chest, stifling my cry as another orgasm rolled through me.

Cash slowly pulled his fingers from me, bringing his fingers to his mouth. "Mmm. You taste good as fuck," he groaned, before pressing a kiss to my forehead.

I smoothed my dress down with shaky hands, trying to gather myself. I went to stand, but my legs felt like jelly.

Cash just watched me, looking entirely too pleased with himself.

"You good?" he asked, rising to his feet.

I nodded, even though my heart was still racing and the ghost of his touch still lingered between my thighs.

"Let me get your fine ass home," he said, tossing some money on the table and taking my hand.

Mike nodded as we passed. "Be easy, Money."

Cash continued to be the perfect gentleman, opening the door like I wasn't just coming apart in his lap a few minutes ago.

I sank into the passenger seat, too caught up in the night to say anything. I replayed every second of dinner, our conversation, his touch, the way he made me feel. It wasn't until we were well on our way that I realized how quiet I'd gotten.

"Why you so quiet?" he asked.

"No reason. I had a really good time tonight," I smiled. Truth was, this nigga had me wide open—and we hadn't even kissed yet.

"Me too." He reached over and rested his hand on my thigh, and something about the way it lingered—I couldn't quite put my finger on it, but things felt more serious between us than when the evening started. I knew he felt it too.

When we pulled up to my building, he came around to open my door.

"You sure you straight?" he asked, rubbing my arm.

"I'm good, Cash. Promise," I laughed softly, hoping it'd ease whatever was going through his head. He nodded, but didn't make a move, just looked at me.

I held my breath. *Was he going to kiss me or what?*

"I'll hit you up tomorrow," he said finally, rubbing the back of his neck as he turned to leave.

My shoulders dropped watching him walk back towards his car.

After a few steps, he spun back around, grabbed me and crashed his mouth onto mine.

Weeks of tension finally snapped as we both finally gave in. I melted into his solid frame as his tongue slid into my mouth. He tasted like cognac and sin, and I knew if I wasn't careful he'd become my addiction.

A soft moan escaped me as his hands dropped to my ass, pulling me closer to him. The kiss was softer than I expected, but the hunger was undeniable. My nipples pebbled and the ache between my thighs flared back to life. I could feel my arousal starting to drip down my legs.

Cash broke the kiss with an unsteady breath, his jaw tight like he was trying to hold himself back.

He ran a hand over his face and shook his head. "You 'bout to be a serious fucking problem for me, woman."

I fought the smile tugging at my lips as I turned toward the door.

The feeling was mutual.

Because I was ready to let Cash Banks ruin my life in more ways than one.

CHAPTER 11
CASH "MONEY" BANKS

STILETTOS WAS PACKED FOR CLYDE'S BIRTHDAY PARTY. ME, Jelani, Slim, and Fontaine had p to celebrate our boy—but I had another reason for being here.

Clyde used to roll with us heavy before his girl got pregnant a few years ago. Now he owned a barbershop downtown in one of my buildings. Not that I needed an excuse to hit the strip club, but it worked out because I needed to catch up with Nairobi.

She hadn't hit me up since I bumped into her with Kyree at the Emerald Bar. I knew she'd been working, but I still needed updates. Aside from this shit with the Eastland Crew, things had seemingly returned to normal. Less ODs and no more missing money which meant the New York plug had probably fallen back. Still, my gut told me that was temporary while he and whoever he was working with were taking time to regroup.

I spotted Nairobi walking the floor with two other dancers. Her tiny neon green bikini top and g-string sat high on her hips, leaving barely anything to the imagination.

Fontaine almost choked on his drink when she came into view.

"Well, well, well. If it isn't the infamous Banks Crew," she said, grinning devilishly as she popped her gum. The red light from the stage flickered over her oiled skin.

"Sup—" Jelani started.

"Bambi," she said smoothly with a wink, stepping into our section.

"Sup, Bambi," he repeated, trying not to stare too hard.

She sauntered over to me, trailing a finger down my chest as she leaned in close.

"You gon' have to pay me for a dance, boss man," she whispered.

Out the corner of my eye, I caught Fontaine's hand tighten around his glass, jaw clenched. My boy was really gone over her.

"You know you driving Fontaine crazy, right?" I said, peeling a Franklin off the stack beside me.

"That man ain't worried about me," she laughed, tucking the bill into her bikini top.

She spun in one fluid motion and dropped into my lap, pressing her back against my chest. The lights flashed overhead as she rolled her hips to the beat of the music. You would've thought she was a dancer for real. I gritted my teeth, willing my dick not to brick up. She twirled again, straddling me and looping her arms around my neck.

"Gotta make it look believable. Kyree has eyes in here," she whispered, grinding slowly.

Fontaine shot up from his seat, nose flaring, like he was ready to risk it all. Slim snatched him back down by his collar before he crashed out.

"You 'bout to have my boy swinging on me tonight," I chuckled. "We need to go before he really starts trippin'."

Nairobi glanced back at Fontaine, slowly licking her lips to mess with him before standing and flipping her hair over her shoulder.

“Private dances are five hundred,” she said loud enough for him to hear, and threw one last look his way before strutting out of the section.

I followed behind, careful not to meet his eyes.

“Nigga, don’t be on no dumb shit tonight,” I heard Jelani warn him.

Nai moved through the club like she‘d worked there for years. Yo Gotti boomed through the speakers as we made our way to the private rooms.

Inside, a single pole was mounted on a small center stage. Nairobi sank into a worn leather against the wall, stretching out like she could finally breathe.

“You ain’t right messing with that man’s head,” I said, dropping down beside her.

“He’s drunk,” she shrugged, slipping off her heels with a groan. “Ugh, my feet are killing me.”

She plopped them onto my lap like I was her assistant and let out a satisfied sigh the second I started rubbing them.

“No cameras in here,” she murmured, closing her eyes. “I deactivated them before I clocked in.”

“So you got something for me, or you just wanted to finesse a foot rub?” I asked, working my hands over the balls of her feet.

She cracked one eye open. “Can’t it be both?” she teased, wiggling her toes in my hands.

“I should go get Fontaine—I bet he’d be on his knees doing this right now.”

“Hm.” She sat up on her elbows, eyes gleaming. “Wonder what your little girlfriend would think if she walked in.”

I paused, caught off guard at the mention of Jasmine.

Nai clocked it immediately and bobbed her head.

"Ohh," she said, a slow smile spreading. "You actually like her. That's cute. But, she's not a little… common for you?"

I shoved her feet off my lap. If it was anyone else, I would've snapped, but she was being petty from me curving her a few months ago.

"Nai, I'm not in the mood for this."

"Fine," she huffed, rolling her eyes. "But you owe me big time for this whole thing. Kyree is so fucking wack, I'm tired of pretending I like him."

I leaned back and remembered how that grimy nigga was grinning in my face at the Emerald Lounge like I was stupid. I couldn't wait to put one in his head.

"It was me, Genesis, Portia, and this new girl, Poppi," she continued. "We pulled up to some mansion in College Park."

"Since when Kyree got a spot over there?"

"It wasn't his place."

"He was meeting someone?"

She nodded. "Finally met the New York plug. Some dude named Marcus. He's apparently a big-time hitter trying to expand down here."

I racked my brain trying to place the name. It didn't ring any bells. We never really dealt with niggas from New York like that. Our plug was from Miami—it was closer and less drama.

"Anyway, it was a few niggas from Marcus's crew, Kyree, and some of your folks that I recognized from the file Fontaine gave me."

I exhaled through my nose. "So they did tighten up."

"A little. After y'all handled Rahmel and Daemon, Marcus has been keeping a low profile. But make no mistake—he's had his eye on Atlanta for a minute."

"I don't care where he's from," I said. "Shit don't move here without me giving it the green light."

Nai stood and drifted over to the pole, hooked an arm around it, and twirled lazily.

"I told you—they think you have too much power," she said, not looking at me. "What don't you get, Money? It doesn't matter how fair you are."

She stopped spinning to fix her eyes on me. "They're still salty about what you did to Rahmel and Daemon. And Marcus has them believing he can take you out—or at least carve out a space for them here."

She plopped back down on the couch and slipped her heels back on.

"You said it was some other BC niggas there. Who?"

"Grizz, Chris, and Derrick."

My stomach sank. They were dudes I considered family. Grizz ran our trucks. Derrick and Chris had been running with us since they were in high school. They were supposed to be solid. I trusted them. At least I thought I could.

"These niggas," I muttered, rubbing my jaw.

"Marcus didn't get into too many details while we were around," Nai said, adjusting her bra strap. "But… he made a hell of a first impression."

"How?"

Her brows knitted together. "Poppi's a little green. Sweet as hell, but was jumpy all night. She accidentally bumped into him and spilled some shit on his shoes. It wasn't that deep. She apologized, of course. But Marcus blacked out. He grabbed her by the throat and slammed her into the wall in front of everybody. He called her everything but a child of God, and was looking around daring somebody to say something."

"Kyree ain't say shit?"

She gave me a dry look. "Come on now. You know that bozo didn't do a damn thing but stand there like a deer in headlights."

"So, nobody did anything after he put hands on a woman?"

"Me." She smiled proudly.

Of course she did.

"I hopped in his face and told him he must've lost his mind putting hands on one of my girls."

"Nairobi..."

"What?" She threw her hands up. "Poppi was hysterical, and the rest of them dudes were useless. I wasn't about to let some crazy-ass man from New York think he can treat those girls any kind of way."

"He get physical with you?"

"He tried," she shrugged. "Puffed up his chest real crazy-eyed like that was supposed to scare me. When he realized that wasn't doing shit, he started laughing. Talkin' about some *'I like you.'*"

She shook her head. "The man's off, Money. Like dead-behind-the-eyes off. He knows the product he's pushing down here is dirty. He knows about the overdoses—he just doesn't care."

I dragged a hand over my chest and tried to rub out the tightness that had settled there. I didn't respect men who put hands on women—that was pussy shit.

"You think Kyree's holding anything in his spot?" I asked.

She sighed, rolling her neck. "Probably. He's dumb, so I'm sure there's a flash drive, a burner phone, or something. But I haven't been over there yet."

"Would you?"

Nairobi crossed her arms. "I'm not fucking him, Money. If it comes to that—add another comma to my fee."

"Nobody's asking you to do all that," I said as I stood and headed toward the door. "See if you can get the girls to go over for another private party. I'll front the cash if that's what it comes down to. Have them keep him busy while you go do your little spy shit."

"We'll see," she huffed.

Fontaine passed me as I left the hall of private rooms.

"You cool?" I asked, stopping him with a hand on his shoulder.

"I'm straight, bruh. My bad about earlier, I just—" he slurred, running a hand down his face. "Why you ain't tell me she was working here?"

"'Cause she's not your girl. Since when you keep tabs on how she moves?" I dropped my hand. "Nai's the homie. We not on anything like that."

"Anymore," he mumbled.

I wasn't about to ask how he found out. I just stepped aside and let him go.

Back in the section, Clyde was drunk off his ass, still making it rain on the dancers.

"You know he went to see *Bambi*, right?" Jelani said, nodding in Fontaine's direction as I sat next to him.

"Ain't got shit to do with me," I replied, putting my hands up.

Slim leaned in. "How bad is it?"

"Pretty fucking bad," I said. "Call a meeting at the farmhouse tomorrow. I'll text you with who all needs to be there. I'm out."

After what Nai told me, the last thing I wanted was to sit around and get drunk. I dapped them up, and didn't even say bye to Clyde—he was occupied with a thick one bouncing her ass in his face.

I took my phone out of my pocket as I headed to my car.

Can I see you?

My phone immediately chirped with a notification as I started the ignition.

Future Wife: Hmm, I don't know. This is giving sneaky link hours...

It's only a sneaky link if it's a secret. You keeping me a secret from someone, Jas?

Future Wife: 🙄 Here you go. Yes, you can come over if your stalker ass isn't already outside.

I smirked, cranked up the radio, peeled out of the lot, and headed to the only place I wanted to be tonight.

CHAPTER 12
NAIROBI CRAWFORD

I SANK BACK INTO THE COUCH AFTER MONEY LEFT. I KNEW Fontaine was about to barge his ass in here any second. My foot tapped as I watched the door, mouthing the words to the stripper anthems blasting through the walls. The click of heels echoed through the hallway as the other girls led clients to their rooms. Plenty of them did extras under the table in VIP, so no one questioned it when I claimed room six for the night.

The door swung open, and he came in scowling, like I knew he'd be.

Light-skinned dudes weren't usually my type, but Fontaine had this *je ne sais quoi* about him. He was 6'4, bald, built like a linebacker—an IT genius, but also a shooter.

He rubbed his head, locking his hazel eyes on me. This nigga was drunk and about to be on some bullshit.

"You came for a dance?" I asked, holding my hand out. I kept my face blank even though my heart was racing.

He didn't say anything, just closed the distance between us until he was towering over me. I stood, placed a hand on his chest, and felt the steady beat of his heart beneath the black Moncler shirt. My fingers slid up to his beard, and I smirked. He'd been growing it out since I told him I liked it. It looked better than the goatee he used to rock.

"Why you keep playing with me, Nai?" he asked, snaking an arm around my waist, pulling me close.

I knew I had a few screws loose because the combination of his cologne and the liquor on his breath had me ready to drop to my knees.

"How am I playing, Bear?" I looked up at him innocently, reaching back to undo the strings of my bikini top.

His eyes dropped to my chest as the flimsy fabric fell to the floor. My nipples pebbled as soon as the cool air touched them. I wiggled out of his grasp and strutted to the pole, hooking my leg around it effortlessly.

"Why you ain't tell me you were working here?" he demanded, eyes glued to me as I did a lazy spin. "And why the fuck was you rubbing up on Money for? I thought y'all was done."

I rolled my eyes. Yeah, Money and I used to mess around. Yeah, I tried to sleep with him the day of the block party, but it was only ever physical between us—nothing like this.

Fontaine was different. He was my Bear.

He never hid how he felt about me—he started flirting with me the moment I met up with him about Kyree. And since Cash and I no longer had our little arrangement, I figured there was no harm in entertaining Fontaine.

This was only supposed to be a three-week job—long enough for me to have a little fun before moving on to my next job. But almost four months later, I was still here… and hooked.

That terrified me. He saw me in a way no one else did.

But this jealousy over Money was getting old, especially

since it was obvious that Money was focused on that little nurse of his.

"Sit," I said, pointing to the couch.

Fontaine glared, but did as he was told.

I didn't break eye contact as I climbed the pole with ease, my body moving in tandem with the music. At the top, I paused long enough to make sure he was watching before I slid down slowly and landed in a split that made his jaw tick.

His hands balled into fists as I went to the strings of my bikini bottoms and took my time loosening the ties. I kicked them to the side, leaned back on my elbows, and lifted my legs while he unbuckled his jeans.

"You still mad?" I asked, spreading my thighs and letting my fingers slide over my wetness. I dipped two inside and moaned, my head rolling back as I started working them. I knew what I was doing to him—having riled him up made it feel even better.

I didn't even hear him move.

One moment I was on the floor—the next, strong arms were lifting me in the air and onto his lap.

"Fuck, Nai," Fontaine groaned, palming my breasts. I whimpered when he took one nipple into his mouth and twisted the other between his fingers.

I couldn't wait any longer—I needed to feel him inside me. Reaching down, I lined him up with my entrance.

"Sit on this dick, Nairobi," he demanded gruffly.

I obeyed, sinking down, moaning as he filled me.

"Shit," we hissed in unison.

"Bear!" I cried out, arching my back as he slammed into me. I caught his rhythm, my breasts bouncing in his face as I rode him.

"Who's pussy is this, Kitten?" he growled, wrapping a fist in my hair.

He wasn't being soft or gentle. And in a twisted way, that was the only way I let him have me.

"Fuck, Bear! Yes!" I panted as he yanked my head back and licked my neck. My thighs were burning, but I refused to tap out.

"Don't make me repeat myself," he warned, smacking my ass.

"Fu– yours. It's yours," I gasped, bouncing harder.

"Exactly. So stop. Fucking. Playing. With me," he grit out, pinching my clit. I screamed his name as my release tore through me, my juices dripping down his shaft.

"Fuck!" Fontaine groaned, digging his fingers into my hips as he came.

I slumped against him and caught my breath while his dick pulsed inside me.

"That fuck nigga Kyree touch you?" he asked as I eased off him.

I grabbed a few baby wipes from a side table, tossing him one before wiping my inner thighs.

"Ew. Never," I scoffed. Kyree was a nuisance, but he hadn't been disrespectful—which I appreciated because Money would be pissed if I killed him before he got the chance.

"Nah, leave the rest of that," he said as I started to wipe between my legs.

I frowned. "But I still got two hours left."

"So?" he shrugged, fixing his jeans. "Your ass wanted to put on a show, right?"

"Bear–" I started.

"No," he said sharply, cutting me off. "You knew what the fuck you was doing, Nai. You're always testing me, poking the damn bear." He stood, rising to his full height. "So since you wanna be on some goofy shit, go back out there and let them niggas smell me on you."

I swallowed hard, fingers fumbling with my g-string. "You know shit's complicated…"

"To *you*. You make it complicated," he said, watching me get dressed. "Bring your ass to my crib tonight, 'cause we're not done."

He kissed me hard, then walked out.

There was no way I could go past his section again—it would be too obvious, and he was already on one tonight.

I exhaled, fixing my wig. Money needed to wrap this shit up with Kyree fast. The sooner he did, the sooner I could leave Atlanta. Fontaine was getting close to breaking through walls that I wasn't sure I was ready to let fall.

CHAPTER 13
JASMINE MILLER

THREE HARD KNOCKS ON MY DOOR PULLED MY ATTENTION from the TV. I turned it down, took a deep breath, and tried to ignore the way my heart sped up.

I almost told him not to come when he texted me. It was after midnight, and I had work in a few hours—but I couldn't stop thinking about him after our date.

I opened the door with a mildly annoyed look.

"Stalker, huh?" Cash teased, leaning against the doorframe.

I shook my head and stepped aside. "Definitely—'cause I never gave you my apartment number," I said, shutting the door behind him. "And I'm not even gonna ask how you got it."

He grinned, showing off his golds. "Can't go giving up all my secrets."

I watched as he took in my apartment. It was a simple one-bedroom that came fully furnished, but I'd done my best to make it home. A vase filled with fresh flowers sat on the dining room table beside a scented candle, and there were a few framed photos of my friends and family on the walls. He paused in front of the one with my arms around my parents.

"These your parents?" he asked.

"Yep." I sank onto the sectional and tucked my legs under me.

He nodded approvingly, kicking off his shoes as he moved closer. "Your mama fine as shit."

I scrunched my face, horrified. "Ew, please don't say that about my mama."

Cash laughed as he plopped down next to me, leaving a little space between us. "I'm saying though. I see where you get it from. The fineness is clearly genetic."

I rolled my eyes, fighting a smile. "Uh huh. So, what brings you to my neck of the woods?"

He leaned back, arms stretched across the back of the couch like he was making himself at home in my space. "I want to see you, just 'cause?"

"Mmhmm." I looked him up and. down, tapping my finger against my lips. "Just 'cause, huh?"

"You don't believe me?"

I stared at him, really trying to feel out his energy.

He looked away first.

"Work shit," he said with a heavy sigh. "Got a lot on my mind and didn't feel like going home."

"You wanna talk about it?" I asked, voice softening.

He turned toward me with a smile, clearly surprised that I said something sweet. "Aww, let me find out you care for a nigga."

I snatched a pillow and tossed it at his chest. "Boy, shut up! See? This why I can't be nice to you now."

I laughed as I started to get up, but he was quick. Cash pulled me into his lap, and I landed on him with a yelp, pressed up against the solid warmth of him.

"You play too much," I huffed, half-heartedly trying to get up again.

"You keep saying that," he murmured, his arms tightening around me. "But you love it here."

Something about the way he held me made my heart slow down. I just stared up at him, getting lost in his dark brown eyes. I was really falling for a whole drug lord at my big age.

His thumb brushed my jaw. "Can I kiss you?"

I nodded, words caught in my throat. His lips touched mine, soft at first, but then he deepened the kiss like he wanted me to feel that shit in my chest.

His hand slid under my shirt and cupped my breast. I moaned into his mouth as he toyed with my nipple, my thighs clenching reflexively.

He pulled back, breath warm against my lips. His fingers were still playing with my nipple, while his other trailed lower until it was pressing against the heat between my legs.

"You not wearing any draws, Jas?"

"Find out for yourself," I whispered, tugging his bottom lip with my teeth.

His fingers slipped past my waistband.

"Fuck," he muttered, dragging through my slick folds. "You stay ready for me, huh?"

I sucked my teeth. "I don't even be thinking about you like that."

"You sure?" His thumb circled the sensitive bundle of nerves, making me jump. "Then why you leaking all over my hand?"

I bit the inside of my cheek, but it didn't stop the moan that slipped out when he pulled his hand free and licked it, his eyes never leaving mine.

"Sit up for me, baby."

I eased off his lap, heart thudding in my chest as I leaned

back into the couch. He dropped to his knees, hooked his arms under my thighs, and tugged my shorts down as I lifted my hips.

"I'm tryna have a late-night snack," he said, nipping the inside of my thigh. "Can I taste her, sweetheart?"

"Bon appetit."

That made him grin. "Spread her open for me."

A shiver ran through me as I reached between my legs and parted my lips with two fingers.

Cash growled low in his throat and dove in. My whole body jerked as his tongue flicked over my clit. I tried to hold it in, but his mouth was too much.

"Money…" I whimpered, running my hand over his head.

He moaned into me, my soul nearly left my body when he added two fingers and curled up so they pressed against my spot.

"This pretty ass pussy," he muttered, eating me like I was his last meal.

"FUCK, Cash—"

He pressed on my stomach with his palm, and I almost blacked out. My thighs clamped around his head, and I cried out, not giving a fuck if my neighbors heard me as I came. He didn't stop until I pushed him away, too sensitive to take any more.

He sat back on his heels, his beard and fingers glistening, looking proud of himself.

I laid there with a lopsided smile on my face, bonnet crooked, but I was too far gone to care.

I reached for his belt as he stood, peeping the heavy print straining against his pants.

"Aht," he said, catching my hands and pulling me up to stand with him. "As much as I wanna bend you over and fuck the shit outta you… not tonight."

I cocked my head. "You scared?"

He chuckled, running his tongue over his teeth as he eyed me hungrily. "Nah, sweetheart. I'm tryna pace myself. You taste too good—I fuck you now?" He shook his head. "I'm already knowin' I'm not coming off you."

My stomach fluttered at the implication, even as my fingers kept fiddling with his belt like they had a mind of their own.

Cash grabbed the back of my neck and kissed me sloppily. I tasted myself on his tongue and wanted more.

"Jas," he said, resting his forehead against mine. "Once I'm inside you? That's it. You mine forreal. I already pistol-whipped a nigga for talking crazy to you. Now imagine how I'ma act when I'm in that thing. You ready for that?"

I rolled my eyes and bent to grab my shorts. "Whatever."

He sat on the edge of the couch, tracking my movements with a quiet intensity that made my chest tighten.

"What you getting into tomorrow?"

"Work. I have to go in for the next four days."

"Aight. Text me when you're on your lunch break, and I'll come scoop you."

I nodded, but still felt a little sting. I wanted him to stay, even though I knew he shouldn't.

"Stop that," he said, wrapping me in a hug. "You're overthinking again. This isn't a sneaky link, Jasmine—I'm not moving like that with you."

There was no deceit in his brown eyes.

"But," he added with a smirk, "I also know you got a queen-sized bed. That's too small for me anyway."

I pushed him off me. "You haven't even been in my room! How you know what size bed I have?"

"Educated guess. I'm wrong?"

"Not too much on my bed," I shot back. "I've had—"

The look he gave me shut me up before I could finish. He smacked my ass playfully on his way to the door.

"Keep playing with me, woman," he said, slipping on his sneakers.

"Yeah, yeah. Goodnight, Cash."

He leaned down for one last kiss, softer this time. A smile lingered on his lips when he pulled back.

"Night, Jas."

♡$♡

I was dragging through my shift, barely functioning after Cash kept me up way past my bedtime. Monica caught me mid-yawn as I tried to power through the stack of charts in front of me.

"Rough night, boo?" she nudged me. "You've been staring at that paperwork for the past five minutes."

I rubbed my eyes. Two cups of coffee—one with an extra shot of espresso—and I was still struggling to keep them open. "Yeah," I yawned again, covering my mouth. "Your man's brother stopped by last night, and—"

Her eyes lit up. "Hold up! Money finally dropped off the dick?"

"You're so damn loud," I hissed, shaking my head. "But… sort of. It was after nearly midnight, and I was acting like I didn't have a twelve-hour shift today,"

Monica screwed up her face. "Sort of? How that work? You either drop off all the dick or none."

Before I could spill the rest of the tea, her eyes flicked past me, and she rolled them hard. I already knew who it was before Dr. Matthews cleared his throat and announced himself like he always did.

"Here this nigga go," Monica muttered.

"Good afternoon, Dr. Matthews," I said sweetly.

"Hey, Nurse Miller," he replied, and quickly turned his full attention to Monica. "Uh, Nurse Pierce, I was wondering if you had a second to check on that patient in 204 with me."

Monica didn't even bother looking up. "I'm pretty sure their labs are already in the system, Dr. Matthews. You can check there."

I pressed my lips together, trying not to laugh. This poor man wanted to talk to her so badly, but she refused to give him the time of day.

"Right," he said, shifting awkwardly. "I figured I'd ask since you're always on top of things."

"Mhm," she hummed, still typing away.

Seeing he was getting nowhere, Dr. Matthews sighed in defeat. "Alright, well… y'all have a good day." He shuffled away, looking like a kicked puppy.

I burst out laughing as soon as he disappeared. "He likes you real bad."

Monica sucked her teeth. "Please. He comes up here acting all innocent, but I got his tea from the phlebotomy girls —he's a man whore."

"Damn, for real?" I wasn't shocked. Young, single doctors stayed sleeping with the nurses.

"Yeah. I don't know why he's all in my face. I don't shit where I eat," she said, giving me a knowing look.

"You don't even work here full-time anymore. Be honest —it's because of Jelani."

"Tuh, no one's worried about Lani." She rolled her eyes.

I frowned. "Oh? I thought you were smitten?"

"Not important," she said, brushing it off. "I wanna hear about your lil night cap."

I snorted. "Chile, we need a girls' night. I didn't even tell you about the date."

"Okay! Come to my place tonight. We can make margaritas and get some carryout."

"Bet!" I grinned, just as my phone vibrated in my pocket.

Big Daddy Cash: Ready for lunch?

"Shit," I muttered under my breath. I'd completely forgotten he was picking me up.

"What?" Monica asked.

"I forgot Cash was taking me out for lunch," I said, staring at my phone.

Rain check? I look like crap, and I'm swamped.

Big Daddy Cash: Nobody worried about what you look like. Bring your pretty ass on. I'm outside.

Monica smirked. "He's outside, ain't he?"

I huffed out a breath and dragged my hand over my face. "Yep. Why is he like this?"

She shrugged. "Jelani's the same way. Go. I'll cover for you if you don't come back."

"Why wouldn't I come back?"

"Maybe he's gonna drop off some midday dick," she teased, snatching the files from me. "Bye! Text me when you want to come over."

I gave her a quick hug, grabbed my stuff from my locker, and headed downstairs.

Cash was leaning against his truck when I came flying through the doors like a bat outta hell.

"Hey," I greeted, slightly out of breath.

He laughed, looking me up and down. "Damn, you alright?"

I flipped him off as he opened the passenger door. "Where we going?"

"One of my favorite spots," he said, pulling off.

I hummed in response and looked out the window. I must've dozed off, because next thing I knew, he was gently shaking me awake.

"Wake up, Jas," he said, stifling a laugh. "You, uh… got a little drool on your chin."

I wiped my mouth, giving him the evil eye. "This is your fault. I wouldn't be tired if you hadn't stopped by so late."

The sun was out, but for once it wasn't humid—a rare blessing. We walked half a block until we reached Marlene's, a mom-and-pop soul food spot with a green and white checkered awning over the door. A hand-painted sign in the window gave it that cozy, Southern charm. The second Cash opened the door, the smell of fried chicken and yams hit me.

"Grab us a table—I'ma holla at Ms. Marlene real quick," Cash said, tapping my ass lightly before swaggering past the line. This man really knew every-damn-body.

The lunch crowd had the place packed, but I spotted an empty table near the middle and sat, watching Cash work his charm. He hugged an older Black woman—clearly Ms. Marlene—and her face lit up as soon as she saw him. The staff knew him, too, dapping him up like he was a long-lost cousin.

He pointed at me from across the room. I gave a little wave, trying not to look awkward. A few minutes later, he came over with two tall cups of sweet tea.

“Ms. Marlene gon’ hook us up,” he said, sliding me a cup.

“You really do know everybody.”

“Her husband, Rodney, used to run with my pops. She used to babysit Jelani and me when we still lived ‘round the way.”

“That’s sweet. Her husband still around?” I asked, tasting my drink. Sweet tea wasn’t my go to, but this one was really good.

“Yeah. He found God after pops got killed. Put his money into this place, became a preacher, and started a megachurch.”

I caught the bitter edge in his voice. “You don’t approve?”

He took a sip of his sweet tea. “I mean… I’m in no place to judge. But a megachurch is just a different kind of hustle to me. He’s just legally hustling for God—selling hope instead of bricks.”

Ms. Marlene appeared at our table with two plates that looked like they belonged in a food magazine—fried chicken, mac and cheese, greens, and thick slices of cornbread fresh from the oven.

“Here y’all go,” she said, eyes twinkling. Ms. Marlene was gorgeous, full-figured, with smooth toffee colored skin that glowed, and her gray hair was pin-curled under a net. I knew Rodney didn’t play about her.

“Thank you. This looks too good,” I said, smiling.

“Appreciate you, Ms. Marlene,” Cash added, slipping her a folded stack of money.

She swatted at his hand. “Boy, you know better—this on the house. Don’t even start with that.”

“Put it toward the next folks in line,” he said, tucking the money into her apron pocket before she could argue.

I watched him, amused. “You’re… interesting.”

Cash raised an eyebrow as he unrolled his silverware. "That supposed to mean something?"

"I'm saying," I replied, unwrapping my own. "I've seen you pistol-whip a grown man, but Ms. Marlene out here treating you like her favorite nephew."

"Didn't I tell you I contain multitudes, shorty?" he winked, biting into his chicken.

I grabbed a wing, and my eyes nearly rolled back. It was juicy and perfectly seasoned. We ate in silence, which was how you know the food was good.

"Jasmine?"

I froze, chicken halfway to my mouth. My eyes swept the crowded restaurant and landed on a tall brown-skinned man weaving through the tables toward us. He was brolic, like he spent every waking moment in the gym, and his long locs were pulled up into a neat bun.

Cash tensed across from me, setting his fork down. "You know him?" he asked under his breath, eyes narrowing.

"I—uh…" I squinted at the man and pursed my lips. "I don't think so."

The man grinned as he approached and let out a low chuckle. "My bad, ma. It's been a minute." His voice had that unmistakable Queens accent. "Marcus."

Oh shit.

Marcus freaking Stokes. He was supposed to be doing twenty years upstate on a RICO. We broke up a few months before he got locked up, and I hadn't heard from him since I told him to stop hounding me from prison.

I stood slowly. "Marcus," I breathed, forcing a smile as he pulled me into a hug, lifting me off the floor like I weighed nothing.

I laughed, startled. "Damn—okay!"

"It's really good to see you, Juicy," he murmured in my

ear. I shifted uncomfortably, moving his hand off me as it crept dangerously close to my ass.

Marcus was no longer the scrawny boy from Jamaica, Queens, who used to drive me around in his beat-up Civic. The man in front of me had definitely leveled up. He'd never been a flashy guy, but here he was iced out—a thick Cuban link around his neck and a big-faced Rolex on his wrist. It didn't match the man I remembered. And it wasn't just the clothes—his whole vibe felt… off. I couldn't put my finger on it, but his energy felt darker. Shit was weird.

He never used to leave New York unless it was to visit family in Trinidad. The nigga didn't even fuck with soul food because he didn't grow up eating it. So what the hell was he doing in a soul food spot in Georgia of all places, grinning like he came in here all the time?

"I didn't know you were out," I said, stepping back. My mind was racing. I needed to hit up Amber. Did she know?

"Charges got tossed a few months ago on a technicality," he said with a dimpled grin that didn't reach his eyes. "I'm down here making some moves. Handling a little business—you know how it go." My skin crawled as his gaze dragged down my body, like he was undressing me. "Still fine as hell, I see."

Cash cleared his throat loudly behind me.

I turned, suddenly remembering that I wasn't alone. "Shit! Sorry. Marcus, this is my friend, Cash. Cash, Marcus. We used to—"

"Yeah," Marcus cut in, eyes locked on Cash. "Me and Juicy used to be real close. Shorty was my lil' nah mean."

Cash's jaw clenched, his hands balled into fists under the table. I sent up a silent prayer that he'd left his gun in the truck.

"Like a million years ago," I added quickly with a weak laugh. "Anyway, good seeing you, Marcus."

"Likewise, beautiful. Yo, your number still the same?"

I hesitated. Lying wouldn't help—Marcus was like Cash, he'd find out anyway.

"Yeah…"

"Bet." He nodded and licked his lips.

He turned to Cash. "You from out here?"

Cash gave a tight nod. "Westside."

"True." Marcus's mouth twisted into a half-smile. "Heard there's a lot of motion out here."

Cash scoffed and glared at him.

Marcus let out a short, dry laugh and turned back to me. "Juicy, I'ma hit you up before I head back to the city. We definitely gotta catch up."

"Sure," I said, sliding back into my seat, wishing I could disappear.

Marcus looked between us, smirking like he knew he stirred up some shit.

I turned to Cash. His whole energy had shifted.

"That's the nigga you said got locked up on a RICO?" he asked icily.

"Yep." I stabbed at my mac and cheese. My appetite seemed to have packed up and left with Marcus.

"Hm." He stood and walked off, returning with two to-go containers. He set one in front of me and started packing up his food.

"You're done eating?" I asked, confused.

"You gotta get back to work, right?" he said without looking up.

"Monica's covering for me, so I'm good to chill," I said lightly, hoping this wouldn't turn into a thing.

"Nah, I got some shit to handle."

"Okay…" I muttered, packing up my food.

The silence followed us all the way back to the car.

"Are you mad at me?" I asked once we were back on the road.

"You good, Jasmine," he said, eyes fixed ahead, his grip on the steering wheel tightening.

"Look, I know that whole thing with Marcus was weird, but I haven't seen him in ten years. It's not that serious."

Cash slammed on the brakes. My body jerked against the seatbelt as cars honked and swerved around us.

His face was hard when he turned to me. "You was giggling and blushing in that nigga's face—and then called me your *friend*?"

"First of all, I was caught off guard! Two, are we not friends?" I snapped back, heat creeping up my neck.

He looked at me like I was speaking another language.

"Oh! I get it now," I said, letting out a bitter laugh. "You think because you spent a little bread on me and ate my pussy that makes you my man?"

We glared at each other until Cash finally let out a hollow laugh. "You right, Jas. My bad." He shifted the car back into drive. "Where am I taking you? Back to work or home?"

I sighed, throwing myself back against the seat. "Just take me home."

I watched the city blur past my window, arms folded tight over my chest. My throat was tight, like the words I wanted to say were stuck there. This was ridiculous, especially after last night. We were really arguing over somebody who held zero weight in my life.

Why was it always something with him?

"This the shit I be talking about," I muttered under my breath. "This is why I don't deal with street dudes. I'm too old for this."

"Nah, you dealin' with me, Jasmine. Don't lump me in with that nigga." He slammed a hand against the steering wheel. "I had to sit there and watch a dude you used to fuck whisper in your ear and try grab your ass in front of me. You think I ain't see that shit?"

I flinched.

"Exactly." He shook his head. "Play dumb if you want to."

My phone chimed in my purse.

(646) 555-3492: What's good, Juicy? It's Marcus. Save this number.

From the corner of my eye, I saw Cash glance down at the screen.

I should've deleted that shit right then. Marcus was a walking red flag and everything in me was scre*aming don't do it*. But Cash had me fucked up trying to puff out his chest like he ran shit.

Me: Done and done

CHAPTER 14
CASH "MONEY" BANKS

IT WOULD BE MY FUCKING LUCK THAT JASMINE'S EX WAS THE same nigga trying to move in on my territory. I wanted to put a bullet in his head so bad, but I'd never disrespect Marlene's spot like that.

Jasmine gave me the silent treatment the rest of the way to her apartment. She sat there with her face screwed up, arms folded, looking out the window like a damn toddler in the middle of a tantrum. Soon as I parked, she hopped out and slammed the car door hard enough to shake the damn frame.

I sat there for a minute and watched her thick ass sashay angrily into her building before leaving. As I began to pull off, I peeped a silver Mustang merging a few cars behind me. I remember seeing one parked out front of Marlene's earlier but didn't think anything of it.

Could've been a coincidence.

Until I switched lanes and a few moments later so did they.

I let out a frustrated breath and reached into the center console for my piece. This nigga Marcus a stalker now too?

I took the next exit and drove aimlessly, weaving through backroads until he finally got bored and backed off.

Still heated, I called Jelani.

"Yo," his voice came through the speakers as I merged back onto the highway.

"I'm headed to the farmhouse. Everybody pulling up?" I asked.

"Yeah, we all here. Why you sound ready to knock someone's top off?"

"Because I am!" I smacked the steering wheel with my palm.

"Aw, shit. Who we fucking up?" he asked giddily. People thought I was the loose cannon, but it was really him they needed to worry about.

"I saw him."

"Who? Kyree?"

"The nigga from New York. Marcus."

"How you know it was him?" Jelani pressed, his voice serious now.

"Because he's Jasmine's ex," I spat. My chest tightened just thinking about the way dude hugged up on her, undressing her with his eyes like I wasn't there. Like she was still his.

"What?!" Jelani shouted.

"We were at Ms. Marlene's, grabbing lunch. And this Hulk-looking motherfucker comes over to the table. As soon as she realized who it was, she was cheesing in his face like I wasn't sitting right there."

"But how you know for sure it's the same dude we dealing with?"

"She told me her ex was doing a bid for a RICO. That lines up with what Nai told me about Kyree's plug—also named Marcus. The nigga straight up said he was down here on business."

Jelani whistled. "Damn. She was really standing there, choppin' it up with him?"

"Catching up like old times," I grumbled.

"She knows how we finna handle him?"

"Nah. But it's whatever. I'm off her since she wanna tell people we just friends." The words tasted bitter as they left my mouth.

"I mean…" Jelani trailed off.

"What?" I snapped, already knowing he was about to say some slick shit.

"Money, she's not your girl. I know you feelin' the nurse. But, bruh—I like Monica, and she's not my girl either."

I clenched my jaw. "What's your point?"

"Nothing," he laughed. "Don't get tight with me 'cause her ex wanna spin the block. The game is the game."

I hung up on him. I wasn't trying to hear that shit.

The weight of the day settled on my shoulders as I pulled up to the farmhouse. Slim and Fontaine were posted outside, passing a blunt between them.

"Sup," I greeted them.

"You straight?" Fontaine asked, dapping me up. Outside of Jelani, he was my closest friend—and he could read me like a book.

"Nah, but we're about to fix that." I nodded toward the farmhouse.

The musty smell of mildew and rotting wood hit me as I entered the decrepit building. I hadn't been out here in months. Most crews used warehouses, but I picked a farmhouse out in the country. It was in the middle of nowhere, and the closest neighbor was two miles away—I didn't have to worry about people hearing screams or gunshots. We only came here when things were about to get messy, like today.

The eight men I'd called were scattered around the room in beat-up folding chairs, chopping it up in low voices.

Nairobi did the background checks before and made sure everyone was clean. Well… almost everyone. There was one loose end that I still needed to handle.

Jelani sat in an old leather recliner, scrolling through his phone, unbothered like he hadn't clowned me on the ride over. Nairobi had switched it up—gone was the jet-black wig from Stilettos. Now, she rocked a sleek brown bob with oversized shades that covered her face. She was off in the cut, but I caught the tilt of her head. Even behind those sunglasses, I knew her eyes were trained on Fontaine who was posted up behind me.

How could I've missed that there was something going on between them?

The murmuring stopped as I stepped into the center of the room. All eyes were on me.

"If you're here, it's 'cause you've been vetted," I started, my voice hard. "But let me make one thing real fucking clear—if word of anything leaves this farm, I'll end you, and make sure your families won't have a pot to piss in."

I let that threat hang as I looked at them.

"I'm sure y'all heard about Rahmel," I went on, pacing slowly. "At first, I thought it was some small shit—someone who just got a little greedy and needed to be handled. But now?" I scoffed. "We got bigger problems. Niggas think they can come at me… my brother." I pointed at Jelani. "Y'all trying to come take the thing Ricardo Banks built."

"That shit's wild to me," I said, slapping my chest. "'Cause I make sure every single one of y'all eats."

Jelani stood, crossing his arms as he moved to stand at my

side. "If anyone got issues with how shit's being run—speak up." His voice was calm, but the message was loud and clear.

The room stayed quiet for a moment before Grizz stood. "Yo, Money. No disrespect, but what the fuck are you talking about?"

My eyes snapped to him. He was one of the ones Nairobi said was at the meetup with Kyree and Marcus. I purposely invited him here, knowing he was moving foul. Like I said, a loose end that needed to be taken care of.

"Loyalty." I deadpanned.

He frowned, looking around. "You just said everyone here's vetted. You know we ridin' with you, so why the threats?"

"Because apparently some of y'all think I've gotten too comfortable," I said, stepping forward. "Like I wouldn't figure out what's going on in my own house. It's like folks forgot what happened after my pops died."

Grizz tried to sit back down like the conversation was over.

"Nah. Stay up," Jelani said. "Since you wanna be the voice of reason."

"I'm good, Jelani," Grizz muttered, hands up. He looked around for backup, but the silence in the room spoke volumes.

I caught Nairobi's eye and nodded. She slid her sunglasses up and strolled to the front, hips switching seductively. Every head followed her like they had just realized she was there.

She handed me the burner, smirking. "Hey, Big Grizz," she purred. "We had fun the other night, didn't we?"

"I—I didn't," he stammered.

I held up my hand while I unlocked the phone and hit play on the video.

Kyree's voice filled the room: *"We know where all the stash houses are, so it's an easy in. With your backing and us knowing everything about BC, we'll be able to snuff them out easy."*

Some girl giggled in the background.

"Hell yeah!" Grizz's voice came in crystal clear. *"I'm ready to get this money wit' y'all, man. I'm tired of running them damn trucks. It's time to get in the field and make some real bread. Money thinks he's running shit with his soft ass—"*

I cut the video off.

"How much he make, Slim?" I asked, keeping my eyes on Grizz.

Grizz looked shook. If he wasn't brown-skinned, I swear he'd be as pale as a ghost.

"Last I checked," Slim said behind me, "$350,000 a year. Not counting bonuses."

I nodded. "Shaun," I called another lieutenant.

His eyes got wide at the sound of his name. "Yeah?"

"How much you make running the Eastside?"

"Shit." He scratched the back of his head. "Maybe like $250k? Give or take."

"Slim?"

"Yeah, he's right."

I turned back to Shaun. "You want a promotion? You can take trucking off Grizz's hands—since he thinks he can make real money being a traitor."

Shaun's eyes bugged out his head. "You serious, Money?"

"Dead ass," I said. "You've been here almost as long as Grizz, and I'm feeling generous today. I'll up the pay to $500,000. How's that sound?"

"Hell yeah, I'll take that shit," he said, trying to hide his grin.

I turned to Grizz. He looked like he was about to shit himself.

"Come up here," I said, motioning him forward with two fingers.

I dragged one of the folding chairs and set it in front of me. He was trembling now, stuck in place.

"Bring your ass up here!" I barked. My voice bounced off the old wood walls. That nigga practically jumped out his skin, stumbling forward, eyes wild, searching for an escape route. Jelani shoved him down into the chair and started tying him up with some rope from the ground.

Slim handed me a roll of black gauze. I took my time, unrolling it slowly and methodically, and began wrapping it around my knuckles. I pulled it taut with each loop until the rough material bit into my skin.

By now, the farmhouse was dead silent, except for the faint buzz of cicadas outside. I paused to tear the gauze with my teeth.

"You think I've gotten soft, Grizz?" I asked calmly, moving to wrap my left hand.

He was a mess—sweat dripped down his face as he hyperventilated. By the time Jelani finished tying him up, he looked like he was on the verge of passing out—and I hadn't even touched him yet.

"Money, come on, man," he said shakily. "I've seen what you've done to niggas. I don't want no problems. I was drunk just talking shit."

"Lani, what you think?" I asked, tearing the gauze again with my teeth.

Jelani sneered, looking at him like he was dog shit on his shoe. "If you gon' talk shit, say it with your chest. Stand on it like a man."

Grizz's head snapped up, his eyes darting between me and

Jelani. "Nah, nah, I swear I wasn't on no disrespectful shit! I just—"

My fist went across his jaw before he had a chance to finish.

"Just what?" I asked, shaking my hand out. Grizz groaned. "Just you thinking I'm pussy? Just you running your mouth? Just you being a bitch ass nigga?"

I hit him again—jab, then hook.

"Which one is it?"

Another blow.

Everything I'd been holding rushed to the surface—lunch with Jasmine. Marcus hugged up on her, both of them playing in my face.

"Money, please…" Grizz slurred, his head rolling.

"*Money, please*," I mocked, yanking his head up. "Nah. I'm soft, right? That's what you said, Gregory."

Nobody in the room spoke or moved. They understood a point was being made.

"Speak up, Grizz. The fuck you gotta say now?" I flung his head down.

Grizz let out a gargled noise. "I'm sor—"

My fist smashed into his face again.

"Fuck your sorry!" I roared, raining blows on him. His soft grunts and the dull smack of knuckles to flesh filled the farmhouse. Blood sprayed across my face, and was getting in my eye. It still wasn't enough to make me stop.

I blacked out. All I could see was Marcus trying to son me like I wasn't Cash-fucking-Banks. Like this wasn't my city.

I kept swinging.

My arms burned, and my knuckles throbbed. But I kept going.

Jelani grabbed me from behind. "He's gone, Money," he said, holding me by the shoulders.

I stood over the chair. My lungs burned as I caught my breath. I wiped my mouth with the back of my hand and turned to the others.

"This—" I pointed to the body slumped in the chair. "—is what happens to niggas who cross me. Maybe Rahmel wasn't enough. So, here's your visual."

I kicked the chair over and spat on Grizz's body. My gaze swept the room until it locked on Derrick and Chris.

"Y'all thought I ain't know you was in on this shit too?" The others scooted back in their chairs to make room for me as I stepped toward them. "I helped get y'all niggas out the mud and run behind this nigga helping the opps?"

Chris started shaking his head. "Nah, it's not like that, Money. Swear—"

"Shut the fuck up."

I turned to look at Slim. He nodded, raised his gun, and pulled the trigger. Two shots cracked through the room. The smell of gunpowder hung in the air as their bodies went limp, falling limp like rag dolls.

I looked around the room again. Most tried to keep their faces neutral, but I saw the fear in their eyes.

"You either with me, or you under me. So, I'ma ask one more time—anybody else got grievances they wanna share?!" My voice boomed through the room, my whole body still buzzing.

Moe hunched over and threw up on the floor.

"Ay! You cleaning that shit up!" Slim barked.

The rest of them shook their heads. The message had been received.

"Good," I said. "A storm's coming. I need y'all to tighten the fuck up. If shit seems off? Tell Slim or Fontaine."

I dismissed the rest of them. Slim, Fontaine, Jelani, and Nairobi stayed behind.

"What we doing with them?" Fontaine asked, nodding at Grizz's body.

As tempting as it was, I couldn't just dump him like I did Rahmel.

"Rodney's pig farm," I said, taking the switchblade from Nairobi and sliced off the gauze. Marlene's husband might've given his life to God, but even the Lord's strongest soldiers were still sinners. He built that pig farm to help Pops back in the day, and even after he opened his church, he kept it running for situations like this.

Pigs don't leave much behind. And they supply meat for Marlene's restaurant—it was like the circle of life if you thought about it.

I flexed my fingers as the gauze dropped to the floor, already thinking about our next moves.

"So what we doing about Marcus?" Slim asked.

I'd hoped that getting rid of Rahmel and Daemon would've been enough to make him back off. His product was garbage and made things too hot for us with all the ODs.

But now, after seeing him in person, my intuition told me that Marcus played dirty. That's probably what got him locked up in the first place.

"Nai, I know you can't stand him, but I need you to bug Kyree's crib. I can't let them hit our houses."

She groaned and rolled her eyes.

"Triple. Rate." She jabbed her finger at me and pulled her shades down.

"What about the nurse?" Jelani asked.

"What about her?"

"She's his ex, right?"

"Hold up," Slim jumped in. "The nurse used to date the opps?"

"Apparently," Jelani said. "Sounds like he's still trying to see what's up with her—"

"Shut the fuck up, Jelani," I snapped, cutting him off. My stomach twisted at the thought of Jasmine being dragged into this. Even though we were beefing, I meant what I said. I wasn't getting her involved. I didn't even want her near Marcus.

Fontaine shifted in the corner. "We could use them hitting the stash houses to our advantage. Once we know which one they're moving on, we clear most of the product out and leave just enough for them to think they hit a lick. That way, they don't know we're onto them."

"True," Jelani agreed. "Moving in too soon could spook them. But if we run the play like Fontaine said, we can flip it and hit them even harder."

I mulled it over. This was a game of chess, not checkers. As much as I wanted to kill these niggas and get it over with, we couldn't just go in guns blazing. They needed to think they had the upper hand.

"Alright," I said. "Nai, bug the crib—sooner than later. Fontaine, tap Kyree and Derrick's phones. Any movement, any meetups—I need to know."

Nairobi nodded. "I got you, boss man."

Everyone knew what was at stake. Marcus thought he could run shit in my city? This was my empire, and he wasn't taking a damn thing from me.

CHAPTER 15
JASMINE MILLER

"Hey, girl, hey!" Monica greeted me, but her bright smile faded as soon as she got a good look at my face.

"Hi," I muttered, stepping inside.

Her apartment was a reflection of her bold personality. Abstract art and colorful wallpaper covered the walls. My favorite part was the pink neon "Happy Hour" sign glowing over her bar cart. She'd rehabbed most of the secondhand furniture with skills she picked up on YouTube.

"What's wrong?" she asked, trailing me into the living room.

"I got into it with Cash," I huffed as I collapsed into her oversized bean bag.

"Girl," she drawled. "Let me get the wine."

She disappeared into the kitchen and came back with two glasses and a bottle tucked under her arm.

"Alright, what happened?" she said, pouring us both a glass.

I took a huge sip and gave her the rundown of the lunch disaster.

Monica's mouth was hanging open by the time I finished. "You didn't say that to him!"

I grabbed the bottle and topped off my glass. "I absolutely did. Like—how's he acting like my man off one date and a little taste of pussy?"

"He did buy you a Versace dress, though…" she pointed out.

"And? Nobody told him to do all that," I scoffed.

"You're not wrong, but calling that man your friend in front of your ex is wild," she laughed.

I threw my hands up. "I was flustered—what was I supposed to say? And honestly… Marcus looked *real* good."

"I mean… Marcus did play in his face, Jas," she said, her voice dropping a little.

"What? How?" I frowned.

"Now you know damn well what it means when a man does that lil' hug-and-lift combo. You said he tried to touch your booty, too? *Girl….*"

I winced.

"Exactly," she said, tipping her glass toward me. "So, even if you were flustered, you came off real giggly. Add insult to injury—he basically asked Cash if he was 'bout that life. Jasmine, please. You cannot be this dense."

I screwed up my face. "Not you defending this man," I grumbled, taking another sip of wine.

Monica snickered as her phone buzzed on the coffee table. She glanced at the screen, rolled her eyes, and silenced it.

"Anyway," I continued, "Marcus texted me while Cash dropped me off. Pretty sure he saw it."

"Bitch, you're messy!" she laughed right as her phone went off again. She groaned and snatched it up.

"What, Jelani?" she snapped.

I raised my eyebrows, watching her face screw up as she listened to whatever he was saying on the other end.

"I have company. I can't talk right now." She closed her eyes, jaw clenched. "What does it matter who's here? Don't you have other bitches to entertain? Get the fuck off my phone."

She hung up and tossed her phone across the couch.

"Trouble in paradise?" I asked.

She snorted and grabbed her wine glass. "Jelani's toxic, and I'm not trying to deal with his shit right now."

"Toxic how?"

She gulped down her wine. "I told him I was cool with keeping things casual, but I made it real clear that if he was seeing other women, just be honest about it. That's it."

I nodded, fully locked in.

"He swears up and down he's not, and to prove it, the nigga starts planning a Miami trip for us. Cool—who says no to a free vacation?"

"So what's the issue?" I asked.

"The issue is," she said, refilling her glass. "While he was here the other night, I heard him in the bathroom whispering sweet nothings to the next bitch."

"Wait—in your house?"

"In my goddamn house," she said, shaking her head. "Talkin 'bout how he misses her and can't wait to see her. Couldn't even wait until he left."

Her voice was laced with disgust, but underneath that, I heard the disappointment and hurt she wouldn't admit to. I didn't know what to say—just a few days ago, she had hearts in her eyes talking about him. Now, she looked like she was two seconds from swinging on him.

She leaned back on the couch and rolled her eyes. "But it's cool. Jelani must've forgot who the fuck I am. Like niggas not in my inbox still pressing me."

"I know that's right."

A hard knock at the door made us both jump.

"Damn, is that the takeout?" I asked.

"I don't think so. I didn't get a notification on my phone," Monica said as she stood and headed to the door. She peeked through the peephole and groaned.

"Open the door, Baby Doll." Jelani's voice came through the other side.

"Why are you even here?" she asked.

He banged again. "Monica!"

I rolled my eyes. "Just open it before one of your neighbors calls the cops." Clearly, causing a scene was a Banks family trait.

With a heavy sigh, she unlocked the door. Jelani wasted no time pulling her into a tight hug, peppering her neck and face with kisses like she hadn't given him her ass to kiss a few minutes ago.

"Ew, Jelani. Get off me," she whined, half-heartedly pushing him away. He whispered something in her ear that made her bite her lip and stifle a giggle.

He kissed her on the mouth, gave her ass a squeeze, then breezed past me without so much as a nod. He disappeared into her bedroom and shut the door behind him.

I gave Monica a look.

She gave me a half shoulder shrug and flopped back onto the couch. "He's drunk. I don't know what he's on tonight."

"But I thought—"

"I'll let him sleep it off tonight and block him tomorrow. I'm over it," she said, waving her hand. She wasn't fooling anybody.

And clearly, this wasn't the first time they'd done this dance.

"Okay… let me get out of your hair then." I stood.

"No, stay!" she insisted. "He'll probably pass out after he showers. He won't even come back out."

I side-eyed her hard. "A shower? He got clothes here? Bye, Monica. Handle your man, and I'll see you later."

"He's not my man!" she protested, standing.

"Uh huh. Okay, *baby doll*."

♡$♡

It'd been two weeks since my fallout with Cash, and he still hadn't reached out—no calls, no texts—not even a damn carrier pigeon. Meanwhile, Marcus had been applying pressure, hitting me up every day to check in, but mostly asking when we could meet up. I kept brushing him off, blaming my work schedule, but I knew that I couldn't keep using that excuse.

Marcus: Why you avoiding me, Juicy?

I swear I'm not. I've got a few weeks left on this contract and I'm trying to stack my bread.

Marcus: Yeah aight. This got something to do with the nigga I saw you with at the soul food spot?

No, he's not my man.

Marcus: So what's the real issue then? Why you can't make time to catch up with an old friend?

Old friend my ass.

I left him on read and swiped to my thread with Cash.

His last message was from the day he picked me up for lunch. I stared at it for a second, lips pursed, debating whether to say something.

I could just say "hi."

No. Fuck him.

I blew out a frustrated breath and tossed the phone into my bag.

It'd been a long ass day at the hospital—there'd been another wave of ODs with back-to-back codes, and the only thing I'd had for lunch was a warm protein shake. I was starving, and my head was pounding. All I wanted was to lie on the couch, bra off, after a hot shower with my phone on Do Not Disturb.

The parking garage was still muggy from the rain earlier. The fluorescent lights buzzed and flickered overhead as I twirled my keys in my hand.

"What the fuck?" I stopped short.

My tires were flat. All of them were slashed to shreds. The back window was shattered. Glass was everywhere—on the pavement, in the backseat.

This had to be a sick joke.

Tears welled up in my eyes as I walked around to look at the damage. Peachtree wasn't in the greatest area, but nobody'd ever said anything about break-ins. Plus, I wasn't stupid—I didn't keep anything in my car worth stealing.

This felt intentional.

I dug through my bag for my phone and called Monica.

"Hey, boo!" she answered cheerfully.

I sniffled. "You at Southside today?"

"Yeah, why? What's up?"

"Somebody slashed my tires," I said, feeling a lump rise in my throat. "And they broke my back window too."

"Jesus. Where you at?"

"I literally just got off. I'm in the garage."

"You want me to call Jelani? He could come up there and—"

"No," I said quickly. "I don't need Cash finding out."

"You sure?" she asked. "You know he'd pull up."

"I know," I said, pinching the bridge of my nose. "But I'm not tryna deal with him right now."

"Okay… You got AAA?"

"I let it lapse," I muttered. "Forgot to update it after my card expired."

She sucked her teeth. "Want me to see if I can get out of here early?"

"Nah," I sighed. "It's fine—you're all the way on the other side of the city. I'll figure something out."

We hung up, and I leaned against one of the concrete columns, breathing hard, trying not to cry. But I could already hear my daddy's disappointed voice in my head.

This is why I told you to make sure your AAA was updated before you left.

I tried Rochelle, but her phone went straight to voicemail.

Calling Cash felt pointless—he probably wouldn't pick up. But on the off chance that he did, I knew he'd be here in a heartbeat, ready to go to war.

But then at some point we'd have to have *that* conversation, and I wasn't in the headspace to do all that.

I looked around the empty garage.

"Ugh!" I let out a frustrated scream and stomped my foot.

I scrolled through my contacts and hit send.

"'Sup, Juicy," Marcus answered on the first ring. I heard the TV on in the background.

"Hey… you busy?"

"Not really. Why you sound like that? You good?"

The first tear fell as I stared at my ruined car.

"Jasmine… talk to me. What happened?" I could hear him mute the TV.

" I-I just got off work and…." I choked back a sob. "All my tires are slashed. The back window is busted. I forgot to renew my AAA, and I'm stuck."

"Where you at?"

"Peachtree Memorial—on the second floor of the parking garage.

"I'm on my way."

♡$♡

I sat in the driver's seat with the door cracked, too tired to move. My scrubs clung to me, damp with sweat, and my eyes still burned from all the crying. Maybe all of this was confirmation that Atlanta was a chop, and I needed to cut my losses and go home to New York. This contract was draining the life out of me, whatever was—or wasn't—happening between me and Cash seemed dead, and now this mess with my car?

Could the Universe be any louder?

Heavy bass filled the quiet garage, headlights sweeping over my car as a black Maserati SUV slid into the space next to me.

Marcus hopped out and slammed the door behind him. He looked like he'd been pretty comfortable wherever he was coming from, based on the basketball shorts and white tank he had on.

"Damn," he muttered, eyeing the damage. "They really fucked your shit up."

I swallowed hard and nodded, wrapping my arms around myself. "I don't even know why. I don't bother anybody."

He studied me for a long second. "You been crying, Juicy?"

"Stop calling me that," I grumbled, looking away.

He pulled me into his arms before I could move. I tensed at first, but let him hold me. I felt myself unravel just a bit, taking in his scent—soap, sandalwood, and a faint trace of weed. He still smelled just like I remembered. I was surprised that it settled something in me.

His laugh rumbled in his chest. "My fault, mama. Old habit."

He let me go and tipped his head toward the trunk. "Pop it and go sit in my car. I'll call a tow."

I hesitated.

"Jas," he said gently. "You called me for a reason. Let me handle it."

I pressed the button and passed him my keys.

He got right to work, his phone cradled between his shoulder and ear, as he used the mini vacuum from my trunk to clean up the broken glass from the backseat.

Thirty minutes later, the tow truck had pulled off. I wouldn't know how much the repairs would be until morning.

Marcus climbed into the driver's seat, started the car, and turned down the music that blasted through the speakers.

"I'll pay you back once I get this situated," I said quietly.

He looked over, frowning. "Pay me back for what? That wasn't shit."

"I'm serious, Marcus. You don't have to—"

"I know I don't," he cut me off. "I wanted to. And anyway, my boy owns the tow company. It's not costing me or you anything."

I sucked my teeth and looked out the window. I hated owing people, and I especially didn't want to be indebted to him. Something told me that this wasn't going to come without some kind of string attached.

"There *is* something you could do."

I turned my head. "What?"

He grinned. "Let me take you out."

I balked as my chest tightened.

I shouldn't have been surprised, but it still threw me. My mind went straight to Cash. Even with us not speaking, he still occupied the corners of my thoughts.

Marcus represented an entire era of my life I'd put behind me. Before my pre-frontal cortex really developed—when I was outside, young, dumb, and running off emotion. I fell for his potential and the fantasy he painted of money, trips, and buying me whatever. All that got old real fast once I realized he was too deep in street life, and I wasn't tryna be nobody's ride or die. I needed stability, not constant stress and anxiety. I wasn't built for conjugal visits or the feds kicking down my door.

And yet… here he was. A whole decade later—a whole lot finer and apparently with the money he'd always dreamed of having.

I wasn't naive. A Maserati fresh out of prison? I already knew Marcus was still into some shit, which made him no different than Cash.

"Jas," he said, holding out his phone. "It's just dinner. It's not that deep."

"Yeah, sure," I said, typing my address into the maps app.

This was fine.

Marcus beamed, squeezing my thigh before he reversed out the spot. I leaned my head against the window, trying to ignore the sinking feeling that came with his touch.

♡$♡

"Ooh! Where you going?" Amber asked when I picked her FaceTime.

I spun one last time in the mirror, looking over my outfit. "Out."

"With your boo Cash?"

"With Marcus, actually," I said, chewing on lip as I waited to see her reaction.

Amber's face bunched up. "Not *thee* Marcus Stokes. Y'all having some video jail date?"

I laughed, sitting on the edge of my bed. "Friend, so much has happened in these past two weeks. I been meaning to call you, but all I want to do after work is sleep."

"Uh, yeah. Because last time we spoke you were dressed in Versace going on a date with Cash."

I gave her the quick run down of events up to my car being vandalized.

"I can't believe you didn't call me!" Amber said when I was finished.

"I know, I know. I've just been so overwhelmed. I'm blown that I'm gonna have to dip into my savings to fix my car, but I guess I should be grateful I have it, right?"

"Yeah, still sucks though. I can't believe Marcus is out. Donny didn't mention it to me."

Donny was Amber's older brother who introduced me to Marcus, they used to hustle together back in the day.

I shrugged. "Maybe he's keeping his word and keeping my hands clean."

Amber clicked her tongue. "Barely. I don't even think that truck company he works for is completely legit, but I mind the business that pays me."

"True," I said, applying another coat of lipgloss.

"So you and Marcus, huh? You think you'd give you guys another shot?"

"I don't know. I don't even really want to go out with him. The physical attraction is still there, but something just feels off. I can't put my finger on it."

"Well it's been a decade and he's not the same person, maybe it's that."

"Yeah, maybe."

A text notification popped up at the top of my screen.

Marcus: I'm here

"Alright, girl. Let me go. He's here."

"Have fun! I need a full debrief after," she said, pointing a finger into the camera.

Marcus's truck was idling in front of the building with its hazards on.

"Hey," I said, climbing in.

"'Sup, mama?" he said, leaning over to kiss me on the cheek. Instead of heading to the exit, he turned into the resident lot and rolled to a stop in front of my assigned space—where a matte black Mercedes coupe now sat, parked in the spot where my Altima used to be.

I looked at him, confused. He reached into the center console and held out a key fob.

"What is this?"

"Your new car," he grinned at me stupidly.

I looked from him to the Benz and back again. "What about my Altima? I just got a quote for the repairs this morning."

"It was old. Plus, whoever did that shit to it knows where you work and what you drive. Who's to say they wouldn't do it again?" He said it like it was the most obvious thing in the world. "How were you supposed to get to work? The bus? Uber? You needed a ride, so I just upgraded you."

A sour taste filled my mouth. The car wasn't even my style. First of all, I'd never drive a coupe. Second of all, something about the oxblood red interior. I just knew my coworkers would immediately assume that I was doing some shady shit.

"It just needed new tires and the window replaced. It was a perfectly good car," I said, trying not to raise my voice.

"Remember I told you I'd buy you anything you wanted once I got my shit together?" he asked, suddenly growing serious. "This is me doing that. I'm trying to make up for lost time with you."

"By buying me a tricked-out Mercedes? I can't drive this to work, Marcus."

His jaw ticked as he stared ahead.

"I'm not tryna make you upset, Jas. I just wanted to do something nice."

I glanced at the car again, forcing myself to swallow the irritation building in my chest. I wanted him to return it and give me back *my* car. It wasn't fancy or new, but it was reliable and low-maintenance. I couldn't afford Mercedes repairs or premium gas on a nurse's salary. He really hadn't thought this through.

But this wasn't the time to push it. Not because I was

scared of him, but because I didn't feel like dragging this night out more than I had to.

I closed my eyes and took a breath, forcing a smile. "Fine. Thank you."

He lit up immediately. It was like my approval flipped some kind of switch.

"It suits you. You'll get used to it," he said, dropping the fob in my hand.

"Mmhm." I pulled out my phone but didn't know who to text. Monica was my girl, but I was sure she'd tell Jelani, and Jelani would tell Cash—and all I needed was that nigga to show up somewhere swinging his gun around again. Amber would probably tell me to sell it for something I actually liked, which made sense, but wasn't really the point.

I bit back another sigh and scrolled through my social media feed instead, halfway listening to whatever he was prattling on about.

Dinner was at a cozy Italian spot Marcus picked. Despite the stunt with the new car, he'd insisted this was a friendly date, so I kept my outfit lowkey and went with jeans and an oversized cardigan since it had finally cooled down. I did a no-makeup-makeup look, and straightened the bundles I'd gotten installed recently.

The hostess led us to our table, where a bottle of champagne sat chilling in an ice bucket.

"You look good," he said as we sat. "Is Italian still your favorite?"

I smiled despite myself, a little surprised. "You remembered that after all these years?"

"You begged me to take you to Del Marco's like every other day," he smirked.

"They had the best veal parm!" I laughed, relaxing a little.

"I've never eaten here, but my boy says this is one of the

best Italian restaurants in Atlanta," he said, pouring me a glass.

I scoffed, taking the glass from him. "I'll be the judge of that. Not everybody does Italian food like New York."

"Facts," he chuckled, raising his glass. "Let's toast—to reconnecting with old friends," he lifted his glass.

My brow furrowed slightly, but I tapped my glass against his anyway with a quiet hum of agreement.

He ordered for us—veal parm for me, because it was my favorite, and a lasagna for him.

"So," he said, leaning back after the waiter left. "What's the infamous Juicy J been up to these last ten years?" he asked. "You were at the hospital when I picked you up—I'm guessing you finished nursing school?"

"Yeah, I finished a year after…" I trailed off awkwardly.

"I got locked up, Jas. We don't have to dance around it," he said with a soft shrug. "But I'm glad you finished school. That's what's up. How'd you end up in Atlanta?"

"Travel nursing," I said. "The contracts down here pay triple what I was making at home, and honestly, I wanted to see what living outside of Queens was like."

"I can dig it." He replied, nodding.

He swirled his drink and tilted his head. "You got any idea who might've done that shit to your car?"

Of course, I spent most of the night trying to figure out who'd be crazy enough to do something so serious, and my mind kept going back to Princess—Cash's ex-jumpoff. I don't know how she'd find out anything about me, but it seemed like when you moved in the circles Cash did, you could find out anything you wanted to for a price.

Still, I wasn't trying to go down the rabbit hole of the mess that had taken over my life. It was easier to pretend that it was just a random act of vandalism, even though I knew better.

"Nope," I said tightly.

"You think it has anything to do with your dude?" he asked as he took a sip of his drink. "What was his name—Cash?"

I ran my tongue across my teeth. "Why would it have anything to do with him?"

He leaned back, one brow raised. "For real, Jas? I know you know what that nigga's into."

"And how would you know?"

Marcus laughed. "C'mon, Juicy. You see the whip. You already know what kind of time I'm on. I know all about Money Banks."

A chill crept up my spine.

"Cash and I weren't serious," I said, straightening in my seat. "And we're not even talking right now. So, I don't know why anybody would be worried about me."

The waiter appeared to let us know our food would be out soon. I offered a small smile and took it as an out.

"I'll be back," I told Marcus, already on my feet. I just needed a minute to breathe and get my head right.

I headed straight for the restroom and handled my business quickly, coaching myself through a few deep breaths. I was mid-exhale when I heard the door swing open behind me.

"I thought that was you."

I glanced up in the mirror and immediately rolled my eyes.

Princess.

She walked in, her honey-blonde boho braids cascading down her back. I looked her up and down, my gaze stopping at the slight swell of her stomach in her tight maxi dress.

"I see your face healed," I said coolly as I reached for a paper towel.

She let out a short laugh. "That's cute. But I'm good—healed and still the prettiest bitch in the room."

She stepped closer, that smug little smirk still on her face. "Funny how things fall into place… especially when you're carrying the right man's baby."

My stomach flipped as bile crept up my throat. Everything clicked.

That's why I hadn't heard from Cash.

He knew. That fuck nigga knew and was too much of a coward to say anything.

I clenched my jaw, forcing myself not to react. "Do you see me here with Cash? What the fuck does any of this have to do with me?" I tossed the paper towel in the trash. "I already knocked you on your ass for talking to me sideways. Keep talking, and I'll do it again."

"And I'll have your ass locked up," she snapped. "Who's gonna save you now?"

She brushed past me into the stall and left me standing there. The little bit of hope I'd been holding onto about me and Cash? Poof. Gone. I wasn't about to be caught up in some baby mama bullshit.

I fixed my face on the walk back to the table, holding my chin up.

It has nothing to do with me.

He's not my man.

They were messing around before me.

Fuck. Him.

None of that settled the tight knot in my stomach.

Marcus glanced up from his phone as I sat. The food had arrived while I was gone, but I couldn't bring myself to eat.

"Everything okay?" he asked, cutting into his lasagna.

I ran a hand through my hair. "I just lost my appetite out of nowhere," I mumbled.

He frowned. "You sick? Need me to take you home?"

I shook my head quickly. Going home meant sitting with my thoughts. If I did that, I'd only end up calling Cash and cussing him out.

"I don't want to go home," I said, eyes still on my plate.

He set his fork down slowly. "So… what you tryna do?"

I looked up. "Let's go back to your place."

His eyes lit up like a kid on Christmas. "Bet." He flagged down the waiter to box up the food.

Princess's confession played on an endless loop the entire ride to the hotel. If she wasn't pregnant, I swear I would've beat that stupid ass look off her face.

I ignored the alarm bells going off in my head as Marcus laced fingers through mine while we walked through the lobby of the Ritz-Carlton. Cash had made his decision, and I had made mine. Jasmine Miller was back outside.

I know it was childish and petty. I didn't even want Marcus like that, but I wanted to have something over Cash—even if I'd regret it later.

The elevator doors opened to a huge suite. The living room alone was bigger than my entire Buckhead apartment, with floor-to-ceiling windows overlooking the Atlanta skyline. Marcus headed straight to the kitchenette. "You want anything to drink?"

"Whatever you're having is fine," I said, sinking into a plush couch.

He raised an eyebrow at me. "It's strong. You sure you can handle it?"

"You're asking this to the girl who used to throw back shots of 151 like water?" I countered with a playful smile.

He chuckled and took another glass from the cabinet. "Aight, big dog."

He poured out our drinks from a black bottle with fancy gold trim. Whatever this was, it wasn't cheap. He brought the glasses over and handed me one as he sat.

I tossed mine back and instantly regretted it. That shit felt like swallowing fire and sent me into a coughing fit.

"I told you," Marcus said smugly, sipping his like it was juice.

"Whatever," I croaked, motioning for more. He laughed and refilled my glass before pulling out a wooden box from the coffee table.

He sparked a pre-rolled blunt, took a long drag, then passed it to me.

I took a small pull as if I could somehow test its strength.

"Don't act scared now," Marcus teased. "You was just talking mad shit a minute ago."

I shot him a look, holding the smoke in for a second, then exhaled slowly. "I got this."

"Nah," he shook his head, grinning. "You gotta take a real pull, mama. That shit gas."

Rolling my eyes, I hit it harder. The smoke clawed at my lungs, burning and making my eyes water, but I swallowed the cough. I wasn't about to have him clowning me.

"Here," I said, passing the blunt back. "Happy now?"

He took it, holding it between his lips while he pulled out his phone. *Love Calls* by Kem filled the suite.

My hand flew to my mouth in an effort to hold back the giggle that bubbled up.

"Why you gigglin'?" he asked, taking another hit before stubbing it out.

"You," I snorted, already high. "Kem? Really? You tryna set the mood and shit."

"Man, whatever," he said, pulling me closer by the thigh.

The giggles turned into hiccups, which made me laugh even harder. Tears streamed down my face as I bent over, trying to catch my breath.

"I'm so–hic—sorry," I wheezed.

Marcus chuckled, reaching up to undo the bun his locs had been in all night. They spilled past his shoulders, somehow making his sharp features stand out more. I looked at him closely, trying to see if the boy I used to know was still in there somewhere.

"You silly as shit," he said, brushing the tears off my cheeks with his thumb.

I leaned into his hand without thinking. That one little touch sent heat curling up my spine—way more than it should've. My laughter faded as I licked my lips, our eyes locking.

"You ever think about us?" he asked, voice distant.

I shrugged, my eyes drifting to the tattoos on his arms. Both were filled with intricately done portraits and bible passages, but what caught my attention were the flowers between them all.

"What kind of flower is this?" I asked, lightly running my fingers over one on his wrist.

He looked at me through heavy-lidded eyes. "Jasmine."

I sucked in a sharp breath and dropped my hand into my lap like I'd touched something too hot.

"I thought about you a lot while I was locked up."

"Mhm. I'm sure you did," I murmured, ignoring the alarm bells ringing in the back of my head again. I wasn't here to reminisce, and I most definitely wasn't about to try and unpack why this nigga had jasmine flowers tattooed all over himself.

I climbed onto his lap and kissed him hard before he

could say something corny and blow my high. The kiss was messy and hungry, fueled by the weed and the two shots coursing through my system. His hands slid up under my cardigan as I reached back to unhook my bra.

"Goddamn, Jas," he breathed, eyes glued to my chest like he couldn't believe I was real.

I let out a low hiss when his mouth closed around my nipple. He flicked it with his tongue, my back arching as he grazed it with his teeth. The weed had every nerve in my body lit up like Christmas.

Laughing, I gave him a gentle shove and fumbled with the button of my jeans. He helped me take them off, and the second I climbed back on his lap, his hand went straight to my panties.

"This shit still juicy as hell," Marcus muttered, rubbing slow circles around my clit before sliding two fingers inside me.

"Shit," I gasped, gripping his shoulders, grinding against his hand.

"I need to be in this pussy now," he grunted.

I slid off him, panties hitting the floor as he pulled off his shirt and jeans. He snatched a condom from the box on the coffee table, ripped it open with his teeth, and rolled it on.

I closed my eyes and touched myself again, trying to ride the high I was feeling.

He slapped my hand away with a growl. "Nah. That's mine."

"Oh!" I yelped as he grabbed my legs and yanked me to the edge of the couch.

He bent to kiss me as he lined himself up with my entrance. I shuddered as he entered me slowly, savoring the feeling of him stretching me out.

“Fuuuck, ma,” he hissed, his locs brushing against my face as his head dropped. “This pussy still tight.”

I moaned, gripping his arms as he delivered steady, deep strokes, like he was tryna mark me. My hand slid between my legs, and I started rubbing my clit hard, chasing my release. Marcus grunted and grabbed my legs, pushing my knees to my chest and thrust harder. I could tell he wasn’t about to last too much longer, and I damn sure wasn’t about to let him nut before me.

“Fuck!” I cried. My pussy clenched around him, another moan catching in my throat as I trembled underneath him.

“Shit, I’m about to nut,” he growled as he gave one last thrust before his whole body stiffened. A low moan came from him as he spilled into the condom and slumped against me, breathing hard.

He collapsed on top of me, chest heaving. Both of us were sweaty and breathless.

After a moment, he pulled out and disappeared down the hall. I lay there, naked, heart still pounding, but not from the afterglow of good dick. The petty sense of satisfaction never came.

It wasn’t bad. But it wasn’t Cash.

I got up, put on my cardigan, and followed the sound of running water to the bathroom. Marcus was already in there, wiping himself down with a washcloth.

“Can I crash here tonight?” I asked, grabbing a fresh washcloth from the counter.

“I didn’t think you were going anywhere,” he smirked, wrapping a towel around his waist. “You can sleep in one of my shirts,” he said, smacking my ass on the way out.

I washed up and wrapped myself in a towel, trying to ignore the unease in the pit of my stomach. I’d wanted this—I wanted Marcus in the moment.

"Good job, Jas," I muttered to myself as I dried my face. I should've had him take me home.

In the bedroom, Marcus had left a plain white tee on the bed for me. I put it on and crawled into bed. He got in beside me, wrapping his arms around my waist.

"Thanks for letting me stay," I mumbled, staring blankly at the wall.

"Mmm," he hummed, already half asleep.

I lay there wide awake, listening to him snore, feeling fifty kinds of stupid. I'd used Marcus to get back at Cash and probably made things worse.

CHAPTER 16
CASH "MONEY" BANKS

I WAS AT CLYDE'S SHOP GETTING A SHAPE-UP WHEN JELANI'S name popped up on my screen. I sent it to voicemail, but a text came through right after.

> Jelani: Pick up, bitch nigga. It's about your nurse.

I frowned. We hadn't talked since our argument, and yeah—I should've hit her up. But between my pride and the bullshit with Marcus and Kyree, I hadn't gotten around to it. Nairobi was finally able to set up a private party so she could plant the bugs in Kyree's house, and Fontaine installed an incognito tracking app on his phone under the guise of a software upgrade.

When the phone rang again, I picked up.

"What's wrong with Jasmine?"

"You still beefin' with her?" Jelani asked.

"We're not beefin'."

"So you talked to her?"

I blew air through my cheeks and pinched the bridge of

my nose. “Lani, you ‘bout to piss me off. Did something happen to her?”

“Monica said somebody fucked her car up… slashed her tires and busted her windows,” he said.

My blood ran cold. I held up a hand to Clyde. “Hold up.”

Clyde froze, his clippers buzzing in the air.

“When was this?” I asked.

“The other night, when she got off work. She’s not hurt or nothin’, but Monica said she sounded real shook—like she was crying and shit.”

“Why she ain’t call me?” I muttered, more to myself than him.

“‘Cause you too busy sulking about her ex being the opps.”

“Whatever, nigga.”

“I’m lying?” he shot back. “Go check on your girl, man.” He hung up.

I flipped my phone face down on my thigh and rubbed my jaw.

Who the fuck would want to come for Jasmine like that? Did she call the cops? How’d she get home if Monica didn’t help her?

Clyde brushed hair clippings from my neck. “Uh oh. What’s the problem?”

“I’m good,” I muttered, rolling my shoulders.

He snorted. “Nigga, I’ve known you my whole life. When you get to tappin’ your foot like that, some shit is up.”

I looked down, not realizing my foot was bouncing.

“Just some shit with my girl,” I said. Jasmine wasn’t technically mine—yet—but Clyde didn’t need the details.

“Hm,” he pulled the cape off. “You fucked up?”

“Why you assume I’m in the wrong?” I stood, pulling out a few bills.

"'Cause I'm a man. And most of the time, we be fucking up," he chuckled as he took the money.

He was right—this was partly on me. If I'd just called Jasmine, we probably would've squashed all this. But I didn't. And now she was out here dealing with this shit on her own.

"Look," Clyde said, reaching for a broom. "I don't know what happened, but as your one married homie? Call her and work it out. That is, if you actually give a fuck. If you don't?" He shrugged. "Plenty of fine-ass women in the city."

"Aight, ol' Master Yoda ass," I said. He laughed and called over his next client.

I sat in my car for a good five minutes before deciding to call Jasmine. When she didn't answer, I called again.

"What, Cash?" she answered, sounding irritated.

"Damn, Jasmine. I'm bothering you? Hello to you too."

She sighed, "I'm tired, Money. I just got home and need to shower."

"What happened to your car?" I asked.

"If you're asking, then you already know," she snapped. "Why do you even care? I haven't heard from you in weeks, and all of a sudden you give a shit?"

"So you not gon' tell me?"

"I'm not about to do this with you."

Two beeps, and the call ended.

I stared at the display for a second before redialing. It went straight to voicemail.

Did this woman just block me?

I must've broken every traffic law flying to her place. She had me fucked up if she thought she could ice me out.

I was still tight by the time I pulled up to her building. I slowed as I passed her parking spot and saw a new black Mercedes sitting there with temporary plates.

Unless she won the lottery in the last forty-eight hours, that wasn't her car.

"I'm buggin'," I muttered. I circled the lot, making sure that was indeed her spot before double-parking in front of the building's entrance. Her car gets fucked up, and now she got a whole new whip without saying anything? The fuck was she on?

I let myself into her building with the copy of her fob I made, fuming the entire elevator ride up to her floor.

"Jasmine!" I banged hard on her door, my voice echoing down the quiet hallway.

A few seconds passed before I heard the locks unlatch. The door cracked open, and there she was—wrapped in a towel with her shower cap on, still damp and looking like she was two seconds from swinging on me.

"Really, Cash?"

"*Really, Jasmine*?" I retorted, matching her tone. "You just gon' hang up and block me?"

She rolled her eyes. "My phone died, and I took a shower."

I pushed against the door, trying to look past her. "You got a nigga in there or something?"

"Can you stop?" she hissed. "No one's here."

"Then let me in."

She wedged herself in the doorway. "We can talk right here."

She was acting like I wasn't welcome in her house, and that only pissed me off more. I stepped closer. "Yo, I'm not in the mood for this," I said, lowering my voice. "I'll cut up in this hallway—try me."

Jasmine glared, but stepped aside to let me in.

"What do you want, Cash?" she asked sharply, slamming the door behind me.

"Where'd you get that car from? What happened to yours?"

"Like I said on the phone—if you're asking, then you already know. There's nothing else to tell." She started to push past me, but I grabbed her wrist and spun her around.

"Where'd the new whip come from?"

She snatched her arm back. "None of your fucking business."

I started pacing in her entryway, rubbing the top of my head. "Why you ain't call me when it happened?"

"Would you even have answered?" She challenged. "I didn't feel like dealing with your bullshit, so I handled it, because that's what grown people do."

"Why didn't you have Monica help?"

"She was at work. And I knew if she told Jelani, he'd tell you—which is exactly what happened."

"So who'd you call?"

Her mouth opened, then shut. Something flashed in her eyes before her face hardened again.

"Who, Jasmine?"

"Marcus."

I nodded slowly. "But it wasn't serious, right?"

"What aren't you getting?" she said, clapping her hands for emphasis. "I didn't have anybody else to call!"

"You fuck him for that new car?" I regretted the words as soon as they left my mouth.

Jasmine's face twisted like I'd slapped her, but she caught herself. Her lips curled in a cold smile as she crossed her arms.

"He bought me the car, and *then* I fucked him. You happy now? That's what you wanna hear, Cash? So you can stay mad? I didn't even ask him for that shit!"

"I didn't—"

She wagged a finger at me. "No. Don't backtrack now. You said what you said. I don't know why you even care. Haven't you been busy with your baby mama?"

I reared back. "Baby mama? The fuck are you talking about?"

"Don't act dumb," Jasmine said, rolling her neck at me. "Princess told me she was having your baby."

I hadn't seen Princess since the night she and Jas got into it at my party. I'd been ignoring her calls and texts for weeks.

"And you believed her?" I asked, squinting.

"She had a bump and everything!"

I rubbed my temples. Dealing with Marcus's shit was already blowing me—now Princess wanted to start some shit too?

With an annoyed sigh, I pulled out my phone, found her name, and put it on speaker.

It rang twice before she picked up.

"Hey–"

"Where you at?" I cut her off. I wasn't trying to exchange pleasantries with this bitch.

"I'm at the shop. Why?"

"Bet. I'm 'bout to come through," I hung up and shoved my phone back in my pocket. "Get dressed."

Jasmine looked at me like I had five heads. "Excuse me?"

"Put some clothes on. Unless you tryna go out wrapped in a towel."

I started toward the living room, but she stepped in front of me and blocked the way.

"You don't get to pop up on me, talk to me crazy, then start throwing out orders like you run shit," she said, jabbing her finger in my chest.

I looked down at her hand, then back up at her face.

"I swear I hate you," she muttered as she spun around and

stormed off to her bedroom, making sure to slam the door behind her.

I sank onto the couch and started flipping through channels.

Jasmine reappeared a short while later in black leggings and a gray crop top, her face still scrunched up as she snatched her purse off the table. "Well?"

I shook my head, chuckling as I turned off the TV and pushed off the couch.

She didn't say shit as we walked to the elevator. When we got in, she posted up in the corner with her lip poked out, arms crossed like a brat the entire ride down.

"Don't slam my shit like you did the last time," I warned when we got to my car.

She sucked her teeth and climbed in, but closed the door softly.

Princess's shop wasn't far from Jasmine's. I pulled up in front of the nail salon, cut the engine, and turned to face Jasmine.

"About what I said earlier…" I pressed my tongue against the inside of my cheek. "I was outta line. I let my anger get the best of me—I shouldn't have come at you like that."

She let out a dry huff, still looking straight ahead.

"Stay in the car," I told her. "If she gets reckless, let me handle it, alright?"

She nodded and rolled the window down.

Through the storefront glass, I spotted Princess laughing with one of her girls. Her friend noticed me and tapped Princess on the shoulder, pointing in my direction. Princess lit up instantly when she saw it was me. She smoothed her shirt and strutted out the door with a little too much pep in her step.

I leaned against the passenger door, blocking her view of Jasmine.

My eyes dropped to her stomach, looking for the "bump" Jasmine mentioned. It was there, barely noticeable, but it was there.

"You got something to tell me?" I asked as she approached.

Her smile faltered. "Um… no?"

"You sure? 'Cause I heard you had some news to share."

I stepped aside, giving her a clear view of Jasmine in the passenger seat.

Princess's smile vanished. Her eyes jumped from me to Jasmine.

"What's *she* doing here?" she asked tightly.

"Don't worry about all that," I said, looking over her shoulder at the shop. Her clients were pressed against the glass, trying to piece together what was happening.

"I… I was gonna tell you," she mumbled, wringing her hands.

"Nah, bitch. Tell him exactly what you told me," Jasmine interjected, leaning out the window. "You had a big-ass smile on your face last night."

"Chill," I told Jasmine without taking my eyes off Princess. "Honestly, it don't even matter. That baby's not mine."

Princess's face crumpled. "How can you say that?" she screeched. "This is your baby, Cash!"

"That's your problem, P," I said, shaking my head. "You think you smarter than everybody. I shoot blanks, shorty. Got my shit snipped a year ago for this exact reason."

Behind me, I heard Jasmine gasp at the same time Princess's jaw dropped.

"I've always wrapped up with you. So what—you was

poking holes in my condoms? That's some grimy shit, even for you," I spat.

"B-b-but…" she stammered, running her hands through her braids.

"But nothing. Go inside and see if your girls can help you figure out who that baby's father is, 'cause I'm not the pappy," I shrugged.

"You know she was out with some nigga last night, right?" she spat, glaring at Jasmine. "She's just using you!"

"Girl, fuck your loose pussy ass!" Jasmine yelled, hitting the button to roll the window up.

I shook my head as I rounded the car to get back in. We pulled off, leaving Princess on the curb looking stuck.

"Ain't no baby," I said finally, breaking the tense silence. "You feel better now?"

Jasmine snorted. "Whatever."

"So we good, right?" I asked as I merged onto the highway, taking us out of the city.

She shifted to face me. "I don't know, you tell me. You're the one who got in your feelings and ghosted me."

"You right," I admitted."My bad."

"Your bad?" she repeated, disbelief lacing her words. "Is it going to be 'your bad' every time you have a temper tantrum? Because that's what the fuck that was. What I look like chasing a grown ass man who can't communicate?"

Clyde's words echoed in my head as I clenched my jaw, fighting the urge to clap back.

"There's more to it than you think," I said. I couldn't just come out and say Marcus was the opps—not after she made it clear she didn't want to be wrapped up in that part of my life.

"What's that supposed to mean?"

I exhaled, staring at the road. "You want to get back with him?" I asked, deflecting.

Jasmine's eyes narrowed as she glanced out the window. "Where are we? This isn't the way my apartment."

"I need to stop past my mother's house, and then we're going to my place."

"What? Why?"

"Because…" I trailed off. Shit, I wasn't even sure I knew why I was doing this. I hadn't brought anyone around Ma in years, and only family ever came through my spot. I just knew this felt right.

♡$♡

"I'll wait in the car," Jasmine said as I cut the engine.

"It's too hot for all that," I said, opening my door. "I just need to grab something—it won't take long."

She looked like she wanted to argue, but instead sighed and unbuckled her seat belt.

"Ma!" I called as I unlocked the front door. Inside, the house was quiet, and still, there was no sign of her anywhere.

"Your mother's house is beautiful," Jasmine said behind me.

"Thank you," my mother's voice floated down the hall. She came from the half-bathroom, drying her hands on a paper towel. A wide smile spread across her face as she approached.

"Cash, baby, why didn't you tell me you were coming?"

"You know I like to surprise you," I said, kissing her on the cheek. "Gotta make sure you ain't got no little boyfriend running around here."

Ma's smile tightened as she pinched me hard on my side, making me flinch. I laughed and turned slightly to Jasmine.

"Ma, this is Jasmine. Jas, meet my mother, Sydney Banks."

Jasmine smiled shyly and extended her hand. "Nice to meet you, Mrs. Banks."

My mother's face lit up as she took Jasmine's hand. "Well, aren't you a gorgeous thing?" she said, pulling her in for a hug. "And you can call me Sydney, sweetheart. I'm a hugger, I hope you don't mind."

Jasmine let out a small laugh, returning the hug. "Not at all, Sydney."

Ma stepped back, looking over Jasmine approvingly before turning to me. "And you brought company?"

I rubbed the back of my neck, feeling slightly awkward. "Last minute decision."

"I bet," she replied, raising an eyebrow, and gestured for us to follow her into the kitchen.

"Can I get y'all anything? Water, juice… something stronger?" she asked, heading to the fridge.

"We're good, Ma," I said, leaning against the counter. "I just came to grab those papers for the building."

"Oh, right," she nodded. "They're in your father's office."

"I'll be back," I said to Jasmine.

She nodded and sat at the island, her gaze wandering around the room.

Coming into Pop's office always felt like stepping back in time. Nothing had changed—his old books and vinyl records lined the shelves; even the decanter, still half-filled with his favorite whiskey, sat on a bar cart in the corner. Ma claimed she used this as her workspace, but I knew she mostly kept it this way to feel close to him.

"You like her, don't you?" Ma said out of nowhere, picking up a manila folder off the desk.

I blinked. "What?"

She sucked her teeth and lightly smacked the folder against my chest. “Boy, you heard me. When was the last time you brought a girl over here?”

I took the folder. “It’s not like that.”

She looked at me skeptically. “Uh huh. So now you out here introducing random girls to your mama now?”

I shook my head, chuckling. “No, ma’am.”

Her expression softened. “Exactly. That’s what I thought,” she patted my cheek gently. “She seems good for you.”

“You said, like, ten words to her.”

“You look at her the way your daddy looked at me,” she said simply. “A mother knows these things.”

I followed behind her as she left the room, still turning her words over in my head. When we stepped back into the kitchen, Jasmine glanced up from her phone, her gaze flicking between us curiously. I could see the curiosity all over her face—she knew we weren’t back there just going over paperwork.

“Aight, Ma. We out,” I said, giving her a quick hug.

Jasmine stood and smiled. “It was really nice meeting you, Sydney.”

“The pleasure’s all mine, sweetheart,” Ma gave her another warm hug. “Hopefully, this one will bring you by for dinner sometime.”

Jasmine gave me a tentative glance. “That sounds nice.”

Ma turned to me with a stern look. “And you—don’t fuck this up, Cash.”

“Here you go,” I muttered. “Yes, ma’am.”

Jasmine was quiet when we got back in the car. I could tell she had a million questions, but she kept them to herself.

“Your mom’s sweet,” she said thoughtfully.

“Yeah, she is,” I agreed, backing out of the driveway.

My house wasn't too far from my mother's—maybe a twenty-minute drive. I'd moved to the suburbs a few years back for the space and privacy. Jelani's wild ass still lived in a high-rise downtown, but I preferred the quiet.

The music on the radio filled the car, neither of us speaking as we were lost in our thoughts. Jasmine was probably trying to figure out the game I was running. And I was still working out why I was letting her see this part of my life.

When we turned down my street, it was hard not to smile at the irony of everything. My crib was set behind a row of perfectly manicured hedges and a gated entrance that gave family man vibes more than a nigga who'd been putting foot to ass lately.

"I don't bring people to my house. Nobody comes here except family and a few close friends," I said.

Jasmine frowned. "You took me to meet your mother… now we're at your house. Is this supposed to make up for the way you acted?"

"Nah," I shook my head. "This isn't a half-ass apology. I'm just…" I took a deep breath, choosing my words carefully. "I want to show you more of me. That's all."

I couldn't remember the last time I'd been this vulnerable with a woman. The words felt raw in my throat.

"I'm not playing games with you, Jas."

She stared at me, searching my face like she was waiting for the catch. Slowly, she turned back to look at the house again.

"Let's go inside," I said, getting out of the car. Jasmine followed, taking in the sprawling white house I called home.

"Your gangsta ass really lives in the suburbs like you got a whole secret family tucked away somewhere," she teased as we walked up the front steps.

"Don't get it twisted. I'm a businessman, shorty," I said, winking as I punched in the code to unlock the door.

She snorted. "Yeah, alright, *Mr. Businessman.*"

I pushed the door open, stepping inside first. "Welcome to my crib," I said, holding it open for her.

My place was nothing like my mom's cozy, lived-in house. I was all about clean lines and open space. The walls were a warm cream color, and I'd had an interior designer hook me up with furniture that had a modern style without feeling cold. It wasn't your typical bachelor pad, though. There were no oversized leather couches or sports posters. Instead, I'd curated a growing collection of work by Black artists. They were pieces that showed a little bit of who I was beneath the flash.

Jasmine walked in, looking around the foyer and up at the high ceilings. The bright hardwood floors gleamed under the sunlight pouring through the big windows.

"Oh, you got big money," she said, sounding awestruck.

I chuckled, locking the door behind us. "I do alright." I tried to sound unfazed, but a small surge of pride swelled in my chest.

She slipped off her sandals and left them by the door, and wandered further inside. She paused at a large abstract painting in the entryway.

"Didn't take you for an art guy," she said, glancing back at me.

"This is just for me," I shrugged, kicking off my sneakers. "I keep this part of my life to myself. Not too many can say they've seen this side of me."

She kept moving, trailing her fingers along the back of the couch, brushing against a glass console table like she was trying to feel the space as much as see it.

Watching her move around stirred something inside me. I wondered what it'd feel like to have her here all the time.

I pushed the thought down and tipped my chin toward the kitchen. "Let me show you around."

We strolled through the house with Jasmine tossing out little comments here and there. I could tell she was impressed by the details and care I put into everything. When we got to the backyard, I showed her the pool and grill set up on the patio.

"This isn't what I expected at all," she said, turning to me.

"What were you expecting?" I asked.

She faced the pool, wrapping her arms around herself. "I knew you were wealthy, but this…" She waved a hand around. "I thought you'd have a flashy penthouse downtown or something, but this is some grown-man shit."

I smiled, stepping closer. "I'm thirty-eight, Jas. I better be on some grown-man shit."

I held out my hand. "I know I'm a little hot-headed—"

"A little?" she cut in, sliding her soft hand into mine.

"Okay, very hot-headed," I admitted, leading her back inside. "But there's more to me than just the nigga you've seen." I gave her hand a squeeze.

"Come on, let me show you the rest."

We headed upstairs, where more art hung on the walls, including framed photos of places I had traveled to.

"Y'all are some mama boys, huh?" she said, stopping in front of a photo of Ma and Jelani on a beach on the Amalfi Coast.

"She means everything to us," I nodded. "If anyone deserves the world, it's her."

"Mhm," she hummed. I led her further down the hall, stopping at the double doors at the end.

"This right here," I said, pushing one open, "this is my sanctuary for real."

Jasmine's eyes widened as she entered the master suite. The room was spacious, centered around a huge California king bed. My walk-in closet and en-suite bathroom were tucked off to the side, but I knew what had caught her attention—the floor-to-ceiling windows and the balcony overlooking the backyard.

"Wow," she murmured, stepping toward the glass.

I sat on the bench at the foot of my bed. "You know, you never answered my question earlier."

"Which one?" she asked, turning back to me.

"Do you want to get back with Marcus?"

Jasmine sighed and leaned against my dresser. "No. I didn't even want to go out with him forreal. I just said yes because he helped me. I know he's down here on some bullshit, and I'm not trying to be caught up in whatever he's got going on."

"But I'm also in this street shit," I reminded her.

"Touché," she said with a half-smile.

"So, what—you saying you like this street nigga better?"

She rolled her eyes and laughed. "Oh my God! Why are you like this?"

I stood, smirking as I closed the distance between us. My fingers hooked in the hem of her top, gently pulling her toward me. "I mean… do you?"

"Nope," she said, popping the *p* with a smirk.

I bent down, placing soft kisses along her neck, trailing up to her ear. "Really?"

My hands slid over her ass, giving it a firm squeeze.

"Nuh-uh," she breathed, gasping when I slipped my hand between her legs and started stroking her through her shorts.

"You're a terrible liar, baby girl," I murmured, grinning as she started grinding against my hand.

“Shut up,” she muttered, yanking me down by my shirt, crashing her lips into mine.

The kiss turned sloppy real fast—like we were trying to make up for every second we were away from each other. Her hands wrapped around my neck as I traced my hands up her sides, memorizing every dip and curve of her body.

A groan rumbled low in my chest as she sucked my bottom lip. I was bricked up, my dick straining hard against my shorts. The moment her body shifted against me, something in me snapped. I grabbed her and backed her into the dresser hard, sending cologne bottles crashing to the floor. I didn’t give a fuck, I needed her.

I yanked her bottoms down, dragging two fingers through her wet folds.

“You already ready for me,” I murmured against her mouth.

“Cash…” she panted, pulling my shorts down and wrapping her hand around my dick.

“Fuck, baby.” My knees almost buckled, nearly giving out as she started stroking me slowly.

I lifted her onto the edge of the dresser. The wood creaked beneath her as she parted her thighs for me. More bottles tumbled to the floor as I pushed inside her slowly, inch by inch.

“Oh my God,” she gasped as her head fell back, eyes fluttering closed.

“Goddamn,” I growled as I began to thrust into her. She felt unreal—she was so tight and warm in a way that made my pulse jump. Like she was made for me.

I gripped her fleshy hips and started stroking her slowly,

letting her adjust to my size. Her soft moans filled the room as she trembled around me.

"Look at me, Jas," I said, my voice rough in her ear. "You feel what you doing to me?"

Her nails raked down my back, sending sparks up my spine. "Shit, Money. Don't stop… please…"

The way she said that name—Money—hit different coming from her, somehow turning me on even more.

"Yeah?" I hooked one arm under her knee and drove in deeper. "You taking this dick like a champ, mama. Like you know this shit yours."

Each stroke was a declaration—if that nigga Marcus thought he was touching her again, I'd put a bullet in his head.

"'Cause it is," she hissed as she wrapped her arms around my neck.

I gripped her jaw and spat in her mouth, then dragged my tongue along her throat and bit down on her neck hard enough to make her gasp.

"And this shit mine. Ain't that right?"

"F-fuck! Yes!" she cried, locking her legs around my waist.

Her cries grew desperate as I circled her clit with my thumb. Her walls tightened around me until she shattered—damn near levitating off the dresser, back arching, legs shaking as her climax rolled through her.

"Fuuuck…." I rasped, using every ounce of willpower I had not to nut.

Jasmine sagged against me, chest rising and falling fast. I slipped my arms under her legs and lifted her off the dresser.

"Where we going?" she asked, voice hoarse, her head resting her on my shoulder.

"I'm not done with you," I said as I carried her to my bed.

I set her down on the mattress and stepped back to take her in. Her hair was wild, lips swollen, and her skin glistened with sweat. But she was still so fucking beautiful.

"Turn around for me, baby," I said, licking my lips. "I wanna see that ass bounce."

She turned around and arched her back slowly. I slapped it, watching it jiggle as her pussy leaked, tempting me to lose control.

"Ain't no other nigga ever gonna have you like this," I murmured as I slid back in. "I'll kill behind you."

She met every thrust, throwing that shit back on me. "Ooh, you fucking me so good, Money…"

"That nigga wasn't fucking you like this, was he?" I grunted, pounding her harder.

"No! Shit—right there—fuck!"

I grabbed her shoulder, pulled out, and slammed back in. "Whose pussy is this?"

"Shit," she choked out.

I slapped her ass again. "Say it, Jas."

"Yours, Money! It's yours!" she screamed, voice raw.

That was it. My vision blurred as my balls tightened.

"Fuck! Fuck!" I roared as I coated her walls. I pulled out, watching our mess drip down her thighs.

Jasmine collapsed onto her back, breathing heavily.

I dipped my fingers between her legs and brought them to her lips. She licked them clean without hesitation.

I couldn't take my eyes off her—my beautiful, nasty girl.

"You know you fucked up, right?" I grinned, pulling my fingers away to kiss her. I groaned into her mouth, tasting both of us.

She propped up on her elbows, still breathless. "How?"

"I'm never coming up off you," I said, kissing her forehead. "We locked all the way in now, sweetheart."

CHAPTER 17
JASMINE MILLER

CASH WASN'T LYING WHEN HE SAID HE WASN'T COMING UP off me. I'd been holed up in his house for two days, living off takeout, orgasms, and wearing his t-shirts that were two sizes too big for me.

He took me back to my place yesterday to grab a few things, but truth be told, I liked wearing his clothes—they smelled like him. Same way I liked waking up tangled in his sheets with his arms around me.

Jelani called earlier, trying to convince him to come out to the club. I wasn't exactly thrilled about it—last time I was there, I ended up throwing hands.

"But you also met me that night," Cash said, flashing me a grin.

I tried every excuse I could to get out of it—said I didn't have anything to wear. He shut that down real quick, said I could show up in a trash bag and still look better than half the chicks in there.

When I told him to go without me, he looked at me like I'd said I was fleeing the state.

"I'd rather be laid up with you, but I gotta show my face

tonight," he said, kissing me deeply. "And if I'm going out, I want you with me. Period."

"I'm sure you can be seen without me," I said, soaping myself up. We'd just finished another round of intense love-making and were showering before heading out.

"I wanna show you off," he said, wrapping his arms around me from behind. His chin rested on top of my head as the steam curled around us.

I sighed, leaning into him. "I can't be out all night. I gotta go back to work eventually." I'd already called out today, and it was looking like tomorrow too.

"Or you could just quit," he suggested, like it was that simple.

I rolled my eyes, wriggling out of his grasp to scrub my body. "I can't just quit. And I thought you said you didn't want a kept woman."

"I don't want a kept baby mama," he corrected, lathering his washcloth. "But I'm tryna keep you."

My hands stilled, feeling a lump rise in my throat. He was just caught up in the moment. Probably still high off the sex.

Swallowing it down, I forced a laugh. "Now you're just talking shit."

"Hm. You don't even like Peachtree—ain't your contract up soon? You can just quit until you find something new."

My chest tightened. I hadn't told him I'd been contemplating moving back to New York after my contract ended.

"I didn't even text Monica to see if she was going," I said, changing the subject.

He hummed, stepping under the other shower head to rinse off.

Cash wrapped a towel around himself when we were done and headed into his closet. I followed, drying myself off and rubbing body oil into my skin. I slipped into my underwear and grabbed my phone off the nightstand.

Hey, boo. You coming to Mansion tonight?

Monica: Thinking about it. Lani been working my nerves though.

When is he not? Just come on so we can talk shit.

A few seconds later, my phone lit up with an incoming call.

"Bitch," Monica greeted me when I picked up. "Why you acting like you not finna be up under Money all night since y'all together now?"

I sucked my teeth. "Whatever. He don't run me."

"Yeah, aight," she tutted. "We'll see. But fine, I'll come out. Maybe I'll find a new nigga and rub it in Lani's face."

I rolled my eyes, knowing that she was holding out hope that Jelani would get his shit together and stop being a fuck boy.

"You know you can just block him right?"

Monica groaned. "Yeah, yeah. Alright, I'll see you in a bit," she said before hanging up.

I rummaged through my duffle bag and settled on a denim short romper and paired it with white knee-high boots. I quickly did my makeup, slicked down my edges, and wrangled my thick curls into a bun.

Cash came out of his closet in dark jeans and a forest green knit shirt, adjusting the Patek on his wrist. The way his fabric clung to his muscles and the tattoos that snaked up his arms made me pause. Every time he walked into a room, he owned it without even trying.

"You look good," I said, giving him a once-over.

He gave me that cocky smile, showing off his open face grills. "You look better," he said, licking his lips. "But you gotta stop looking at me like that, Jas."

I bit my lip, holding his stare in the mirror. The clean, spicy scent of his cologne wrapped around me, hitting me so hard I was damn near drooling.

"What you mean?"

"I mean, I'mma end up tossin' you on this bed if you don't quit it," he said, stepping up behind me. "And I know you'd love that. Too bad Hassan's already here. You ready?"

"I can't believe you just have a driver on call like that," I said as we went downstairs.

Cash shrugged. "It's better than dealing with a car service."

Outside, Hassan stood by the black G-Wagon, giving Cash a nod as we approached.

"Money," Hassan greeted, dapping Cash up before turning to me with a smile. "Jasmine." He said my name like we'd known each other for years, even though it was our first time meeting. I wasn't surprised. I was sure everyone in Cash's circle knew about me by now.

Cash helped me into the truck, his hand found my thigh as soon as his seatbelt was on. As Hassan backed out of the driveway, my phone vibrated.

I glanced at the screen, and my stomach dropped.

It was Marcus.

I shoved it back into my bag before Cash could see. I had no intention of calling him back. The car he bought sat untouched in my spot. I knew it was only a matter of time before I had to deal with him and dead this shit completely. But not tonight.

Right now, I was focused on how good things were and

leaning into that. Resting my head on Cash's shoulder, I laced my fingers in his as the downtown Atlanta skyline came into view.

♡$♡

Mansion was packed when we pulled up. Cash got out and exchanged a few words with Hassan after he parked. He came around to help me out, and I felt eyes on us as we bypassed the line and walked straight to the entrance.

Cash kept a firm grip on me as we moved through the tight bodies toward the short flight of stairs that led to VIP. This section was smaller than the one at Palladium—fewer people, less privacy. I spotted Slim and Fontaine chilling on a couch.

"Aww shit." Jelani popped up, grinning. He hugged Cash, then slung an arm over my shoulder, pulling me aside. "You know we basically related now, right?"

I raised a brow. "How you figure?"

"'Cause you're officially my brother's girl, and you met Ma. That's major—he doesn't just bring anybody to meet her."

I laughed, playing along. "Is that so?"

"Yup," he nodded like it was gospel.

I looked around. "Where's Monica?"

Jelani jerked his head toward the restroom. "She's been in there for a minute. I think she's mad at me."

"What'd you do now?" I asked just as Cash's arm slipped around my waist, pulling me back into his orbit. "What you drinking, baby?"

"Tequila soda," I said, smiling.

He kissed my forehead and went to find a bottle girl.

Monica came stomping out of the restroom, swatting Jelani's hand away when he reached for her.

"Girl, come dance with me before I smack this stupid boy," she huffed, grabbing my wrist.

I glanced at Jelani as she pulled me toward the stairs. He rubbed the back of his neck, looking like he knew he fucked up. I shook my head as we headed down into the sea of people.

The DJ was playing an early 2010s mix that had me feeling nostalgic. We found a little space to move, hyping each other up as we started dancing. She turned and started twerking on me. I grabbed her hips and caught the beat.

"Ay!" I laughed, giving her ass a playful slap.

Someone brushed against me, and I turned, smiling, expecting to see Cash, but my heart dropped when I saw Marcus's cocky grin.

"Juicy!" he shouted over the music. "Been a minute!"

"Hey, Marcus," I said weakly. Monica slid beside me instantly, clocking the shift in energy.

"You okay, friend?" she asked, eyeing him suspiciously.

I nodded stiffly as Marcus leaned in, slipping his hand around my waist.

"You been hiding from me?" he murmured in my ear.

My mouth went dry. I needed to get away from him before Cash spotted us.

"Jas, let's go back upstairs," Monica urged, tugging my arm.

Marcus tightened his hold on me. "It ain't even gotta be all that." He leaned closer, brushing his nose against my cheek.

"I just wanna know why you been duckin' me, mama."

I pressed a hand against his chest, trying to push him back, but he wouldn't budge.

My eyes flicked towards our section. *Here we fucking go.* Cash and Jelani were practically floating down the stairs, looking ready to fuck some shit up. People instinctively moved out of their way, creating a path as they pushed through.

"Lord, this about to be some shit," Monica muttered.

"The fuck is this?" Cash growled, his eyes locked on Marcus.

Marcus smiled, eyeing Cash unbothered. "Oh, you ain't tell me you was here with your little *friend*, Juicy," he said, finally letting go of me.

I wasted no time backing up. "Actually, Cash is my man," I said firmly, stepping beside him.

Marcus's face twisted in anger. "Your man? You dead ass? 'Cause the other night—"

"Don't get popped saying slick shit, my nigga," Cash cut him off as he stepped in front of me.

"Take the L and leave, bruh," Jelani warned, moving Monica behind him. "I promise, this ain't what you want."

Marcus's eyes darkened, but he put his hands up and backed away. "Y'all got it," he laughed, his eyes flicked toward me. "I'ma holla at you, Jasmine."

Cash started toward him, and I grabbed his shirt before he could go after him.

"Fucking clown," Jelani muttered as Marcus disappeared into the crowd.

"Always some shit when we out with y'all," Monica mumbled, pushing away from Jelani when he tried taking her hand.

Cash was visibly heated as we made our way back to VIP. Slim and Fontaine sat up straighter when they saw him, like they were waiting for the green light. I sank onto a couch, trying to steady my breathing. Monica dropped down beside me with a sigh. Cash stood near the railing, fuming as he looked out over the crowd, like he was trying to track Marcus's movements on the dance floor.

The bottle girl came over with our drinks. I took mine and threw it back, hoping the tequila would wash away the sick feeling out of my chest.

"What the fuck was that?" Monica whispered.

"My nut ass ex," I muttered, fishing my phone out of my purse as it buzzed again.

Marcus: [1 video attachment]

I clicked it without thinking, expecting some bullshit.

But I wanted to throw up the second it loaded.

It was us in his hotel suite.

Him on top of me. My legs around him.

I didn't even know he recorded it.

Another text came through.

Marcus: Should I send this to your nigga?

The phone slipped from my hand and hit my thigh.

"Jasmine."

I looked up, heart hammering, and saw Cash standing over me. I snatched the phone and shoved it into my purse before he could catch a glimpse of the screen.

"Come talk to me," he said, moving toward a secluded corner.

I rubbed my hands on my thighs and stood.

"The fuck was that?" he asked once we were out of earshot.

"What was what?" I fumed. "You think I wanted him all up on me like that?"

"I didn't say that—"

"You didn't have to." I looked up at the ceiling, fighting the tears threatening to fall. "We just got past this, Cash. I'm not about to do this back and forth."

He caught my arm as I turned to walk away.

"Jas—don't do that." His voice softened.

"You're insecure about a nigga that's a non-factor. If that's where we're at, maybe I need to go back to my place."

"Nah. We're going home together," he said.

I wanted to scream. He reached out and pulled me into his chest, wrapping his arms around me. I let myself melt into him—like being this close might quiet the noise in my head.

"I'm sorry, baby," he said against my temple. "I don't like that shit. He knows what he's doing, pushing up on you to get a reaction outta me. It's not insecurity, it's about respect."

I nodded, resting my head against him. I heard him, but his words did nothing to settle the knots twisting in my gut.

Marcus could ruin everything with one tap—and Cash didn't even know.

He kissed my hair and held me tighter like it was settled.

How could I make this disappear without blowing up in both our faces?

CHAPTER 18
MARCUS STOKES

"WHAT YOU KNOW ABOUT MONEY'S GIRL?" I ASKED KYREE.

We were at his spot, going over some last-minute shit before hitting one of BC's stash houses. I didn't need anything from them. We had more than enough from our own suppliers, but it was time to see if Kyree was really built for this. He was going against the people he'd been riding with since he was fifteen. The nigga talked real tough, and tonight would show me if he could hold his weight as my second down here.

He took a long pull from the blunt, cheeks puffed out before letting the smoke out through his nose. "Not much," he said, passing it to me. "Just heard she's some nurse bitch."

If I wasn't trying to keep my connection to Jasmine quiet, I'd beat this nigga's face in with my gun. Jasmine wasn't some bitch, even if her head was a little twisted right now. She didn't deserve to be talked about like that by some young dude with no clue who he was running his mouth on.

Still, I couldn't wrap my head around how she went from me back to Money practically overnight. The math wasn't mathin'. I really thought I was close to getting her back.

The night I met her at Donny's kickback, I knew Jasmine was different from any other female I'd dealt with. She was beautiful, smart, solid—real wifey material. I felt like I could breathe around her—really be myself. But back then, I was just a corner boy out in Queensbridge, trying to get put on while she was focused on nursing school. What future could we have had for real?

So nah, I wasn't mad when she broke up with me. Shit hurt, but I held no ill will toward her. She stayed on my mind, though. I never stopped thinking about her, not once. I kept hustling and moving up the food chain, telling myself I'd spin the block on her when I had something real to offer. I wasn't trying to be some hood nigga with lofty dreams. I wanted to build something with her.

That RICO charge almost took all of that away from me. But prison turned out to be a blessing in a weird way. Shit broke me down and built me back up stronger, smarter. I learned more behind those walls than I ever did in the streets.

I had to put a couple niggas in the ground along the way. But that was the cost of building the life I wanted. It was the price I was willing to pay for her.

Everything I did was for Jasmine—to get her back where she belonged by my side. She was my soulmate. No one was gonna take that away from me. I thought about her every day I was in that concrete box, not on some *the one that got away* type shit, but about what we had and what we were supposed to be.

I needed her on me permanently. I found one of the best tattoo artists on the yard and had him ink jasmine flowers down my arms and across my chest. It wasn't that cheap, dirty, prison ink. My boy hooked me up with detailed professional-grade work. The flowers wrapped around my older tattoos, blooming over angels and scriptures like they were always meant to be there. It took five sessions, and I made sure I blessed his books to show my gratitude. Now Jasmine would forever be part of me, claimed in ink.

These other niggas inside were fighting for scraps, trying to stay alive, and whole time I was learning how to build. The OGs put me on to how the real bosses move. They put me on with their suppliers, taught me how to clean money, and how to make the system bend in my favor.

Shout out to my lawyer. After years of digging—and paying niggas off—he figured out that the Feds used illegal wiretaps. That technicality gave me a second chance. I might've been gone for ten years, but the day I stepped out those gates, I felt it in my bones—God was giving me a second chance. And this time, wasn't shit coming between me and what's mine.

Everything was already set up and waiting for me when I got out. I wasn't 'bout to be no corner boy again. Fuck that. I was running shit. City officials, cops, DAs—I spent years paying off the right people and lining their pockets. I was never seeing the inside of a cell again.

Ever.

"Why you ask?" Kyree asked, side-eyeing me.

I shrugged, "Saw them at the club the other night. Thought she might be useful."

He didn't need to know the truth.

First thing I did after I got out was hit Donny, her best friend Amber's older brother. He'd been out the game for a minute but still had his ear to the streets. More importantly, he'd been keeping me abreast of Jasmine's moves. He'd told me when she'd graduated from nursing school and when she'd passed her board exams. That's how me and her even met. Donny vouched for me then, and still fucked with me now.

I was shocked when he told me Jasmine was down in Atlanta. But when he added that it was some young niggas down there trying to make some noise? Without a doubt, I knew that was God opening a door for me. I had the money, the product, and the muscle. It was time to expand anyway, and Jasmine gave me the perfect excuse to come down here.

Within a week, I had her routine mapped out.

I knew she'd be at the soul food spot 'cause I had one of my young boys trailing her that day. What I didn't expect was for her to be hugged up with Money Banks.

Kyree stayed gassing that nigga up like he was a mix of the boogeyman and the messiah.

"Nothing moves unless Money says so."

Yeah, aight.

Every king has their weakness. You just needed to be patient enough to find it. When I saw the way he looked at Jasmine—how his eyes lit up when she talked—I realized we had something in common.

She was his soft spot. The same way she'd always been mine.

I knew hugging up on her and letting him know I'd had that pussy before him would get under his skin. I saw how tense he got, how his jaw ticked. That nigga wanted to put hands on me, but he wasn't about to show his ass in his people's spot. I'm sure they had a real cute chat after I left.

But when Jasmine kept brushing me off and dodging me like I was a fucking bill collector, I knew I had to turn up the pressure.

Fucking up her car wasn't about scaring her. She just needed to be a little shook up. Enough to second-guess being in Atlanta and getting wrapped up with that nigga. I figured it was a fifty-fifty shot—either she'd call him, or she'd call me.

And when we ended up back at my place, I thought I had it in the bag.

The pussy I'd been fantasizing about and jacking off to in my cell for years… it was better than I remembered. Being inside her again felt like everything aligned. I was back where I belonged. I'd won. Her body told me before her mouth ever would.

Then she ghosted me—went back to that nigga like what happened between us meant nothing. Said Money was her man, like I wasn't her first love.

Like I only imagined the spark reigniting between us. Like it wasn't fate we'd reconnected. Like she couldn't see how far I'd come since the last time I saw her. Bought that bitch a new car and she left it sitting in the lot like she was ashamed of it. The fuck did she think this was?

That shit had me tight.

I sent the video to wake her up out of whatever fantasy world she was living in. Jasmine needed to remember what we were. What we still are.

I knew once she saw it, she'd realize she couldn't just walk away from me.

"You want a dance, daddy?" Poppi purred, slithering into my lap.

I don't know why they kept bringing her around. She was cute, but smelled like she bathed in that old Victoria's Secret body spray girls wore in high school—Love Spell or some shit.

"I'm good, ma," I muttered, pulling on the blunt. She didn't move, just kept herself parked in my lap, eyes locked on the blunt in my hand like a fiend.

"You good, mama?" I asked, blowing smoke in her face. "Why you eyeing my shit like that?"

She giggled, tucking a loose strand behind her ear.

"Poppi!" Bambi called from down the hall.

Poppi hopped off my lap like twelve was coming and scurried off to the room in the back.

Bambi wasn't the biggest chick, but she was the one all the girls listened to. She was the baddest too—tall, long legs, beautiful deep brown skin, and a face too fine to be hanging around niggas like this. She danced sometimes, but mostly brought the girls where Kyree told her they needed to be.

She hadn't fucked with me since the incident with Poppi.

Shorty spilled some liquor on my vintage Jordans. They were deadstock that I flew out to L.A. for. Priceless shit. I blacked out a little and ended up shaking the shit outta her.

Not my proudest moment… but it was the principle.

Bambi was the only one who said shit. Her ass got right in my face and told me I had her fucked up if I thought I was gonna manhandle her girls.

I backed off.

Not 'cause I felt bad, but out of respect. I saw it in her eyes—she wasn't scared. I knew if I bucked at her, she'd put up a fight. And I liked that.

Once it was me, Kyree, and his boys, alone in the room, I got back to business.

"Your guys ready?" I asked.

Kyree leaned back with a heavy-lidded smile. "Been ready. This finna be an easy lick. There's no less than $50k of product at the house. Money's been slacking, so it should only be two, maybe three niggas inside."

Shit sounded too good to be true. From everything I'd heard, Money ran a tight ship. But Kyree had been BC for years, so I had no choice but to trust his intel.

I leaned forward, resting my elbows on my knees. "Good. Make that shit clean. I don't want no loose ends."

Kyree nodded, eyes lighting up, eager to prove himself. I

just hoped that he wouldn't be on no show-off shit because that's how people got killed.

CHAPTER 19
JASMINE MILLER

"I THINK YOU CAN GIVE ME ONE MORE, JAS," CASH GROWLED.

I clawed at the sheets, back arching as he drove into me. He was stroking me so deep, my thighs burned as he pushed my knees closer to my chest.

"Fuck, baby!" I cried out as my body shuddered, pussy spasmed around as my climax crashed over me.

Cash cursed low under his breath, thrusts growing erratic before he stilled, pressing into me as he finished with a deep groan.

I melted into the mattress, breathless and a little dizzy. He pulled out and disappeared into the bathroom, returning a moment later with a warm washcloth. I reached for it, but he ignored me, gently parting my thighs and wiping between them himself.

The small gesture—how careful he was, how soft—made something twist in my chest. An aching kind of tenderness I didn't want to acknowledge.

"I'm so happy you're snipped down there," I said, sliding back against the pillows. "Because I'm pretty sure I'd be pregnant by now."

He gave me a look as he slid into his briefs. “Just say the word, and I’ll get it reversed.”

I rolled my eyes. “You’re not serious.”

“Why would I joke about that?”

I studied his face, searching for some hint that he was playing. But he wasn’t. He never was when it came to us. It threw me off. I never knew what to do with that kind of certainty. Lately, I’d been catching myself wondering what it might feel like to say yes.

“Stop staring at me like I’m running game on you, shorty,” he said, climbing back into bed and kissing my neck. “I’m already Big Daddy, I can be baby daddy too.”

I laughed and nudged him off playfully just as his phone chimed on the nightstand. He leaned over me to get it.

“Yo,” he answered, tucking the phone between his shoulder and ear, as he pulled on his basketball shorts and disappeared into the closet to take the call.

I headed into the bathroom to wash up, still feeling the afterglow buzzing in my body. I tossed the washcloth into his hamper, climbed back into bed, and grabbed my phone.

I scrolled through social media, trying to enjoy how good I felt, but my mind drifted to the larger problem at hand—I hadn’t told Cash about the video. I barely even processed it myself before Marcus’s psycho-ass sent me another one this morning. This time, the video was zoomed in at a tighter angle and focused on my face, so you saw every expression I made while he fucked me.

I felt sick all over again just thinking about it. I didn’t respond and deleted it immediately. Same way I ignored the first one. I wanted to block him, but couldn’t. That would probably really set him off, and he’d send it to Cash off principle.

It was cruel and calculated. The Marcus I’d known

would've never done something like this. I didn't even know what his angle was. Surely he didn't think this would get me to go back to him.

Cash came back in the room and sat at the edge of the bed, his brows pinched together deep in thought.

"Everything ok?" I asked, glancing up from my screen.

"Work shit," he muttered.

I pursed my lips. "That sounds like code for shady shit you can't tell me about."

He laughed dryly. "Actually… I can. Has to do with your boy Marcus."

I set my phone down, feeling my heart start to pound. "Should I be worried?"

Cash shook his head. "Nah, I'm not worried about you and him. But that nigga and I got beef."

"This doesn't have anything to do with me, does it?" I asked, sitting up and wrapping the blanket around me tighter.

"Not really," he said, inching closer. "But your sexy ass being in the mix doesn't help," he added. "What do you know about him being down here?"

"I didn't ask him," I admitted. "But judging by his car, I figured he was still in the game—just leveled up."

"Well, he leveled up and brought dirty product with him." Cash's face hardened. "His shit is behind all the ODs."

My stomach dropped. "Are you serious?"

It'd been bad for months, so bad the mayor was calling it a public health crisis. The ER barely made it through a shift without at least two overdose cases—and most of them didn't make it.

"Yeah." He dragged a hand over his head. "Long story short, I've been trying to figure out for months where that shit was coming from. We finally traced it to him. I didn't know who he was until he said who he was at Marlene's."

I didn't know what to say. It was one thing to be in this world, but to knowingly sell something that was hurting so many people?

What kind of man had Marcus really become?

"When I went out with him…" I paused, trying to figure out a way to tell him without saying too much. "He knew who you were."

Cash's eyes darkened. "What exactly did he say?"

I took a deep breath. "He asked if I thought what happened to my car had anything to do with you. I asked him what he meant by that, and he said he knew all about the infamous Money Banks."

Cash sat up, expression cold. "What else?"

I swallowed hard, my mind flashing to the video again.

"Nothing," I said flatly. "Just that he knew who you were. That's it."

Cash tilted his head, studying me like he could tell something was off.

I looked away. "So… what happens now?"

"That first time we went out, you told me you weren't trying to get wrapped up in this lifestyle. I'm still trying to honor that," he said. "I'm handling it."

"But?"

"That nigga is grimy. I don't like the way he moves. And now that he knows we're together, I wouldn't put it past him to use you to get to me."

I stiffened. "What are you saying?"

"I just want to take some precautions," he reached for my hand. "I'd tell you to stay here, but I already know your stubborn ass gon' tell me no. So, I'm putting a detail on your building."

"To do what? Watch the damn parking lot?" I scoffed. "He's not gonna snatch me up, Cash."

"This shit not funny, Jasmine," he said, giving me a hard look. "It's my job to protect what's mine," he said.

"You don't think you're overreacting? How long you plan to keep this up?"

"'Til I put that nigga down," he said with a shrug.

"Cash…"

"The game is the game, love. He knows just like I do. I'm sure he's thinking the same about me."

$

Monica and I trudged through the parking garage after finishing a grueling twelve-hour shift. Another wave of OD cases came in today, and Cash's warning about Marcus kept replaying in my mind.

"What's up with you and Jelani?" I asked, tossing her a look. She'd told me she'd gone on a few dates and was even being friendly to Dr. Matthews. I didn't know if she was trying to get Jelani out of her system or if she truly moved on.

Monica shrugged, twirling her keys in her hand with a tired smile. "Other than him not leaving me alone? Nothing."

"So you're over him for real?" I asked, digging out my own keys from my purse.

She hesitated. "I mean… I'm not completely over him. But I know he's definitely not good for me."

"So you blocked him?"

"No…" she shook her head. "I can't deny that I like him, but trust? Yeah, not so sure about that, you know," she sighed as she unlocked her door. "Maybe he needs a few years, and he'll calm down like Cash."

I snorted. "Cash? Calm? You got jokes, Mo'."

"You know what I mean," she smacked my arm. "Cash knew he wanted you. There were no mind games. You saw how quick he shut that shit with Princess down. Now, baby brother? That one be talking 'bout being done with other bitches, but can I trust him after he was being messy in my crib?"

I thought back to Jelani's face at the club when he realized how badly he fucked things up with Monica.

"I don't know, sis. He was looking like a kicked puppy when you kept blowing him off at Mansion."

She rolled her eyes. "Please. He's just mad 'cause he can't get what he wants. And don't be defending him just because you're in good with the family now."

"Girl, bye!" I laughed, heading toward my car. "See you Wednesday."

Monica paused. "You sure you don't want a ride to your car?"

"I'm good. It's just down there." I waved her off and pulled out my phone to call Cash.

"'Sup, beautiful." His voice had me cheesing immediately.

"Hey," I said softly. "I just got off and heading to my car." Ever since he told me about Marcus, Cash wanted me to call and check in with him after I got off. I thought it was overkill, but I humored him. I walked down the steps to the lower level, where I was parked.

"You coming over?"

I sighed. "No, I'm exhausted. I don't have the energy for the drive, babe."

Cash's house was almost thirty minutes from the hospital, while my apartment was only ten.

"That's why I keep telling you to let Hassan pick you up and drop you off," he scolded.

I rolled my eyes. "Having my building watched isn't enough? I don't need a driver too. I'll be over tomorrow... unless you want to come to my place."

He sucked his teeth. "And sleep in that small ass bed? Tuh.

I let out a tired laugh, but it faded when I saw a figure leaning against my car.

"Cash," I whispered, walking slower. "There's someone by my car."

"What? Jas, go back inside the hospital. Where's Monica?"

"She left already." My voice was barely above a whisper. My heart began hammering as I squinted and froze.

Marcus.

"Baby, let me call you back." I ended the call and slid my phone into my pocket.

He was leaning against the new BMW X4 that Cash bought me. He'd gotten rid of the gaudy Benz Marcus bought me, saying there was no way I was driving around in something another man gave me. That much we agreed on—I didn't even like it. He sold it and dropped the money in my account. I still felt like a BMW was a bit much, but at least this felt more like me.

"What's good, Juicy?" he drawled with a smug smile that made my stomach turn as he pushed off the car's hood.

I adjusted my bag on my shoulder and took a cautious step back.

"What are you doing here, Marcus?"

He lifted his hands. "You been ignoring my texts. Figured it'd be better to come speak in person—without your nigga interrupting us."

"I've been working," I scoffed, trying to keep my voice

even despite the growing sinking feeling in my stomach. "It's late, Marcus. I'm tired. Whatever this is, it can wait."

He continued moving closer to me until I was backed up against the car next to mine.

"See you got a new whip," he said and nodded toward the BMW. "My shit wasn't good enough for you?"

The air around us felt thick. I swallowed hard and glanced around the empty garage. "Marcus, please. Just let me go home. We can talk some other time."

"You know," he said as he rubbed his jaw, " I thought we had a nice time together. Then, just like that—" he snapped his fingers, "—you ghost me and get back with *that* nigga? Explain to me how that works, ma?"

Was this nigga out his rabid-ass mind? What the actual fuck was happening right now?

"It wasn't like I planned any of this. It just happened," I mumbled. I felt hot, sweat rolled down my back—every nerve in my body screamed at me to run, but it felt like my legs were bolted to the floor.

"So, that's it?" he sneered, his gaze narrowed, and his eyes darkened. "I waited ten years for a second chance with you, and you just toss me aside like what we had was nothing?"

He reached out and grabbed me. His fingers dug into my arm.

"Marcus, you're hurting me," I whispered, tears stinging my eyes.

"You hurt me first." There was an unhinged quality to his voice now.

My phone started vibrating in my pocket.

A slow smile curved on Marcus's face. "I bet that's him."

"Don't—" I started, but he'd already snatched the phone from my pocket.

"Yerrr!" he answered, putting the phone on speaker. "What's good, my guy?" His eyes never left mine.

"Who the fuck is this?" Cash asked angrily.

"Come on now," Marcus grinned. "You know who this is."

"Put Jas on the phone, Marcus," Cash growled.

"Sorry, my wife can't talk to you right now."

"*Wife?!*" Cash and I exclaimed at the same time.

Marcus disconnected the call and slid the phone into his pocket. "Time to go home, Jas."

"Marcus wha—"

He pulled me into him, his breath hot against my ear. "I waited a decade for a second chance with you. I'm gon' make you see that we belong together, baby. Believe that."

Before I could pull away, he pulled a dirty white cloth from his pocket and clamped it over my face. A sickly sweet smell flooded my nostrils and burned my throat.

"Wha—" I tried to speak as the world around me blurred.

"Shh…" he murmured, catching me as my legs gave out. "I'm gonna fix this."

CHAPTER 20
CASH "MONEY" BANKS

"FUCK!" I SLAMMED MY FIST ON THE COUNTER WHEN Jasmine's phone went straight to voicemail for the hundredth time.

I called Jelani. He picked up on the first ring. "Yo."

"He took Jasmine," I gritted as I headed for the safe upstairs.

"Wait—who?" his voice sharpened. "Yo, turn that shit down!" he barked at someone in the background.

"Marcus," I spat, pressing my thumb to the keypad. The safe popped open with a click. I put the phone on speaker and checked both chambers of my guns before shoving them in the waistband of my pants. "I fucking told her that nigga was grimy."

"What you need me to do?"

"Call Slim. Tell him to hit that nigga's shipment tonight." We were supposed to wait another day or two, but if Marcus wanted to start a war, I'd give him one. "I put a tracker on her phone a few weeks back. If it's still on her, I can ping her location.

"You put a tracker on her phone?"

"Now's not the time to judge me, nigga," I said as I shoved my feet into my sneakers. "I'm calling Nairobi. She needs to bring Kyree in. Time to wrap this shit up."

I hung up and grabbed my keys. My heart hammered against my ribs, rage swelling in my chest at the thought of something happening to her.

If Marcus violated her, he was gonna regret the day that RICO got tossed.

CHAPTER 21
JELANI BANKS

"I GOTTA GO," I TOLD SHEA AFTER HANGING UP WITH Money.

She sat up in the bed, the sheets slipping down to her waist. "What's going on?" she asked, handing me my t-shirt.

"My brother needs me. It's an emergency." I grabbed my wallet and keys off the nightstand.

"But you'll come back after, right?" she asked hopefully.

Truthfully, I shouldn't have even been here. But Shea was a pretty face with a fat ass and deep throat. Ever since Monica started curving me, I'd been hitting her up more often than I'd cared to admit.

Monica. Shit. I should call her about Jasmine.

"Nah. But I'ma holla at you," I said, walking out of the room. I rushed through the front door, hopped in my car, and called Slim as soon as the Bluetooth connected.

"'Sup," he answered.

"Some shit went down with the nurse. Money said hit that nigga's shipment tonight," I said, backing out of the driveway.

"The fuck? I don't know if I have enough time to get everybody together."

"Make that shit work. Marcus snatched Jasmine, so you already know Money finna burn shit down behind her. Get it done and call me when y'all in position,"

"Shit," Slim muttered. "Yeah, aight. I got you. I'll hit you back."

I cut through traffic, praying I wouldn't get pulled over for speeding. I needed to hit my condo for some heat. I dialed Monica next. She sent me to voicemail twice, but finally she answered.

"What do you want?" she asked. I could hear the impatience in her voice.

"Jasmine's missing," I said, cutting off a slow car.

"What? I just saw her when I got off work." I heard rustling and a low voice in the background.

"Yo, who you got over there?" I snapped.

"Lani, you just told me Jasmine's missing, and now you're worried about who's here? You a nut ass nigga, you know that?"

"Damn right I wanna know who's at my girl's crib," I shot back.

She sucked her teeth. "Are you calling 'cause you want my help? Want me to call the hospital?"

"I'm actually 'bout to come get you. We'll go together."

"I'll meet you there."

"Monica, have your thick ass ready in thirty. And tell the nigga you got over there your man's coming through—and I'm a shooter. Don't play with me." I hung up and floored it.

I double-parked in front of my building and put the hazards on. I stormed through the lobby and punched the elevator button to my penthouse. My phone vibrated, and I answered without checking.

"Her phone is still pinging at the hospital," Money said tightly.

I'd never heard my brother worked up about anyone like this before. No woman had ever gotten under his skin the way Jasmine did. He didn't say it out right, but the way he moved when he talked and acted around her made it obvious. That nigga worshipped the ground she walked on.

He was in love.

"I'm picking up Monica and heading over there. I'll see if I can get footage and find her phone," I replied. "You hear from Nai?"

"Yeah. She's gonna bring Kyree to the crib. I'm taking him down to the basement. Come through when you're done at the hospital."

"Bet. Slim's rounding up the crew to hit the shipment. He's not happy about it, but he knows what it is."

"Good," Money replied, ending the call.

I stood in the entryway of my condo, heart racing as adrenaline pumped through me. We'd been to war before, but this wasn't that. This wasn't business. We didn't know what we were walking into, what resources Marcus had, or what he'd do after his shipment was destroyed.

"I hope she's worth it, bruh," I muttered aloud as I stormed into my office. I flipped open the hidden panel and punched in the code. There was a soft click, and then the bookshelf split open to reveal my gun cache. I grabbed the duffle bag on the floor and started tossing shit into it—handguns, extra clips, knives, gloves, and a small med kit.

I needed to be prepared for anything.

By the time I was back at my car, my chest was tight, my mind spinning with a hundred different ways this could play out. If Marcus hurt Jasmine, Money was gonna burn all this shit down.

The drive to Monica's was a blur. I kept wondering just how far my brother was willing to go to get his girl back.

As I pulled up, I spotted Monica already sitting in the lobby of her building. I honked twice to get her attention.

"I'm only here because of my friend," she grumbled as she got in.

"And because you missed me," I teased, leaning over to kiss her cheek.

She mushed me in the face. "Don't even start."

"Can't help it," I grinned, pulling onto the street.

She glanced over, her expression softening. "It was Marcus, wasn't it?"

"How you know?"

"That nigga gave me weirdo vibes at the club. The way he was looking at her..." She shuddered. "Something was off. But she kept telling me he was harmless."

"Hm," I hummed. "So, who you had over at your place?"

She scoffed. "Here you go with this shit again."

"What you mean?" I asked, tightening my grip on the steering wheel.

She turned to face me, narrowing her eyes. "One minute, you act like we go together, and the next, you're laid up with one of your bitches. I'm sure that's what you were doing before you picked me up."

I pressed down on the gas when the light turned green.

"Exactly," she said, shifting in the seat. "Like I fucking thought."

I huffed out a frustrated breath. "I told you—I'm sorry."

"Yeah, you *are* sorry," she muttered.

"I've been trying to show you I'm serious, Mo'." I said, pulling into the hospital lot. "It's just hard to balance everything."

She sucked her teeth. "Balance? Jelani, the only thing you

know how to balance is a bitch on your dick. And you can keep doing that, 'cause I had a life before you and I'll have one after you. It's not like there's a shortage of niggas outside."

I didn't say shit because I couldn't argue with the truth.

"Can't keep your dick in your pants, but ready to knock somebody's head off if they look at me. Like I said—a nut ass nigga."

Monica hopped out as soon as I parked, like she couldn't wait to be out of my presence.

"Yo! Mo', wait up."

She paused long enough for me to catch up. "This is about Jasmine, not us. Save whatever sob story you got for later." She spun on her heel and kept walking. Even with her face all screwed up, she was so damn pretty.

I ran my hand down my face as I followed her. "You don't gotta act like this," I muttered under my breath.

She gave me another dirty look. "Lani, shut the fuck up and focus." She plastered a smile on her face as we reached the reception desk.

"Hey, Ms. Wanda," she chirped at an older Black woman behind the counter.

Ms. Wanda looked up from her phone and smiled over her readers. "Monica! What you doing back here? I thought you got off already. Forget something?" She side-eyed me curiously. "And who's this? Your boyfriend?"

Monica jumped in before I could answer. "Uh, actually, Ms. Wanda, I think I left my badge somewhere. Just wanted to check if it ended up with security. Who's down there tonight?"

Ms. Wanda flipped through a stack of papers. "Looks like Richie."

Monica's smile stayed perfectly sweet, like she wasn't just cursing my ass out. "Thanks so much, Ms. Wanda!"

"Why you ain't introduce me?" I fell in step beside her and hooked a finger in her belt loop. She slapped my hand away and pressed the elevator button.

I really hated the silent treatment from her. I cleared my throat. "Baby Doll—"

"Don't call me that," she snapped, giving me another hard look as the elevator doors slid open. We stepped inside, and she hit the button for the lower level. She stared ahead, arms crossed, tapping her foot impatiently as the numbers ticked down.

She moved with purpose toward the security office when we reached the basement. I trailed behind her and watched as she pushed open the door labeled *Peachtree Memorial Security.* The room was cramped, lined with filing cabinets and glowing TV monitors. Richie, a Black man in his mid-forties, was chillin' at the desk with his feet kicked up. He looked up and smiled when he saw her.

"What's up, Mo' baby?" he greeted her, a little too warmly for my liking.

"Hey, boo," she cooed, batting her eyelashes. I rolled my eyes, but Richie's ass ate that shit up. "I need a huge favor. It's an emergency."

He sat up, so transfixed on Monica that he barely noticed me. "What you need?"

"Something happened to Jasmine," she said. "She got snatched in the parking garage, and we need to see the footage."

Richie's smile vanished. "Jasmine got what?! You need to call the police."

Monica shook her head. "This ain't for them, boo. I know

this breaks every rule in the book, but I wouldn't ask if it wasn't serious."

Richie finally looked over at me and sized me up. "Who's this?"

"Her—" I started, but Monica balled up my mouth in her hand.

"Jasmine's boyfriend's brother. He's helping me."

Richie's face tightened. "Monica… If anybody finds out, I could lose my job."

This was getting us nowhere. I reached for the piece tucked in my waistband and leveled it at him. "We don't have time for all this."

Richie jumped up and reached for his service weapon, eyes wide.

"Jelani, put the damn gun down!" Monica said, throwing herself between us. "Richie, chill!"

"Monica, what the hell is going on?" Richie demanded, eyes wide.

I rolled my head and squared my shoulders. I was losing patience. "Say, man, just pull up the fucking footage so we can go."

The gun in his hand trembled—he wasn't built for this. The nigga probably never fired that thing in his whole career.

"Please, Richie," Monica pleaded.

He hesitated, eyes flicking from her to me, and nodded.

Monica sighed in relief. "Thank you! We clocked out around 8:00 p.m. We were on the third floor in the garage."

Richie dropped back into his chair and started typing.

We stepped behind the desk as the footage loaded. He toggled through the timestamps until he landed on 8:00 p.m.

"There," he said, tapping the monitor.

The grainy footage showed Monica and Jasmine entering

the garage and talking. After a few seconds, the feed froze and skipped.

Richie frowned. He rewound the video and pressed play, but it froze again in the same spot.

"That's weird. It shouldn't be doing that."

"Y'all got any other cameras on that floor?" I asked.

He typed again, switching to a second feed. This one was corrupted, Motoo.

"Fuck," I muttered.

Richie slumped back in his chair with a defeated look. "Sorry, Mo'. Looks like the whole feed's corrupted."

"How's that even possible?" Monica asked, looking at me.

"Marcus probably hacked the system," I muttered, pulling out my phone to text Fontaine. "Let's go."

"Thanks, Richie. And sorry for all the fuss," she smiled apologetically and walked out ahead of me.

I turned to him, giving him a hard look. "Next time you reach for your weapon, make sure you're ready to shoot, 'cause I don't miss." I rapped my knuckles on the desk and followed Monica out.

CHAPTER 22
MONICA PIERCE

JELANI WALKED IN AND HANDED CASH A PHONE. "THE footage from the hospital was a dub, but we found her phone."

I tried not to gawk. Cash's place was something straight out of one of those fancy home decor magazines. If this was how he lived, I could only imagine what Jelani's condo looked like.

Cash gave me a curious once-over as he closed the door. "What's she doing here?"

"Your dumb ass brother refused to take me home 'cause he thinks I'm finna call my new jumpoff," I huffed, shooting Jelani a dirty look.

Cash raised a brow at him. Jelani shrugged. "She can stay up here while we're in the basement."

"Oh, *hell* no!" I snaked my head, jabbing a finger in his chest. "You dragged me out here, and I'm supposed to sit upstairs like a kid? You got me fucked up, Lani! I have a right to know what's going on. Jasmine's *my* friend." I glared, daring him to say something.

Besides, I didn't even have anyone serious over earlier—just some old work I was debating putting back in rotation.

Cash shook his head and walked off.

"Can you chill?" Jelani whispered as we followed him downstairs.

I elbowed him. "I *am* chill. But you not about to have me upstairs alone while you do god knows what."

Cash led us through a maze of a basement. We passed his home gym, a small screening room, and a few other closed doors before stopping at one.

He turned to look at me, his brown eyes cold. "If anything you see tonight leaves this room, that's your head."

My stomach dropped. I glanced at Jelani, unsure how to respond.

"Money, she's not gonna—"

Cash held up his hand and cut him off.

"I don't care about whatever you got going on with my brother, or that Jasmine's your friend. It's my job to protect this family at all costs."

I swallowed hard and nodded slowly. "I hear you, Money. I get it."

"Good," he said, unlocking the door.

The room was bare. Clear tarp covered the floor, and a metal table and chair were in the center. The sharp, sterile scent of industrial cleaner hit me immediately. I felt like I was back at the hospital.

I forced myself to keep my face blank as I looked around. There was a man slumped in the chair with his hands chained to the table. His feet were tied to the chair legs.

A woman with platinum finger waves slid off a deep freezer in the corner. She was bad as hell in her black jump-suit and heels. She looked a little too put together for whatever the hell was about to go down here.

She smirked as we walked in, looking me up and down. "Really, Jelani? You brought your girlfriend?"

I frowned and started to respond, but Jelani quickly grabbed my elbow and steered me to a folding chair.

"Sit here, Baby Doll," he said in a low voice.

I resisted the urge to smack him and tell him to kiss my ass, but now wasn't the time.

The woman turned to Cash and clapped excitedly. "So, we waking his ass up?"

Cash nodded. She crouched next to the man and pulled a syringe from a small black bag on the floor. She jabbed it into his thigh, and seconds later, he jerked upright, eyes flying open with a sharp gasp like someone had poured ice water on him.

"Bambi?" His voice cracked as he looked around wildly. "What the—Where am I?" His chest heaved as he looked around in panic.

"That's not my name," she said coolly, patting his head.

Cash stepped up beside her with an icy grin. "Kyree, you've never been to my house before," he said, spreading his arms. "Welcome."

A chill ran down my spine at the amusement in his voice.

Kyree's eyes went wide again as he yanked against the chains.

"You can stop all that," the woman drawled. "There's no point struggling. You're not going anywhere."

"Yo, Money, wh-what the hell? Why you g-got me tied up like this?" Kyree stammered.

Cash's smile dropped. "You tell me," he said, keeping his voice even. "What would make me bring you to my house, especially when you've been MIA for months?"

I glanced at Jelani. He stood next to me with his arms

crossed, watching like this was the most normal thing in the world.

"On everything, I don't know what you're talking about," Kyree's voice cracked.

Cash let out a tired sigh, pinching the bridge of his nose. "Kyree, please don't piss me off. You're here, so you already know you're not leaving alive. Cut the shit."

He picked up a hunting knife from the table, turning it so the light caught the blade's edge. Tracing a finger down the blade, he locked eyes with Kyree.

"Where's Jasmine?"

Kyree blinked, his face twisting in confusion. "Who?"

Cash brought the knife down in a fluid motion, slicing clean through Kyree's pinky.

Time stretched. For a second, Kyree just stared at the blood spurting from his mangled nub like his brain hadn't caught up yet.

That woman must've given him adrenaline because it took another few seconds before a raw, gut-wrenching scream tore from his throat.

I flinched, my heart hammering, but I forced myself not to look away.

This was the Money Banks that niggas feared.

"What the fuck?" I muttered.

Kyree's voice broke through his sobs. "Who the fuck is Jasmine?!"

"Wrong answer." Cash stepped back, unfazed by the blood pooling on the table. "Let's try this again. I don't have time to waste, and you don't have much left."

The room was quiet, save for Kyree's cries. I was starting to think that staying upstairs wouldn't have been so bad. Jelani said that someone would be getting roughed up on the ride over, but clearly, we had different definitions of what that meant. I'd seen some things as an ER nurse, but this was some next shit. I shifted uncomfortably as Cash paced.

"I know you been working with Marcus to push his shit down here," he said. "And apparently, you think I have too much power, and you wanted something for yourself. Ain't that right, Nairobi?"

He looked over at the woman, who was leaning against a wall, inspecting her nails.

Nairobi glanced up, rolling her eyes. "Now, why would you tell him my government name, Money?" She sucked her teeth. "Kyree, baby, do us all a favor and tell the man what he wants to know. He gets real long-winded when he's pissed."

Cash reared back. "Me? Long-winded?"

"Tuh. Nigga, you be giving soliloquies and shit," Jelani chuckled.

Were they cracking jokes like a man hadn't just gotten his finger chopped off?

"Man, fuck y'all," Cash flipped them off, turning back to Kyree. "Point is, you really thought I didn't know what you were up to, when I've known for months. Rahmel snitched you out, you know." He cocked his head. "You need a better team if you're going to try and move in on my shit."

"Money, I was just trying to help the nigga set up shop here," he blubbered, tears and snot streaking his face. "I was gonna put you on, I swear!"

"Uh huh." Cash lifted the knife again. "Why would you help some random nigga push shit in my territory, Kyree? And his shit dirty. I don't need you or anybody putting me on to shit."

"I don't—" Kyree started, but the knife came down straight through the middle of his hand.

This time, the scream was instant.

I squeezed my eyes shut and gripped Jelani's leg as Kyree's cries echoed off the walls.

Cash pulled out his phone, tapping it to pull up his lock screen.

Oh, he had my girl as his wallpaper? This nigga was gone over her for real.

"You seen her before?" he put the screen in Kyree's face.

Kyree squinted, blinking weakly as he struggled to focus. His face was pale from the blood loss.

"Yeah," he mumbled. "I saw her with you at Emerald Lounge a while back." His voice trailed off as he slumped over.

"Nai, hit this nigga again," Cash ordered.

Nairobi pulled another syringe from the bag and walked toward them.

My nurse instincts kicked in. "Careful, you don't want him having a heart attack," I muttered.

"I got this. Thanks," she replied dryly as she jabbed the needle into Kyree's thigh.

He jerked awake, coughing as the adrenaline kicked in again.

Jelani knelt beside me. "They know what they're doing," he whispered. "He won't die before we get what we need."

"So you've never seen Marcus with her?" Cash asked, holding up the phone again.

Kyree shook his head vehemently. "No. He barely paid attention to the girls Bambi brought around." He winced as Cash yanked the knife out his hand. "He did ask me about your girl once."

Cash's face darkened. "What'd he ask?"

Kyree swallowed, struggling to steady himself. "He just wanted to know if I knew anything about her… I told him I didn't know who she was, just heard she was some nurse bit—"

The metal table clanged as Cash's fist smashed down on Kyree's injured hand.

"Watch your fucking mouth," he growled.

Kyree screamed, his body shaking from the pain. "Aight, aight, I'm sorry!" he panted. "That's all I know! He just said that maybe she could be… useful. I don't know nothin' else!"

Something clicked.

New York.

I don't know how I knew, but I felt it deep in my gut. It made too much sense.

BC was too deep in Atlanta for Marcus to hide out here. But he could move freely in New York. If he had the money, he could've easily chartered a flight with no one knowing.

"They're in New York," I blurted, shooting up from my seat. All heads turned to me. Nairobi raised an eyebrow, halfway impressed.

"What makes you say that?" Cash asked.

I shifted closer to Jelani. "Marcus has nobody here, and y'all got too many eyes on the streets," I said. "Even if it's not BC, everyone knows the local crews are loyal to you. If I were trying to get her away from you, that's where I'd go."

I could see the gears turning in his head.

"Nai, call Fontaine and tell him to check the most recent charter flights out of the city," he instructed. "Lani, call West. Have him get a plane ready. And take Monica home—she don't need to see this next part."

Jelani gave a quick nod, then motioned for me to follow him. I hesitated and glanced back at Kyree. He was shaking now—tears and snot running down his face. My heart twisted despite knowing he'd fucked up royally by betraying Money. Nothing could save him now.

Jelani's hand closed around mine."Come on," he said, pulling me towards the door.

Pop.

My breath caught in my throat at the sound of a single, muffled gunshot. It echoed in my head, but I kept putting one foot in front of the other.

It's not like I hadn't seen the effects of violence up close. I'd patched up plenty of gunshot wounds and stabbing victims working at Peachtree Memorial. It was wild seeing the shit happen in real-time.

The image of Kyree's face stayed with me all the way to the car.

I slid into the passenger seat and moved on autopilot as I buckled my seatbelt. "So now what?"

"Now I take you home," Jelani replied as he pulled out of the driveway.

"And Jasmine?"

His jaw ticked. "You heard Money—we're going to New York. Even if we gotta burn through the five boroughs, Money ain't leaving till he gets her back."

I let out a heavy sigh and leaned back against the headrest. The rush from earlier was quickly wearing off. My limbs felt heavy, and my head was foggy. The adrenaline had faded—the effects of the ten-hour shift I worked before this came crashing down on me like a freight train.

My home girl had gotten snatched up by her psycho-ex, and I just witnessed a man get tortured right before being killed.

What the fuck was my life right now?

"You know I'd do the same for you, right?" Jelani said after a stretch of silence.

I looked over at him, too tired to argue or overthink it.

"Okay," I mumbled, barely able to keep my eyes open.

When they opened again, Jelani was parked in front of my building.

"We're here," he said quietly. I rubbed my eyes, looking at him.

Ugh. I hated how damn fine he was.

"Thanks." I needed to get out before he said something that would have me rethinking my decision to cut him off.

Jelani's hand caught mine as I reached for the door handle.

"Mo' wait…"

I sighed, shaking my head. "Lani, can we not? I'm tired. Tired of fighting you."

"Nah, listen," he said, his voice held a sincerity I'd never heard from him before. "When I get back from New York, I need it to be me and you, Baby Doll. That's all I wanted to say."

He didn't let go of my hand, and I didn't pull away.

"I can't keep doing this shit with you," I said. "Today, you want me tomorrow, you're out doing whatever. You're all over the place, Jelani."

"Seeing Money tonight made me think about who I'd go that hard for. And it's you, Monica. I know I'm a mess, but I don't want to lose you."

His lips were on mine before I could process what he said.

This wasn't one of those other kisses he'd given me in the past—the ones that were usually charged with heat and frustration. This was different. It was softer. Sweeter. Like he was finally putting all his cards on the table.

Jelani's hand slipped to the back of my neck and eased me forward until there was no space left between us. I moaned as his tongue swept over my mouth and my fingers twisted around his locs.

Everything that pissed me off about him faded away into the background. None of it mattered, and I let myself get lost in him.

When he finally pulled away, he rested his forehead on mine. My lips tingled from his kiss.

"I only want you, Baby Doll," he murmured.

Part of me wanted to argue, to tell him he was full of shit. But the dampness in my panties said otherwise.

So I just nodded.

He let me go but gave me one last, soft peck. "Go get some rest," he said.

I almost asked him why he wasn't coming up with me, but decided it was better this way.

Jelani's gaze never left me as I got out of the car. I felt it on me as I walked to the lobby door. I didn't look back.

I was on autopilot until I was back in my apartment. I exhaled deeply as I closed the door behind me. I pressed my back against it and shut my eyes, caught somewhere between relief and hating myself for wanting him all over again.

One thing was for sure—if this nigga broke my heart, I'd kill him.

CHAPTER 23
JASMINE MILLER

MY EYES FLEW OPEN LIKE I'D JUST BEEN YANKED OUT OF A dream. My heart raced, and my head pounded like I'd gone too hard the night before. Everything felt off—hazy, disjointed, like I couldn't wake up fully. Attempting to piece things together only made the throbbing worse.

Groaning, I reached out toward the nightstand for my phone, but my fingers grazed nothing but sheets. I frowned as I blinked into the dim room. Thin slivers of sunlight slipped through the curtains, casting faint lines of light across the room.

Cash didn't have blackout curtains.

I squeezed my eyes shut and tried to push past the ache in my skull. Bits and pieces of last night filtered in—leaving work with Monica, calling Cash, and then… *Marcus*.

My stomach twisted as the coldness in his face flashed in my mind.

I rolled out of bed and stumbled toward the windows. Sunlight poured in when I yanked the curtains open, making me cover my eyes to block the glare.

My jaw dropped once my vision adjusted.

Central Park was sprawled out twenty stories down.

New York? This nigga brought me back to New York?

I clutched my stomach as I turned to take in the room. One wall was all windows, overlooking the city, and a king-sized bed sat against a charcoal-gray wall. Everything looked cold and expensive, like a showroom.

At the foot of the bed were a few suitcases. I looked down and realized that I wasn't in my scrubs. Someone had changed me into one of my own pajamas.

A chill ran down my spine.

Marcus had been in my apartment and gone through my things while I wasn't there. Undressed me. How long had he been planning this?

My bladder tugged at my attention, and I made my way toward an open bathroom door. My chest tightened. My toiletries neatly laid out on the counter—all my skincare, my bonnet, my fucking toothbrush, all there like I was here for an extended stay.

I sat on the toilet and stared at my hands shaking in my lap. I flexed my fingers as I took a few deep breaths in an attempt to settle my nerves.

"What the fuck, what the fuck, what the fuck…" I whispered to myself.

After using the bathroom, I splashed some water on my face, and downed a few aspirin I found under the sink. This whole thing felt surreal—like I was moving through a nightmare I couldn't wake up from.

Back in the bedroom, I couldn't stop the tears from falling as I sank onto the edge of the bed and put my head in my hands.

I should've taken Cash's warnings seriously—should've told him about the videos. But no, I stupidly held out hope that Marcus had some redeeming factor.

A soft knock at the door made me sit up.

"Amber?!" I blurted, staring at my best friend as she walked in holding two steaming mugs of coffee.

"Surprise," she said, offering me one with a weak smile.

"What are you doing here? Did you help this nigga kidnap me? And where the hell are we?" I fired off questions as I took the coffee from her.

"Ay Dios," Amber muttered, setting her mug on the nightstand. "Jas, you deadass? You think I'd help that man snatch you?"

"I don't know! Up until twenty-four hours ago, I didn't think he was even capable of doing this!"

She sat on the bed beside me, nudging at the coffee in my hands. I took a small sip while she spoke.

"He called Donny when he got here with you last night. Donny called me. We're at his penthouse. Marcus's been super erratic since he got back, so I convinced him to let me stay here with you. I told him you'd rather see my face first than his."

"Facts," I grumbled, taking another sip. "Do you have your phone? I don't know Cash's number by heart, but maybe I could DM Monica or something."

Amber shook her head. "His driver made me hand it over before I came upstairs."

"Fuck." Tears welled up again, my throat tightening as my frustration boiled over. This was too much.

Amber pulled me into a hug, rubbing my back. "Hey, hey, listen. He didn't touch you—other than carrying you up here. I changed you and stayed with you last night. I just went down to make coffee, that's why I wasn't here when you woke up."

Her words helped a little. But they didn't change the fact that Marcus had still violated me.

"Thank you," I murmured.

"For what?"

"For coming. For staying with me." I shook my head. "I don't even know what to think. Is he even here?"

"Yeah, I'm here."

Amber and I both looked up to see Marcus standing in the doorway.

"Bitch ass nigga!" I yelled, shoving my mug into Amber's hands and launching off the bed. Rage shot through me as I slapped him across the face with everything I had.

"You kidnapped me! Are you out of your fucking mind!"

Amber threw her arms around my waist and pulled me back before I could swing again.

Marcus barely flinched. He rubbed his cheek slowly, looking at me like I was a toddler throwing a tantrum. "You're not a prisoner, Jas."

"Word? Then give me my phone," I demanded. "Let me go home if I'm so 'free'."

I tried lunging at him again, but Amber locked her arms around me tighter, dragging me back toward the bed.

"You are home," Marcus said, stepping further into the room.

I stared at him in disbelief. "Do you hear yourself? You sound insane! Give me my shit, Marcus."

His mouth twisted into a smirk. "So you can call your little *boyfriend*?" he scoffed. "Yeah, not happening, mama."

My hands balled into fists, nails digging into my palms. Every word out of his mouth made me want to spit in his face.

"Your man went and blew up a huge shipment last night," he continued bitterly. "Probably after he figured out I had you. But I ain't even trippin' off that."

I glared at him; my nerves were shot, and I was hanging

on by a thread. "The fuck does y'all beef have to do with me?"

"Everything," he said, eyes darkening. "Money has a monopoly in Atlanta. Niggas too pussy to check him—why should one man have all that power?"

He scoffed. "That's why I brought you here. To get you away from all that while I get my shit established down there. Plus, New York's home. It's where you belong. With me."

He started pacing and motioned around the room. "Don't you see how far I've come? I did all of this for you. You just need to be away from that nigga to see it."

I shot Amber a look, and by the way her face was twisted up, I knew I wasn't the only one who thought he'd lost it.

"We broke up ten years ago!" I snapped. "We can't just pick up where we left off. I don't even know you anymore."

Marcus tilted his head like I was being unreasonable. "I guess this is a lot to take in, but you'll see. It was always supposed to be me and you. I'm done waiting. You're *my* woman. My wife."

"I'm not your fucking wife!" I shouted as I jumped up from the bed. My blood was boiling now.

"And those videos you took of us without my consent?" I stepped in closer and mushed his forehead hard. "How could you do that? You're disgusting."

Marcus's mouth twitched, and in an instant, his hand was around my throat, slamming me against the wall so hard my teeth rattled. I gasped and clawed at his wrist, but he only tightened his grip, cutting off air.

"Marcus!" Amber screamed, pounding on his back, and tried to tear him off me.

Finally, he let go and dropped me like nothing happened.

I crumpled to the floor, coughing and blinking through

spots in my vision. My throat and lungs burned as I sucked in mouthfuls of air.

"I let that shit slide when you smacked me 'cause you're upset," he said as he shoved his hands into the front of his hoodie. "But don't ever put your hands on me again."

He turned and walked out, slamming the door behind him like he was the one who just got choked out.

I dragged myself to my feet, rubbing my neck with shaky hands. My whole body was buzzing with pain and rage and fear that I wasn't ready to acknowledge.

"Jas—" Amber said as she bent to help me.

"I'm fine," I croaked, brushing past her and collapsing onto the bed. I didn't have any tears left—just a hollow ache growing in my chest.

"Jas, give me Monica's IG," she whispered. "As soon as I'm out of here, I'll send her a message."

"You're gonna leave me?"

"There's no way to use my phone here," she held my gaze. "Trust me. I know he's on one right now, but I don't think he'll touch you again."

I nodded and told her Monica's handle. "You better come back. I swear I'm liable to kill him if he comes back in here talking that crazy shit again."

Amber laughed and hugged me. "I got you," she promised, holding up her pinky.

"Always," I finished, hooking mine around hers.

She slipped out, and the silence of her absence weighed on me. I scanned the room, and my eyes landed on a flat screen mounted to the wall. I grabbed the remote off the dress and turned it on, needing some kind of distraction. I could still feel the ghost of Marcus's hand around my neck.

News 12 prattling on in the background didn't help.

I flopped back on the bed, wincing at the soreness in my

neck. I stared at the ceiling as Marcus's words looped through my mind.

"It was always supposed to be me and you."

And by the crazed look in his eyes, I knew that he meant that, and that was the part that shook me.

Ten years locked up had clearly broken something in him. He'd created a twisted fantasy in his head. He *truly* believed that I belonged here. His delusion was scary—not because he was angry, but because in his mind, this made sense.

I drew in a shaky breath. I couldn't afford to panic. I had to keep my shit together. Amber said she'd be back. I just had to hold out until then.

And in the meantime, all I could do was pray that Cash found me sooner than later because I wasn't sure what Marcus would do if he went too far off the deep end.

CHAPTER 24
CASH "MONEY" BANKS

"CAN YOU SIT DOWN?" JELANI ASKED, KICKING HIS FEET UP on the coffee table in our suite at the Mark Hotel. The nigga was acting like we were on vacation. "All that pacing making me dizzy."

"Then stop watching me," I snapped. It'd been forty-eight hours since I last heard from Jasmine, and I was close to losing my shit. Slim had come through and blown up one of Marcus's major shipments, which put a huge dent in his operation. Snatching the shit would've been too easy, and the city didn't need any more of it on the street.

Jelani chuckled, tossing his phone on the couch. "My nigga, I know love got you acting out of sorts, but you're the one who taught me—when you lose control of your emotions, you lose control in the game."

"Love?" I scoffed, even though the tightness in my chest made it clear he'd hit a nerve. "Who said anything about love?"

He cocked his head with a smug grin. "Bruh, you gonna act slow now? We ain't here because he's moving in on our shit. We're here because that nigga took your girl. It's personal, if this ain't love, I don't know what is."

I rolled my eyes. "It's the principle," I muttered. "Niggas can't just push their shit in my city and think that there won't be consequences."

"Yeah, aight. You keep telling yourself that," Jelani laughed. "Meanwhile, I bet your nurse is giving that nigga the blues. Hopefully, Fontaine will have updates soon."

Fontaine had been glued to his laptop since we touched down. Slim was out in Brooklyn with the Gotham Reapers, sorting out logistics and talking about checking in on some old work before heading back. Which meant, for now, it was just me and Lani.

Jelani clapped his hands, pulling me from my thoughts. "We should go out and get some food."

"We can order room service," I grumbled, sinking on the couch beside him.

"Money, my nigga, I love you, but you need some fresh air." He gave me a rough slap on the back. "Sulking around not gonna bring Jas back any faster."

He was right, but it felt wrong going out when Marcus had her locked up somewhere.

"C'mon, we're in New York. Might as well make the most of it till it's time to knock that nigga's head off." He stood and stretched. "I won't even make you pay."

"I wasn't paying anyway. Your bougie ass got me paying for this suite like we're on vacation," I said.

Jelani tossed a pillow at me. "Shut yo' grumpy ass up and get dressed."

I hated feeling out of my element. I was used to being the one called for favors—not the person calling for one.

I'd hit up one of Pops' old friends, Creed Dennis. OG Creed was the founder of the Gotham Reapers Motorcycle

Club and was as thorough as they came. If anybody knew who had real motion out here, it was him. His son, Creed Jr., CJ, ran the crew now, but OG's name still held weight.

When we arrived in New York, CJ met us at the hotel and gave us the rundown on Marcus. Word was, he built his crew while he was locked up, recruiting dudes he used to hustle with, calling hits on the outside, and moving weight on the inside. By the time his charges were thrown out, he had a whole operation waiting. Now, he practically ran Queens and Brooklyn. But with the Reapers having a presence in all five boroughs, both OG and CJ assured me they'd keep tabs on Marcus's people while I focused on getting Jasmine back.

After a quick shower, I threw on black jeans and a black sweater. Jelani had already called a car service, and by the time I grabbed my phone and coat, it was pulling up outside.

I couldn't focus—I barely noticed the traffic or the small talk Jelani tried to make. My knee bounced the whole ride like my body was trying to channel the tension bottled up inside. Weed wasn't doing shit to mellow me out—I was a rubber band stretched to its limit. On my mama, I was putting a bullet in the next person who even coughed wrong around me.

I should've done more.

Should've insisted that Hassan take her to and from work and tightened up security. Maybe I should've told her what Marcus had done to that one dancer to spook her. The nigga's a certified nut, and I still let her brush it off because I didn't want to be that guy. I didn't want to control her; I respected her boundaries and independence.

Because of that, she was gone.

Then the part I wouldn't say aloud continued to wiggle its way into my mind—*what comes after?* When this nigga is dead, and I get her back. Her contract was almost up. Was she thinking about coming back to New York? I wasn't trying to do that long-distance shit. Could I convince her to move in with me?

I let out a low chuckle and shook my head.

Damn. *Maybe I did love her.*

"What you over there daydreaming about?" Jelani asked.

I took a sip of water. "Tryna figure out how you managed to get us a table when they're clearly booked out," I said.

"Money talks. Plus, being a charming ass nigga don't hurt either."

I chuckled as our server came to take our orders.

"Welcome to Maxwell's. I'm Emma. I'll be taking care of you tonight," she said. Jelani and I rattled off our drink orders to her.

"Great, I'll put those in for you now," she said as Jelani's phone buzzed on the table.

"Hello?" His face immediately tensed. "Yo, slow down, Mo—" He sat up straighter. "Send me a screenshot. Now."

He placed the phone down with a frown.

I already felt the shift in his energy. "Everything good?"

"That was Monica. Jas' home girl, Amber, hit her up on IG. She said she's seen Jasmine… she's safe."

Amber… I'd heard that name before. That was Jasmine's best friend. How the fuck did Amber see her? Shouldn't she be doing more to help? Why wasn't she hitting me up or sending us Jasmine's location?

I opened my mouth to press Jelani for more when something in my peripheral caught my attention. My stomach dropped when I turned my head.

Jasmine.

My baby looked incredible—the champagne colored dress hugged her curves, and her curls were big and wild, the way she wore them when she couldn't be bothered to fuss with them.

But her body language was way the fuck off.

There was no light in her eyes. Her shoulders were stiff, mouth in a tight line like she was holding back a scream.

And this nigga Marcus had his hand on the small of her back, steering her through the restaurant like she was his puppet.

"What are you looking at?" Jelani asked, following my line of sight. "Shit."

My whole body tensed, blood roared in my ears—I was ready to dead this right here. Right now.

Jelani grabbed my arm. "Cash. We can't do this here."

"She's right fucking there," I gritted. I couldn't look away. Jasmine slid into the booth next to Marcus but kept distance between them. He whispered something in her ear that made her scowl.

"This ain't our city," Jelani muttered, glancing around. "He probably got security, and it's just the two of us."

Jasmine turned, like she felt me watching. Her eyes widened when they landed on me. She looked away quickly, her fingers trembling as she reached for her glass of water.

I noticed the bruises on her neck—they were faint but clear as day.

The fuck did he do to her?

I pushed back from the table. "I'm going to the bathroom."

"Sit your ass down," Jelani hissed.

"I can't sit here and pretend like I don't see her." My voice cracked as the pressure started to mount in my chest. My girl was right there. I could feel her pain from across the room, and all I wanted to do was make him pay for every second she'd had to spend with him.

"Then let's leave," Jelani said, peeling off two blue faces and tossing them on the table. "We do this the right way. We're not making a scene here."

I looked over one last time. Marcus was so consumed with her that he didn't notice where her attention was. His arm was slung over her shoulder as he kissed on her like they were this picture-perfect couple. But her eyes glistened with unshed tears, and I swear she flinched every time his lips touched her.

She shook her head, just the slightest. But I caught it.

Being that close to her and having to walk away almost broke me.

"Get me the fuck out of here."

Turning my back on her felt like betrayal, but staying would've been worse for both of us.

CHAPTER 25
JASMINE MILLER

I'D NEVER WANTED TO SCREAM SO BADLY IN MY LIFE.

My heart shattered as I watched Cash and Jelani leave the restaurant. He was right there —close enough to tear this place apart if I'd just given him a sign. But he didn't know what I knew.

Marcus never traveled without security. If Cash had made a move, it would've been a bloodbath.

"You're not drinking your wine?" Marcus asked casually, sipping his Old Fashioned. I didn't understand how he was acting like this shit was normal, like he hadn't just choked me out twenty-four hours prior.

I stared down at the glass. My throat ached when I swallowed, and the skin along my neck was slightly bruised and tender. I tried to cover up the marks as best I could, but they still peeked through.

Did Cash see them?

For a moment, I pictured myself having a reality TV moment and throwing the Sauvignon Blanc in Marcus's face, but I couldn't afford to cut up in here. He already told me he had NYPD paid off. Running, or attempting to get help, was pointless.

I grabbed it and chugged it down. "Happy?" I flashed him a fake smile.

He chuckled, swirling the ice in his glass. "I don't know why you got such an attitude. It's a nice night, we're out, and you look amazing." He leaned back and tipped his chin at me. "You know how much that dress cost?"

The wine settled in my stomach like acid. "Like I give a shit. You could've gotten it from SHEIN for all I care." I rolled my eyes.

I didn't even bother hiding the contempt in my voice. My whole body was on edge like I was expecting him to go apeshit again. Marcus insisted on painting this delusion of us being together, and I refused to play along.

What made it worse was the realization that, technically, I could stand up and walk out of here. Same way I could leave his penthouse, but he was too connected—I didn't know how deep his web went. It was a mind fuck that made me feel small and pathetic.

And I didn't care what Amber said earlier. There was no trusting a man this volatile.

His smile slipped, his eyes darkening for a beat before the mask snapped back into place. "You and that fucking mouth, Jasmine."

Our server appeared with our food, temporarily breaking up the tense moment. Marcus had ordered for both of us, because why wouldn't he? My stomach growled as they set the plate of roast chicken and truffle mac and cheese in front of me. I shifted uncomfortably in my seat. I was hungry, but I didn't trust myself to keep anything down.

Seeing Cash tonight—knowing he was here, that he came for me—was the only thing keeping me from falling apart.

Marcus twirled his pasta with his fork. "Eat," he ordered. "You not about to be starving yourself to spite me. I hear your damn stomach."

I leaned forward and rested my head in my hand. "Have it wrapped up," I grumbled. "I'll eat it in my room."

"You're being a brat," he snapped as he shoved a forkful of food in his mouth.

"Brat? You mean hostage? I don't even want to be here—you could've left me at your house."

"*Our* house," he corrected. "You should get used to us being together. What you not getting, Juicy? You're Mrs. Marcus Stokes now. Or are you the type that wants her last name hyphenated?"

"Okay, Marcus," I muttered flatly. This nigga was trying to be funny, and it was no use arguing he was off his fucking rocker.

I nursed several glasses of wine instead of eating—anything to drown out the sound of him droning on about bullshit. My untouched food was boxed and handed off to one of his security guards, who followed us like we were under Secret Service protection. By the time we headed back to the car. I was tipsy enough to need Marcus's arm just to stay upright. Was this some sick joke? That I had to lean on the same man I was trying to get away from.

$

"Jasmine."

I'd mostly sobered up by the time we got back to the penthouse and darted off to the room as soon as we got off the elevator. I needed to wash the whole night off me. I scrubbed my body raw, ignoring the ache in my neck. I threw on some pajamas, collapsed into bed, and stared at the chandelier overhead while the TV droned on softly in the background.

I didn't bother sitting up to acknowledge Marcus's presence.

"What?" I said, keeping my eyes locked overhead.

The mattress dipped as he sat at the edge of the bed. "What if I let you see your parents?" His voice had a coaxing sweetness to it, like he was offering me a gift instead of a leash.

My heart skipped a beat at the thought of seeing them, but I refused to let it show. "Knowing your ass, it's not that simple. What do you want?"

"Be my date to a charity gala in two days."

That made me turn my head to look at him. "Parading me around in public like a trophy isn't going to change the way I feel about you."

He let out a long, exaggerated sigh. "This could be work if you stopped fighting me."

"Mhm," I hummed. He was about to give me one of his tired-ass speeches.

"I built this life for us," he started.

I rolled my eyes.

"I didn't have the motion back then like I do now. You want a Birkin? I got you. A chartered flight to Bali? I can make it happen."

I sat up, heat rising in my chest. "Is this what this is about? You trying to live out some weird fantasy you've been holding onto for a decade? We broke up because you were too busy chasing the bag, and I needed to go back to school. End of story."

I dropped out of college at nineteen and had no real sense

of direction. It wasn't until I hit twenty-five that I finally got serious and decided to pursue nursing. Once I was in the thick of the program, I was drowning in classes and practicals, and Marcus was deep in the streets. What we had just fizzled out. There were no hard feelings—it was just the natural progression of things. A few months later, he got locked up.

"But now you don't have to work," he said.

I leaned back into the pillows. "You don't get to make that decision for me."

"Oh, so it's cool for you to get wrapped up with the biggest drug dealers in Atlanta, but someone you grew up with is out of the question?"

I slammed my hand against the bed. "Stop bringing Cash into this!" My voice cracked with anger. "You actin' like I got with him because he was a dealer. Newsflash—I had a roster full of niggas in Atlanta before I met him! It just—" I clapped my hands for emphasis, "—fucking happened. I even told him about you. Not by name, but he knew our history."

I exhaled and sank back down, the fight draining out of me. "At this point, I'd be better off without either of you," I muttered.

Marcus went quiet.

"If you want to see your parents, Amber will take you," he said finally. "But no funny shit. Donny put a tracker on her car, and my people will follow you. If I even think your parents know what's going on, I'll hurt them."

The way he said it so casually sent a chill down my spine.

He stood to leave. "I'd hate to do that to you," he added softly.

CHAPTER 26
NAIROBI CRAWFORD

"BEAR," I MURMURED AGAINST FONTAINE'S SWEATY shoulder.

"Hmm?"

"We gotta get going," I said as I kissed the top of his head.

He groaned like a spoiled child and rolled himself off me. "Shower with me?"

"Nuh uh. We'll be late if we do all that," I smirked, even though the ache between my thighs almost made me reconsider.

When Money said we were heading to New York, Fontaine didn't even ask.

"I already got us a junior suite," he said on the ride to the airport. "You gon' be sneaking in my shit anyway."

We still hadn't defined our situation. Did he care? Of course. But this thing between us was too strong. No matter how many times I told myself I'd fall back, I kept ending up in his bed, with him buried deep inside me.

I hit the shower, letting the hot water clear my head, and threw on jeans and a hoodie.

When I came out of the shower, Fontaine was in his boxers, hunched over his laptop, glasses low on his nose.

I picked up my purse and slid on my sunnies. "Go wash up. I'll meet you upstairs."

He glanced up over the rim of his glasses. "Arriving at different times ain't gonna make it less obvious."

"Maybe not," I shrugged. "But it doesn't make it *super* obvious."

"Yeah, aight," he said, rolling his eyes before going back to work.

Before going to Cash's room, I stopped at one of them overpriced delis for a breakfast sandwich. I almost got one for Fontaine, but caught myself.

It still tripped me out that I'd been riding with them for five months. Most contracts didn't last this long, and if I weren't so close with Cash, I probably would've been gone already. Rescue missions weren't my usual gig either, but a job was a job. Niggas would die, and I'd still get my money.

"Look who decided to finally show up," Jelani teased when he opened the door.

I brushed past him. "Here you go," I said. "My bad for wanting to get some food before we got started."

"Is that all?" he replied, closing the door behind him. I wasn't even going to think about what he meant by that.

He leaned in. "Heads-up—Money's been in a mood all morning."

Sunlight spilled through the oversized windows of their suite. It was unnaturally quiet—normally, the guys would be talking shit before we got started. Jelani would be getting on Money's nerves, but the vibe in here had me second-guessing if I should even open my mouth. And I don't get rattled easily.

Cash stood by a window in the living room, hands in his

pockets, staring down at the street as if he could will Jasmine to appear among the thousands of people below.

Slim was lounging in an armchair, eyes closed, looking completely unbothered.

"Slim," I called to him, wanting to break the silence. "You end up linking with ol' girl in Brooklyn?"

Slim cracked an eye open as a slow grin spread across his face. "Sure did," he said.

I unwrapped my sandwich and glanced over to Cash, who still hadn't acknowledged my presence.

"Where's Fontaine?" Money said finally as he turned from the window.

Right on cue, there was a hard knock at the door. Jelani hopped up to answer it.

Fontaine strolled in, his book bag slung over one shoulder, with a man I didn't recognize trailing behind him.

"My bad, y'all," Fontaine said, dropping his bag on the floor. "Needed coffee."

Cash turned his attention to the stranger. "CJ," he said with a nod.

"What up, Money?" CJ stepped forward to dap up him and Slim.

"Damn, Money, it's like that?" I teased, mid-chew. "Can a lady get a little respect?"

"My fault, Nai," Cash exhaled, running a hand down his face. "Slept like shit last night."

CJ dropped on the couch next to me, forcing me to scoot over. That Brooklyn arrogance oozed off him as he ignored the side eye I gave him. The man knew he was fine as hell, though—smooth nutmeg skin, full lips, and a fresh Caesar fade that I knew he got lined up every week. His biker vest proudly displayed the Gotham Reapers symbol, and hung open to show off his solid build under a fitted long-sleeved shirt.

He turned, flashing me a dimpled smile and a playful wink like he knew I was grilling him. I rolled my eyes and popped the last of my sandwich into my mouth.

Jelani dragged another chair into the room, sighing heavily as he sat. “We saw Jasmine and Marcus last night.”

“What?” Slim sat up straight.

“We went to get dinner, and apparently so were they,” Jelani said grimly.

My pulse kicked up. “They see y’all?” I asked.

“Jas did,” Cash said, finally stepping away from the window. “Marcus didn’t. I swear on Sydney—I’m ready to put a hole in that nigga’s head.”

Fontaine was already pulling out his laptop. “About that… I found some shit this morning you need to see.”

Cash made his way over, hovering over Fontaine’s shoulder as he typed. I couldn’t see the screen, but I watched Cash tense up, eyes narrowing.

“The fuck am I looking at ?”

“A marriage certificate,” Fontaine said slowly.

“Fuck,” Slim muttered.

Cash straightened and let out a hollow, humorless laugh. He looked like he was two seconds from crashing out. “She ain’t marry that nigga.”

“He forged her signature,” Fontaine confirmed. “But it’s filed, it’s official on paper.”

A chair went flying across the suite, crashing against the wall as Cash exploded. “This why he called her his wife?” he shouted.

I dragged my teeth across my bottom lip. This whole thing made my skin crawl. I knew Marcus wasn’t someone to take lightly. I’d still thought about how he blacked out on

Poppi over some sneakers. He'd come out of prison broken in more ways than one.

CJ whistled as he stretched his arms along the back of the couch. "That nigga came home on one. Can't say I'm shocked."

Cash paced the length of the suite, both hands locked behind his head. "When can I kill this nigga, yo?"

"He's taking her to a gala in two days. We can move then," Fontaine said.

Cash ran a hand over his waves. "Fuck he doing taking her to a gala?"

"Apparently, Marcus is one of the councilman's biggest donors," Fontaine explained.

Slim snorted. "A dirty ass politician in bed with a dirty ass nigga. Sounds about right."

"Oh, he's showing her off," I said. "Especially if they're married—this is some weirdo power play."

Men like Marcus pissed me off the most—corny niggas who believed their money and power made them untouchable.

Fontaine looked up from his screen. "It's gonna be tight. The whole event will be-crawling with private security and law enforcement.

"And we don't have BC manpower here," I added. "So there's no room for fuck ups.

CJ shifted beside me, his knee brushing mine as he leaned in. "Guess that's where my people come in. Stir up a little chaos an' shit."

There was no mistaking the flirtiness in his voice as his eyes slid over me. "That just happens to be my specialty."

A soft laugh slipped out before I could stop it. This man was bold.

I crossed my legs and lifted my chin. "Is that so?"

"Yeah," he murmured, leaning in until his lips almost brushed my ear. "I'm very interested in learning what *your* specialty is, mama."

"Ay, yo!"

Fontaine's voice cut through the room. He was on his feet, chest all puffed up, looking about to put CJ through a wall.

CJ raised his hands with a grin. "My fault, my fault. This you, bruh?"

I cocked my head and arched a brow at Fontaine. He stared back like I'd crossed some invisible line. Between Cash crashing out and whatever this little pissing contest was turning into, I was about to barf from all the testosterone in the room.

"I'm sending y'all the bill if you niggas fuck the room up," Jelani grumbled.

Cash stepped in and murmured something in his ear. It clearly worked because Fontaine sat back down, but continued glaring at CJ and me.

"CJ, chill on Nairobi," Cash deadpanned. "She's really handy with a knife and a gun."

CJ chuckled, licking his lips as his eyes darted back to me. "Oh, word?"

I rolled my eyes, turning back to the others. Across the room, Slim frowned as his gaze bounced between me and Fontaine, probably connecting all the dots.

I cleared my throat. "So, the Reapers will provide a distraction…" I wasn't about to be the center of attention.

"Right," Fontaine said, voice clipped. "Slim will be with the Reapers for the diversion. I'll send out the hotel layout tonight and work on scrambling their cameras."

"Why not just cut the lights?" Jelani suggested.

"Too much confusion," Fontaine replied without looking

up. “Security would lock that place down. A blackout at a gala full of city officials? That’s a recipe for disaster.”

“You don’t think we can handle it?” I pressed.

He looked up. His face was calm, but I could see the fire in his eyes. “Did I say that? I’m just saying too many unknowns.”

“Fine,” I conceded. “If I can get the burner to Jasmine, we’ll still be able to find her if things go left.”

Cash shrugged. “Works for me.”

“Thanks, boss man,” I smiled, throwing Fontaine a pointed look.

“Whatever,” Fontaine scowled.

For the next few hours, we worked out the plan. I’d roll into the gala with Cash and Jelani as arm candy, keeping an eye on Jasmine until she slipped off to the bathroom, where I’d hand off the burner. If anyone got in our way, we’d drop them.

I hung back once Slim and CJ left. Fontaine stormed out as soon as we finished. I already knew he was going to be on some bullshit whenever I got back to the room.

“Is she worth all this?” I asked Cash after Jelani dipped off to his side of the suite.

Cash was by the wet bar, pouring himself a drink. “Why you ask?”

“‘Cause I’m about to drop a stack in Saks on a dress that’s going to end up trashed before the night’s over.”

He chuckled and sank into the armchair across from me with a distant look.

“She’s worth it,” he said before taking a sip. “But I’m tapping out after this.”

I damn near slid off the couch. “You serious?”

He nodded. “Deadass. I knew Jas was my wife the second

I laid eyes on her at Palladium. I was drunk as fuck, but I knew."

"You know you sound crazy, right?"

"I'm almost forty, Nai. The hell I look like doing this forever? I'm tryna have the life my parents never had. I can handle myself, but I can't be worried about somebody sliding on her every time I turn around. I'll clean the money. Jelani can hold down the rest."

I whistled and shook my head. "Damn. Never thought I'd see the day Big Money Banks was ready to hang up his jersey."

He gave a lazy shrug. "Fontaine would do the same for you."

I blinked, forcing out a laugh. "The hell are you talking about?"

Cash drained the rest of his drink and set the glass down. "Come the fuck on, Nairobi. Y'all thought nobody noticed? That shit at Stilettos? The way y'all sat together on the plane? His little outburst with CJ just confirmed it." He leaned back in the chair. "You really thought y'all were being low?"

Well shit. "It's not—" I started, my voice catching in my throat.

He cut me off. "Shorty, I know you, and I know him. I know y'all are sharing a suite."

My mouth went dry. "How?"

Cash rolled his eyes. "Fontaine's not the only person who can hack into a hotel's database. Stop playing."

I shot to my feet. "I'm leaving when we get back to Atlanta."

"And he'll just come after you."

He might.

But if he did, I'd just have to show him how good I was at disappearing.

CHAPTER 27
JASMINE MILLER

I DECIDED TO FOLLOW MY INTUITION FOR ONCE AND SKIP seeing my parents. One look at me at my mother would've immediately clocked that something was off. She had this look she got whenever she was sniffing out bullshit—lips pursed, eyes squinted. I'd fold in seconds.

Worse if my daddy found out. He'd show up at the penthouse waving his .44 before my mama had NYPD on the line.

Nobody else needed to be dragged into this mess.

So I told Marcus I changed my mind and braced myself for another tantrum. Instead, he surprised me by calmly handing me his black Amex and told me Amber could take me shopping for the gala. I was going regardless whether I'd taken him up on his stupid-ass excuse of an olive branch.

Seeing Cash the other night gave me a little bit of hope. He was somewhere in the city working on a solution. Until then, I had to keep it cute and play along. But if the nigga put his hands on me again, I was definitely swinging back. Even if it got me killed.

Amber and I drifted through Saks, like we were two

besties on a carefree shopping trip and not that I was a hostage in broad daylight. I tried on dresses and cracked jokes, but the whole thing felt surreal. It was as if I were watching all of it happen outside of myself.

"You tryna stay in Atlanta?" she asked as we headed to the shoe department.

I shrugged. "Who knows. My contract with Peachtree is almost up, but I've been MIA for damn near a week. Pretty sure they fired me. Then Cash and I just got serious and now…" I waved a hand. "This whole mess. Chile, maybe I need to go back to square niggas."

Amber snorted as she picked up a pair of heels. "You don't even believe that."

I let out a short laugh. "You right."

Atlanta was supposed to be a temporary chapter. But being with Cash had me wondering—*what if it wasn't?*

He made me curious in a way I hadn't let myself be in a long time. Curious about what life would look like if I stayed and built something real with him.

Because, despite how wild this all was, I liked Cash. *A lot*. He made it damn near impossible not to.

He wasn't bluffing when he said I could quit my job. Most women would've jumped at that without a second thought. I mean, who wouldn't? It's rare to find a man who wants to give you ease with no strings. He didn't offer it to control me—he just wanted to give me peace. At his core, that man was a protector and provider. His showing up in New York proved it.

Being with him felt almost too good—but not in some fake fairytale way. More like an answer to a prayer I didn't even know I'd sent up.

Cash was who Marcus thought he was—who he thought

his money and power made him. But Marcus was trying to force me to love him by demanding my obedience. My submission. Cash just wanted me.

Was it love? Or was I dickmatized and under duress?

Honestly… probably a little bit of both.

♡$♡

I was still in bed when I heard the door creak open the next morning.

Marcus walked in with a breakfast tray, still acting like we were playing house—eggs, a bagel, and a glass of orange juice, all arranged perfectly.

"You should eat," he said, setting it on the nightstand.

I just stared at him. He usually left the tray outside the door. If he was in here, it's because he wanted something.

He walked over to the window and opened the curtains. "Big night tonight. Excited?"

I flipped him off behind his back, then climbed out of bed without a word and headed for the bathroom.

I took my sweet time brushing my teeth, washing my face, purposefully moving slowly in the hope that he'd be gone when I came out.

But there he was—perched on the edge of the bed with an envelope next to him.

"Here," he said as he stood, holding it out to me.

I narrowed my eyes. "What is it?"

"Just look."

My gut already knew it was going to be some bullshit. I snatched it from him and opened it.

State of New York Marriage License.

His name. His signature.

My name.

A signature that was supposed to be mine—except it looked like it had been signed by a drunk toddler.

I bit down hard on the inside of my cheek, fury crawling up the back of my neck.

"We're married now?"

He smiled and nodded. "You're officially Mrs. Marcus Stokes."

I laughed because it was the only thing keeping me from breaking the breakfast tray over his head.

"This doesn't mean shit, Marcus."

I ripped the paper in half.

Then again. And again. Until it was just scraps in my hand.

"Fuck you," I gritted as I tossed it in his face.

His nostrils flared as he snatched the glass of orange juice off the tray and hurled it across the room. It hit the wall with a loud crack, sending juice and glass everywhere.

My heart was pounding, but I didn't flinch. I refused to let him break me.

I let out a bored yawn. "You done?"

He ran his tongue along his teeth and looked away, chuckling. "I'm making big moves with important people in this city. It looks better when you're married. You need to stop trying me and get with the fucking program. It's been days, no one's coming to save you."

He turned on his heels and walked out, slamming the door behind him.

The tears came soon after. I slid down to the floor and folded in on myself as the sobs tore loose. I cried until my throat burned and exhaustion wrapped itself around me like a weighted blanket. Eventually, my body gave out, and I passed out right there on the floor.

When I woke up, the sun was dipping low behind the skyline, casting the room in a haze of golden light. A sticky patch of dried orange juice clung to the floor near my food, and the untouched breakfast tray was still on the nightstand.

I got up slowly myself to my feet and started cleaning—wiping the wall and floor, picking up the glass as best I could since there was no broom. I was practically done when a sharp knock at the door made me jump.

Before I could answer, it swung open, and two Black women walked in carrying kits. They looked like they were on a mission.

"We're here to get you ready," one said.

"I'm Dyamond," said the thicker one with a heavy Brooklyn accent. "Hair."

"I'm Keisha," the other added, wheeling her case into the center of the room. "Marcus said we need you done by six."

I stood there, hair a tangled mess, eyes puffy, still holding a crumpled paper towel. "I need a minute," I mumbled and headed into the bathroom to shower.

"Get it together," I whispered to myself as I stepped under the water. My chest ached, another wave of helplessness crashing over me. I hated feeling so small. So fucking pathetic because there was nothing I could do but wait this out. A fresh set of tears ran down my face as I pressed my forehead against the tile.

Marriage?

I choked back another sob. "Cash, where are you?"

By the time I stepped out and wrapped myself in my robe, my hands had stopped shaking, and my eyes were… less red. I practiced a smile in the mirror—fake, but good enough to pass if they didn't press me too hard.

In the bedroom, Dyamond had her tools laid out across the dresser, curling irons already heated up. Keisha was scrolling through her phone, her makeup case flipped open and ready. Both of them had a calm, non-nonsense vibe, like they'd see it all and then some.

"You good?" Dyamond asked as I slid into the chair.

"Yep," I said, forcing some cheer into my voice. "Let's get this show on the road."

"What we doin' with your hair?" she asked.

"Honestly, I don't care. Do your best or worst, I'm at your mercy," I joked.

"Nah, sis, you gotta give me more than that!" she said, planting her hands on my shoulders. "Councilman Dorsey's galas are like that! And your man's getting honored. Girl!" She patted me lightly. "Don't worry, by the time I'm done, that man's gonna be on his knees."

I almost threw up at the thought.

Keisha walked over to the garment bag hanging on the closet door. "This the dress?"

I nodded, unzipping it to show her. I'd settled on a v-neck, sequined gown, with a high slit. She studied it for a few seconds before nodding confidently. "Bet. I got you."

For the next three hours, they worked their magic. Keisha brought out her mini Bluetooth player and queued up her "Bad Bitch" playlist. We jammed to Meg the Stallion and Latto, and at some point, a bottle of champagne appeared, which I gladly sipped on to calm my nerves. Dyamond and Keisha were funny and easy to talk to, and neither pried too much into my personal life. It was the first real interaction I'd had outside of Amber, and it felt good.

"Voila!" Dyamond stepped back and handed me a large hand mirror.

I gasped at my reflection. She'd given me a quick weave

styled in long Hollywood waves that fell perfectly down the middle of my back. Keisha did her thing with my makeup—a soft, matte brown smoky eye, and a sexy nude lip.

"Damn, y'all are good," I murmured.

Keisha smiled. "You're gonna have them gagged tonight. You're already gorgeous, girl! All we did was make you a badder bitch."

"Marcus ain't gonna be able to keep his hands off you," Dyamond laughed.

I let out a weak laugh, but shuddered internally. They didn't need to know that I'd rather fling myself off the roof before that happened again.

Once they left, I slipped into the dress and YSL heels I'd bought with Amber. Standing in front of the bedroom's full-length mirror, I took in the complete transformation. I looked good, *really* good. Damn sure didn't look like what I'd been through. If I was a weaker bitch, it'd be easy to get sucked into this delusion he was forcing on me.

"Wow."

I turned as Marcus stepped into the room. As much as I wanted to two-piece him, I couldn't deny that the man was undeniably handsome. He'd come a long way from the Timbs and baggy jeans he used to wear. The tux he wore looked custom, and his long locs were braided into an intricate fish-tail braid down his back.

"You look incredible," he said.

"Thanks," I replied flatly, ignoring the adoration in his eyes.

He walked over with a smug look and held out a small velvet box. "I want you to wear this tonight."

He flipped it open. Nestled inside was a thin gold chain with a diamond-encrusted *M* charm.

My stomach twisted. "I'm not wearing that."

"It's not a request," he said firmly, removing the necklace from the box. He stepped behind me and clasped it around my neck.

His breath hit the side of my face, warm and laced with bourbon. "Now everyone will know who you belong to."

My fists curled at my sides, bile rising in my throat as he came back around, pulling another box from his pocket. This one held a gaudy, platinum eternity wedding band with huge emerald-cut diamonds that screamed "new money." My jaw went slack.

"You're not serious."

He didn't even blink. "You're my wife, remember?"

Every part of me screamed to kick him in the nuts, but I remembered what happened that morning. With gritted teeth, I let him slide the ring onto my finger.

It was tacky and loud. Just like him.

"Perfect," he said as he admired it.

I exhaled slowly and swallowed down my anger. "Let's just get this over with," I muttered, shoving past him and walking out of the room.

He caught up with me at the door, where one of his ever-present security flunkies was posted, peering down at me through dark sunglasses. He didn't even blink as I screwed up my face and flipped him off.

"Why you got all these secret service ass niggas around?" I asked once we were in the elevator.

Marcus looked over, clearly surprised that I was speaking to him unprompted. He adjusted his bow tie with a slight smirk. "You do enough grimy shit on the way up, you tend to be a walking target. Comes with the territory."

♡$♡

Hudson Hall was one of those places every New Yorker knew about but very few ever stepped inside. It was a historic landmark reserved for the city's elite and hosting the most exclusive events. Tickets for something like this were easily a thousand a pop.

The gala was in full swing by the time we arrived. News vans lined the street outside, cameras flashed, as paparazzi and reporters swarmed guests for pictures and sound bites. The moment Marcus got out of the limo, an Asian reporter shoved a mic in his face.

"Mr. Stokes! Mr. Stokes! How does it feel to be one of tonight's honorees?"

I took my time getting out, trying to avoid being in frame, but he caught my arm and pulled me into his side with a practiced smile.

"Truly, it's an incredible feeling, Janice," he said smoothly. "I'm honored that Councilman Dorsey chose me for such a prestigious award. But if you'll excuse us, we need to head inside."

He guided me towards the steps without giving me a chance to pull away.

Inside, jazz music floated through the grand lobby, as servers in crisp white uniforms weaved through the crowd with trays of champagne. I discreetly snatched a glass and tossed it back, hoping the alcohol would dull my irritation.

Marcus, on the other hand, was in his element. He worked the room, shaking hands and schmoozing with what felt like every politician and socialite in the city. I trailed behind him, wishing he'd at least let me sit down.

"This is my wife, Jasmine," he announced to every person we walked up to.

I wanted to throw up each time the words left his mouth. After a few hours, faces started to blur together, and my cheeks were sore from the fake smiling. I was over it.

"Do I need to talk to all these people? My feet are killing me," I said, leaning closer to him as another balding politician and his mistress walked away.

His expression softened, and for a split second, I caught a glimpse of the Marcus I used to know. "Go sit by the bar. I'll get you when it's time to eat."

Finally. He didn't have to tell me twice. I dropped his hand and headed straight for the bar. The second my ass hit the stool, I sighed in relief. These damn stilettos were killing me—I don't know why I let Amber talk me into buying them.

I ordered a cocktail and scanned the room. All the designer gowns and suits, the laughter, the power in this room, and not one person in here could do shit for me. Even if they wanted to, Marcus had his claws in too deep—nobody was about to cross him.

"Well, this makes my job easier," a smooth, silky voice purred next to me.

I turned and locked eyes with a dark-skinned woman who looked like she'd just stepped off a couture runway. She was the epitome of a bad bitch—rocking a silvery blonde fade and a bronze-colored dress that gave her an almost ethereal glow.

"Do I know you?" I asked warily.

"Not exactly." Her lips curled into a sly smile when she spotted the necklace resting against my collarbone. It widened as her gaze shifted to my hand, catching the ring before I could move it into my lap.

"Oh, he's gonna *love* that," she drawled with a soft chuckle, gently taking my wrist. Her cool fingers turned my hand over as she studied the ring, then brushed the pendant.

"Who?"

"Money," she said with a mischievous glint in her eye.

My breath hitched. *Money*. I opened my mouth, ready to shoot off a dozen questions. Before I could, she closed her hand around mine.

"Shh," she said softly. "Just listen. Can you do that?"

I nodded stiffly, my eyes darted to the crowd to search for Marcus.

"Good." Her voice was almost soothing. "Now drink and keep your eyes forward."

I'd all but forgotten the drink I'd ordered. I took another sip.

"When they seat you for dinner," she continued. "Wait ten minutes, then excuse yourself to the bathroom. I'll meet you there and explain the rest, okay?"

Movement in the crowd caught my attention—Marcus was making his way toward me. I nodded quickly, but when I turned back to the woman, she was already gone.

"Who were you talking to?" Marcus asked, looking at the chair she'd just been in.

I blinked blankly. "Huh? Who are you talking about? The bartender?"

He narrowed his eyes. "That woman with blonde hair," he pressed.

"Oh." I waved a hand dismissively, bringing the drink to my lips. "I don't know, she was complimenting my dress."

"Hm." He didn't look convinced. "They're about to seat us for dinner."

He hooked his arm in mine and led me through the crowded ballroom. Around us, the air was filled with chatter and clinking glasses, as the jazz band continued to play. I felt myself pushed into another guest, as someone bumped into Marcus hard.

"Watch where you're—" Marcus snapped, but the words died on his lips as the man turned to face him.

"'Sup, bitch ass nigga?" Cash grinned.

My heart sped up with a familiar giddiness when I saw him.

Cash looked too damn good in his black suit, his open-faced grills gleaming under the light of the chandeliers. His hair was freshly lined up, his beard trimmed and moisturized like he just stepped out of the chair. The iced-out watch on his wrist only added to his aura. He looked every bit of a boss.

Marcus tensed and glanced around, but folks weren't paying us any mind.

"The fuck are you doing here?" Marcus hissed, keeping his voice low.

Cash shrugged. "I heard they were honoring dirty ass niggas tonight. Figured I'd pull up and see for myself."

Finally, he looked at me. His gaze dragged over me hungrily until he saw the necklace. I watched the heat in his eyes turn to something colder. His jaw ticked when he saw the wedding band. I looked away and instinctively curled my fingers.

I wanted to say something. To explain that Marcus made me wear it, but the words wouldn't come.

Marcus's grip on my arm tightened. "You can't do shit here," he gritted.

"And neither can you," Cash said. "You good, baby?"

I nodded, but my heart felt like it might pound its way out of my chest.

A voice boomed over the mic. "Alright, you gorgeous,

beautiful people. The powers that be would love for everyone to find their seats so we can get dinner started."

The dance floor began to clear as guests brushed past us to get to their tables. Marcus used the commotion to drag me away, but I could feel Cash's eyes burning into my back as we walked off.

At our table, Marcus mumbled something about a phone call and stormed off. It was clear Cash's appearance had thrown him off.

I was left sitting with a bunch of strangers, nodding and smiling through introductions, but my mind was elsewhere. *Ten minutes*. I needed to meet the woman, but without a watch or phone, I had no idea how much time had passed. *Fuck it*. Marcus was gone. If I was going to take a risk, now was the time.

"Excuse me," I murmured, sliding my chair back.

I moved quickly through the stragglers on the dance floor and slipped out of the ballroom and into the lobby.

A large hand grabbed my arm. I spun around to find one of Marcus's security towering over me.

"What?" I snapped, masking my nerves with irritation. "Y'all gotta escort me to the bathroom? Are you shitting me?"

He didn't respond. Just narrowed his eyes as he tapped his earpiece.

"She says she needs to use the bathroom," he said flatly. "Do I need to go with her?"

I scowled as he listened to whoever was on the other end.

"Copy that," he said, shoving me forward. "Looks like I do."

I rolled my eyes and yanked my arm from his grip. "I don't know where you think I'm going," I said. "I don't even have a fucking phone."

He scoffed and posted outside the bathroom door as I pushed it open.

"Five minutes," he called after me.

I flipped him off and let the door slam behind me.

The restroom was empty except for a woman washing her hands at a sink. She smiled politely and dried her hands before walking out.

I paced for a few seconds before ducking into a stall with a sigh. "Might as well go while I'm here," I muttered to myself.

A loud bang rattled the door. "Hurry up!" the guard barked.

"Fucking relax!" I yelled back as I headed to the sink to wash my hands.

Where was she?

Muffled voices came from the other side of the door. My heart jumped in my throat as the woman from the bar strolled in, her heels clicking against the tile floor. She checked her lipstick in the mirror.

"I saw Cash," I whispered.

She laughed dryly as she shook her head. "That nigga can't help but showboat." She pulled a small phone out of her clutch and handed it to me.

"Don't make any calls from it," she said sharply. "But answer if it rings."

I took it from her and slipped it into my bag. "What's your name?"

Indecision flickered in her eyes before she finally answered. "Nairobi."

"Nairobi," I repeated softly.

"Jasmine!" Marcus's voice boomed from outside the door.

Nairobi tipped her head towards the exit, signaling for me

to leave. I smoothed down my dress, squared my back, and pushed the door open.

"I hope she's worth it." I heard her mutter under her breath as I walked out.

Marcus snatched my arm the second I was within reach. "We're leaving," he barked.

"What? We didn't even eat," I protested, stumbling to keep up. "What about your award?"

"Fuck that award," he gritted. "Your nigga trying to start some shit tonight."

I dug my heels into the floor and forced him to stop. "Are you scared?" I asked, crossing my arms.

He pinched the bridge of his nose. "No, I'm not fucking scared, Jasmine. But I'm not doing this bullshit here with him tonight."

"But you both said you couldn't touch each other here," I reminded him. "You think leaving is going to make a difference? He won't stop until you're dead."

"Mr. Stokes!" We turned to see a frazzled young woman in heels rushing towards us.

Her light brown cheeks were flushed as she caught her breath. "Oh, thank God! They're about to start honoring the recipients. You need to get back to your table."

Marcus gave her a phony apologetic smile. "Tell the Councilman I'm very sorry, but my wife's not feeling well. We've got to go."

I perked up. "But I feel better!" I batted my eyelashes at him, knowing damn well he wouldn't act up in front of the Councilman's staff. *He wanted to play? Let's fucking play.*

"Your stomach, babe." His voice was tight.

"Must've been something I ate, but I took care of it in the bathroom," I chirped, patting my stomach. "I wouldn't want you to miss your big moment. This award means so much to you, *babe*." I stroked his face.

The woman's shoulders relaxed as she let out a relieved sigh. "Thank God. The Councilman would've been really upset if you left now." She glanced nervously at Marcus, like her job depended on him staying put.

I squeezed his hand and started back toward the ballroom with a bright smile plastered on my face. "We wouldn't miss it for the world." My grip on his hand tightened enough to let him know I wasn't backing down. *Fuck with me if you want to.*

CHAPTER 28
CASH "MONEY" BANKS

TONIGHT, I WAS GETTING MY GIRL BACK AND DEADING THIS shit with Marcus for good. Showing up at the gala was reckless because he knew my face. I didn't give a fuck. Plus, the nigga wasn't stupid about to start shit in a room full of politicians and power players. It didn't matter how many of them were in his pocket—he couldn't touch me.

Seeing me would send him spiraling because he'd know something was up. It would eat at him all night, trying to figure out when I'd make my move. Tonight was ending with only one of us walking out alive, and it wasn't going to be him.

I adjusted the tie of my black Armani suit in the mirror. For a last-minute buy with rushed alterations, the shit was fire. It was about to get messy tonight, but I was stepping out looking like a king.

Satisfied, I went out to the living room and found Jelani by the window with his phone pressed to his ear.

"I'm finna tear that puss—" He cut himself off mid-sentence when he saw me. "Baby Doll, I'ma call you back," he ended the call and tucked his phone away. His locs were pulled up in a neat bun, and he wore a suit identical to mine.

"You and Monica finally official?" I asked, cocking my head.

He looked down. "We working on it."

"And that means?"

"That we working on it, nosy ass, nigga," he laughed and brushed past me toward the door.

Manhattan was buzzing as we stepped out into the cool fall evening. Nairobi leaned against the limo, looking like she'd rather be somewhere else. Her bronze Grecian-style dress shimmered against her skin, the high slit showing off her long legs. She looked like a siren with her hair slicked back, just waiting to lure a man to his death.

"Where's your man?" Jelani teased, pulling her into a quick hug.

"See. You play too much, Jelani," she said, smacking him upside the head.

He laughed, rubbing the spot. "That nigga almost burst a blood vessel yesterday."

"He good?" I asked, holding the limo door open for her.

She rolled her eyes as she slid into the limo. "How about we focus on getting your girl back before y'all start interrogating me."

Jelani and I climbed in after her. As soon as the door shut, the privacy divider went up.

Nairobi handed us our burners. "Jasmine's phone is in my clutch." She patted the sequined bag beside her. "I'm finna dip once we're inside. Marcus might recognize me without the wigs."

"When the Reapers pulling up?" I asked.

"Slim said 9:00 pm," Jelani replied, sliding a clip into one of his guns.

"Good." I ran through the plan for the hundredth time in my head. "Nai, once shit gets poppin', grab Jas and get her to the safe house. I'll handle Marcus myself—he's not leaving out that bitch alive."

The weight of what was about to happen finally hit me. I'd done this shit before— takeovers, crushing rival crews—it's how I took control in Atlanta. But this was different. This wasn't about money or territory—it was about her. When I told Jas she was mine, I meant that shit. Marcus had fucked around and was about to find out what happens when you touch what's mine.

Nairobi stared out the window with an unreadable expression. Jelani's leg bounced as he distracted himself on his phone. I cracked my neck and rolled my shoulders, centering myself as the limo slowed, pulling up in front of Hudson Hall. Spotlights danced across its steps, the building glowing under the evening sky.

Jelani buttoned his suit jacket, locking eyes with me. "Ready?"

Showtime.

♡$♡

I glanced at my watch—8:45 p.m. Fifteen minutes before we flipped this bitch on its head. I wasn't supposed to approach Marcus and Jasmine, but I couldn't help myself. Not like that nigga could do shit to me anyway. The look on his face was priceless. And Jasmine... Damn, my baby looked like a fucking star. Until I saw that necklace. Marcus was trying to do everything he could to claim her, but she would never be his.

Jelani was in hustle mode, chopping it up with a couple of real estate investors at our table. We were here for one thing, but business was business, and from the easy smile on his face, my brother was in the zone.

"Nah, y'all gotta come check us in Atlanta. We've got a few commercial properties I think you'll love," he said to an older white man in a tailored gray suit.

I smirked to myself and took a sip of my Old Fashioned. This is what I needed to see. The business would be solid in Jelani's hands. No matter what went down tonight, the future of the Banks Crew was secure.

Jelani took the man's phone like they were old friends. "Here, take my number," he said, and gestured toward me. "This is my older brother, Cash—our CEO,"

I gave the man a quick nod, lifting my glass. "Pleasure."

The man was saying something about being impressed, but I was pulling out my phone to check my messages.

Nai: Jasmine has the burner.

Good. Everything was moving like it should.

"How's everyone feeling tonight?" The MC said over the mic.

On stage now was a middle-aged Black man in a crisp black tuxedo, mic in hand. He flashed a polished politician's smile as the room turned its attention to him.

"Hope y'all are enjoying yourselves so far," he continued, his voice rising above the quiet clatter of silverware.

Slim's voice crackled through the earpiece. "Ten minutes."

I swirled the ice in my glass as I looked over at Jelani. He'd just wrapped up his conversation with the investor and gave me a sharp nod. He'd gotten the message, too.

The MC adjusted his tie. “Tonight, we’re honoring some of the best and brightest folks of our great borough. Before we begin, let’s give a big thanks to Councilman Dorsey’s office for hosting this annual event.” The room broke out into applause.

He smiled and waited for the applause to die down before he continued. “As many of you know, a portion of the proceeds from tonight’s ticket sales goes toward funding STEM and creative arts programs for public school students here in Queens. So, give it up for yourselves!”

A light round of applause rippled through the room.

“And we’re incredibly fortunate to have the beautiful 2022 Miss Manhattan, Hannah Brockman, here to present our first award.”

The spotlight shone on a blonde woman on stage in a navy blue evening gown. She definitely had the whole pageant queen thing down pat—a dazzling, megawatt smile with bleach white veneers that I was sure came straight from Türkiye. She air-kissed the MC and took the mic.

“Good evening, everyone,” she beamed. “It’s truly an honor to be here amongst such distinguished guests and to celebrate some remarkable individuals.”

I tuned her out, spotting Marcus’s and Jasmine’s table near the stage. Marcus had his arm slung possessively over Jasmine’s chair, focused on his phone instead of the woman who was set to present him with his award. Jasmine’s shoulders looked tense as she tried to keep herself from physically touching Marcus.

“…and it is my honor to present the Entrepreneur of the Year Award to Mr. Marcus Stokes,” Hannah announced.

“Three minutes,” Slim said as applause filled the room.

Marcus stood and straightened his suit jacket with a forced smile. He bent to kiss Jasmine, but she turned her head, subtly nudging him toward the stage. His face twisted for a split second, but he quickly recovered as he plastered on a fake-ass smile.

Hannah handed him the glass plaque, and they posed for a quick photo before he turned to the mic. You would've thought the nigga just won an Oscar the way he was cheesing.

"Thank you, thank you," he started. "This award isn't just for me— it's for everyone who's made mistakes and worked hard enough to find their redemption."

The room quieted down. Everyone was ready to eat up his bullshit.

"My journey hasn't been the easiest," he went on. "I come from a broken home, and like so many kids in my position, I found solace in the streets. I made a lot of mistakes—ones that could've cost me everything, including my life. My incarceration was a wake-up call to do things differently, so when I was exonerated, that's what I did. I clawed my way out of a hopeless situation because I realized my past didn't have to define my future. And now I'm standing before you all not only as a self-made businessman, but as a testament that second chances are real."

"Man, shut the fuck up," Jelani muttered under his breath.

I coughed to cover my laugh.

"There's someone special I want to thank tonight," Marcus continued, turning his gaze to Jasmine. The spotlight followed and landed on her. My hand gripped the edge of the table so hard that I felt the muscles in my forearm strain. The sound of my glass hitting the table snapped me out of it—I'd slammed it down without realizing, earning me a few curious glances from nearby tables. Marcus didn't even notice—his ass was too busy soaking up this moment.

"Jasmine, my *wife*, my rock," he said, pausing dramatically. "Baby, you've been the light for me when things were dark. This award is yours as much as it is mine."

My chest tightened. *Baby? His rock?* My leg started bouncing under the table, two seconds away from seeing red. How was Jas his lifeline? Like he hadn't just swooped in and taken her from a life she was building, *we* were building. There was no honor in controlling someone you claimed to love.

I was more than ready to put this nigga down.

Marcus stared at Jasmine. She made no move to acknowledge anything he said. She just sat there with her back straight, the silence stretching longer than it should.

He cleared his throat, trying to pick up where he left off, but I didn't hear any of it.

The only thing that kept me from losing it completely was Jasmine knowing wasn't with this shit at all.

This fucking dickhead.

BOOM!

The explosion outside rocked the building. Crystal chandeliers rattled overhead, swaying dangerously as gasps filled the room.

BOOM!

The lights flickered, and the gasps turned to full-blown screams as glass shattered somewhere in the distance. The low rumble of motorcycles got louder.

Security and a handful of cops sprinted towards the exits, their radios crackling as they tried to assess the situation. Panic spread through the crowd—chairs scraped against the floor as people scrambled to their feet and rushed for the emergency exits.

I cracked my knuckles as an eerie sense of calm washed over me. Jelani sat back in his chair and checked his watch, completely unfazed.

On stage, Marcus gripped the podium, stuck as chaos erupted around him. His gaze darted across the room until it landed on me. A slow smile spread across my face as I raised my glass and tilted it slightly towards him in a mock toast. The expression on his face twisted between rage and fear before he stumbled back and pushed through the people who'd rushed the stage.

Fontaine's voice came through the earpiece. "Fifteen minutes until the cavalry's here. Y'all need to move."

Jelani drew the Glock from the holster under his jacket. He flicked off the safety and rolled his shoulders as he stood. "Let's get your nurse back."

Gunfire erupted before I could respond, setting off another wave of screams through the room.

I tapped my earpiece, crouching low, keeping my head on a swivel. "Nai, where you at?" I pulled my gun from its holster. Outside, the Reapers' motorcycles revved louder, and another explosion went off, shaking the floor beneath us.

"These Reaper niggas are out here with rocket launchers, bruh," Fontaine said in disbelief over the earpiece. "What the fuck?"

"Yeah, I hear it," I said, ducking behind a toppled table. The gala had turned into mayhem—the screams and glass breaking was deafening.

"I'm looking for your girl," Nai said in a clipped tone. A grunt followed, then a gunshot cracked in the background.

A fresh round of gunshots went off, this time inside the ballroom. I peeked over the table and froze.

A man in a black Halloween mask with glowing red Xs over the eyes and matching red stitching across the mouth stood in the middle of the room. He looked like something out of a nightmare, waving an AK-47 over his head and firing rounds into the ceiling.

These Reaper niggas were unhinged.

Most of the crowd had cleared out by now, but a few stragglers huddled under tables, clutching each other and covering their mouths to stay quiet.

"They called the SWAT team," Fontaine said. "They're fifteen minutes out."

"Fuck," I muttered. We didn't have enough manpower to handle a whole SWAT team.

"We good. SWAT ain't shit," CJ's voice crackled confidently through the earpiece. "Get your girl, Money. We got you out here."

I wasted no time, bolting from the ballroom into the main hall. Hudson Hall was a mess—glass littered the floor, and the smell of smoke was thick in the air.

I pulled out my phone and opened the tracker app installed on Jasmine's burner. The blinking dot on the screen moved steadily toward the garage.

"They're headed for the garage!" I barked, sprinting towards the stairwell. A man stepped in front of me with his gun drawn.

Pop.

He dropped before I could raise my weapon. I looked over my shoulder to see Jelani lowering his gun.

"Good looks," I said, stepping over the body, continuing towards the stairs.

At the stairwell door, Nai was struggling with another of Marcus's security guards. She kneed him in the balls and was reaching for the knife strapped to her thigh.

Pop! Pop!

I let off a few rounds and dropped him.

"I had that," she snapped, panting.

"Teamwork," I retorted, yanking open the door.

We flew down the stairs and burst into the parking deck just as Marcus was shoving Jasmine into an idling Yukon.

"Marcus!" I bellowed, gun raised.

He froze, turning to face me, his expression twisting into an angry snarl.

I took a step forward. "Let her go!" I ordered

"Fuck you," he spat. He yanked his piece from his waistband and aimed it at me. "Ain't nobody fucking scared of you, Money!"

"This shit's between me and you. Leave Jas out of it."

Marcus sneered, dragging Jasmine forward. "She don't even want to go back with you! Go on, tell him!"

Jasmine's tear-streaked face looked at me. No words came out of her trembling lips.

Marcus shoved her hard. "She said it herself—she'd be better off without either of us. So what now, huh? You take her, and she gon' leave your ass anyway. Then what?"

I shook my head. "And you over here snatching somebody who ain't want your ass in the first place," I fired back. "You're a fucking clown, Marcus. Now, I don't like repeating myself. Let. Her. Go."

Marcus laughed again. "You not gon'—"

Bang!

He jumped back as the warning shot ricocheted off the concrete near his foot.

"I won't miss next time," I warned.

Jasmine used the moment to slam her heel down on Marcus's foot.

"Shit!" He hissed. His grip loosened enough for her to wrench free and scramble away from him.

I charged him, slamming my shoulder into his chest. Both of us went down.

"Fuck off me!" he growled, throwing an elbow into my ribs. I ignored the pain flaring through my side as we both scrambled to our feet. I shrugged off my suit jacket as I rolled my shoulders.

Marcus squared up before lunging and swung for my face. I ducked and moved to hit him, but he caught me first with a punch to my gut that knocked the wind out of me.

"This all the infamous Money Banks got?" he taunted, as I staggered back. "You soft, nigga."

I wiped my mouth, spitting on the pavement. "And you New York niggas talk too fucking much."

I was ready when he rushed me again—this time, my fist into his nose. Blood poured down his face. Adrenaline surged as I grabbed his jacket and slammed his head against the truck's window.

Marcus groaned, but still fought to break free. I yanked him up, ready to ram his head again, but he twisted out of my grip and dove for the gun on the ground.

"Nah, nigga," I snarled. My hand closed around his collar as his fingers brushed the handle of the gun. I pulled him back with everything in me, sending us both tumbling to the ground.

Out the corner of my eye, I saw Jelani start to move, but Nairobi threw her arm against his chest—this wasn't his fight, it was mine.

Marcus landed on top of me. Stars exploded behind my eyes as he punched the side of my head. I put my hands up to cover myself as he rained down punches.

"This who you chose, Jasmine?" Marcus spat, his face inches from mine. "This weak ass nigga?"

Blood roared in my ears. I hated the sound of Jasmine's name in his mouth.

With a guttural yell, I bucked my hips and shoved him off

me. He staggered back, spitting blood to the floor with a wild look in his eyes.

"That all your bitch ass got?" he said with a bloody grin.

We ran at each other again, neither of us willing to back down. I caught him mid-stride and slammed him into the side of a parked car so hard the impact set off the car alarm. Marcus was stronger than I'd anticipated, but I had more to lose.

I pinned him against the car and kneed him in the stomach. Marcus keeled over as I threw punch after punch into his ribs— the fight draining from him with each blow I landed.

"Again, this all you got, nigga?" he laughed weakly.

I growled and threw him to the ground. His head bounced off the concrete. He rolled over, choking on more blood, struggling to get up. My chest heaved as I stared at him. Even in his fucked up state, I could see the hatred in his eyes.

"Why won't you just stay down?" I muttered.

His eyes darted again to the gun lying a few feet away.

"Nuh uh," I kicked it out of his reach before he went for it.

I grabbed him by the collar and slammed him into a concrete pillar. "You should've never come to Atlanta."

"Cash!" Jasmine's frantic voice rang out.

I turned to her and saw the fear all over her tear-streaked face. She didn't need to watch this drag out.

With a roar, Marcus shoved me back and swung wildly at me.

I hit him with a hook to his temple, bringing him down again. He groaned as he struggled to get back up, but I was ending this now.

I walked over and picked up the gun. He was on his knees now, swaying.

"Fuck you," he spat, his voice hoarse but defiant.

I nodded slowly. "Gotta give it to you—you ain't a beggin' ass nigga," I leveled the Glock with his head. "I respect that."

Marcus glanced over at Jasmine through swollen eyes.

"Tell Kyree I said, 'what's up."

The shot went between his eyes. His body jerked and collapsed onto the concrete with a heavy thud. He'd get no last words.

I stepped over his body and fired again, watching the blood pool under his head.

It was done.

CHAPTER 29
JASMINE MILLER

MARCUS WAS DEAD. *MARCUS WAS DEAD.*

The realization finally hit me as I stared at his lifeless body. Bile rose in my throat as I stumbled back and threw up. My knees buckled as the little salad I'd eaten earlier splattered onto the ground.

My head spun and my vision blurred. I'd seen dead bodies before, working in the ER. Shit, I'd been there when a few patients took their last breath. But watching somebody's life get snatched in front of you was different. My body shook as I dry heaved, gasping for air.

"Hey, hey." Cash's deep voice broke through the fog. His arms wrapped around me and pulled me upright. "I got you, baby. I got you."

I looked up at him through a haze of tears. His face was pretty beat up—he had a nasty gash above his eyebrow, a busted lip, and dirt smeared across his cheeks. But he was here. He was real.

"You hurt?" I asked, my voice barely above a whisper. I reached for his face, then moved down to his chest. He flinched when I brushed against his ribs.

"This ain't shit," he grunted.

"Yo, hate to rush y'all, but we gotta move. Now," Nairobi said.

Cash nodded. "We'll take the Yukon." He jerked his head toward the truck still idling nearby. Everything happened so fast, I'd forgotten all about it.

"Where's the driver at?" Nairobi asked, looking around the garage.

"That nigga took off soon as Money and ol' boy started tusslin," Jelani said.

"At least he left the keys," Cash said. He tightened his hands around my shoulders, steadying me. "You good to walk?"

I nodded even though my legs still felt shaky. We moved toward the truck. Jelani slid into the driver's seat, Nairobi hopped in next to him, and Cash climbed in the back with me.

"You just gonna leave him like that?" I asked. I didn't know the rules to any of this shit, but leaving him there felt… wrong.

"Yeah," Cash said. He pulled close and planted a soft kiss on my forehead. He sounded cold and indifferent. "He'll be another casualty of tonight's shit. Don't worry about it."

Jelani revved the engine and drove the truck out of the parking garage. Outside was pure insanity. Two cars were on fire, the dark smoke filling the night air as firefighters worked to douse them. EMTs rushed around, loading the injured on stretchers and into waiting ambulances.

A cop stepped in front of the truck before we could merge onto the street. My heart jumped into my throat. This was it—we were about to get arrested. I was about to go to prison. We looked guilty as fuck—dirt smudged on our faces, Nairobi had blood on hers. I prayed he wouldn't see Cash in the back, who looked the worst out of all of us.

Jelani rolled down the window and turned the charm on, feeding the officer some story about us just wanting to get home. Whatever he said was good enough because the officer waved us through without a second glance.

I exhaled, my eyes glued to the chaos outside. My body felt heavy, like all the adrenaline that had kept me moving had finally left. By the time we hit the highway, exhaustion had me slumped against Cash's chest. The steady rhythm of his heartbeat grounded me, even as my feet throbbed from those damn heels.

"Wake up," Cash whispered, shaking me gently. My eyes fluttered open, and I squinted at the sight outside the tinted window. We were parked in the driveway of a large, well-lit cabin surrounded by towering trees. There were no other houses around.

I yawned. "Where are we?" I asked groggily.

"Somewhere safe," Cash replied. "We're gonna stay here for a few days till shit dies down." Jelani and Nairobi were already out of the truck.

I reached for the door handle, but Cash stopped me. His warm fingers brushed against my skin as he yanked the necklace off. I inhaled, remembering the look on his face when he first saw it. I didn't say anything. Instead, I opened the door and kicked off my heels before I stepped out. The gravel pressed into my bare feet, every step sending a dull ache up my legs, but I pushed through.

Inside, Slim was sprawled on an oversized gray couch, one leg propped on the coffee table while a movie played on the flatscreen TV. He looked over and lifted a hand in greeting, like this was just another day at the office.

The place felt like a well-kept Airbnb rather than a safe house with its polished wooden floors and modern furniture.

I noticed Fontaine and Nairobi hugged up in a corner as

Cash led me upstairs. The master suite was spacious and simple—a king-sized bed and a dark dresser that complemented the furniture downstairs. Thick curtains lined the tall windows.

"What about my stuff?" I asked as I glanced around the room. "Everything's still in his penthouse."

"You'll get it tomorrow," Cash said, lowering himself carefully into an armchair. He winced as he pressed a hand to his side. "Nai grabbed you some things in the meantime." He nodded toward a pile of shopping bags near the bed.

"Thanks," I murmured. I leaned down to kiss him, but he pulled back slightly, his eyes dropping to my hand.

I followed his gaze and froze—the ring.

Without saying a word, he reached for my hand and gently slid it off.

"Go shower," he said, looking at me with an expression I couldn't place.

I frowned. I wanted to question him, but pressed my lips together, grabbed the bags, and headed into the en-suite bathroom. I was surprised to see it was stocked with everything I could need—a shower cap, body wash, shampoo, even a small jar of whipped shea butter that smelled faintly of mango.

Steam filled the bathroom as I stepped under the hot water. It was a little too hot, but I didn't care. I needed to wash away any evidence of tonight. So I got to work, scrubbing my skin until it felt raw, trying to free myself from the weight of the night—the past week—off me.

I sighed, blinking back tears—no more of that. I'd done enough crying for the last year, and I was tired of it.

Once I dried off, I reached for the shea butter. The sweet mango scent calmed me—it reminded me of my personal collection of body oils that I had at home. While I rubbed it into my skin, I made a mental note to thank Nairobi. She'd thought of everything, including the new pack of underwear and a soft pajama shorts set that I put on.

In the bedroom, Cash was still sitting in the armchair. His head was leaned back as his hand rested lightly over his ribs. His eyes were closed, but I could tell that he wasn't asleep.

"Cash?" I called softly.

He opened his eyes, but there was no warmth in them.

"Let me take a look at your ribs," I said, stepping toward him. "They might be broken."

He sat up and grimaced. His hand was still pressed to his side. "I'm fine, Jas," he grunted roughly. "They're just bruised."

He pushed himself to his feet and brushed past me on his way to the bathroom. The sound of the shower filled the silence in the room.

I didn't know what else to do, so I went down to the kitchen to get something to drink.

Most of the lights downstairs were off, except for the ones in the hallway and kitchen. Jelani and Slim were on the couch watching the evening news.

"We're reporting live from Councilman Dorsey's Gala, which came under attack this evening. Multiple injuries have been reported, and there were a few casualties, including businessman, Marcus Stokes, who had just been awarded Entrepreneur of the Year..."

I turned away, tuning out the rest, and opened the fridge. It was fully stocked with juices and sparkling waters, but I needed something stronger to take the edge off.

"What you lookin' for, nurse?"

I jumped slightly. Jelani was leaning against the kitchen island, watching me.

I rolled my eyes and closed the fridge. "How the hell do you move so quietly?"

"I called your name," he shrugged. "You didn't answer, so here I am."

"Where's the liquor?" I asked, opening cabinets, looking for a glass.

Jelani cocked his head, studying me. "For you or Money?"

"Me," I said. I pulled out a glass and set it on the counter.

Jelani pursed his lips before rounding the island to open a lower cabinet. When he stood back up, he held two bottles—tequila and rum.

"Pick your poison."

I grabbed the tequila and poured myself a heavy shot. I tossed it back, no chaser in sight.

"Damn, Jas," Jelani chuckled. "The fuck got you drinking like that?"

I shook my head and poured myself another shot. "How can you just be okay with all of this? Like this shit is normal."

He leaned back on the counter, crossing his arms over his chest. "I mean, coming to New York City to rescue my brother's girlfriend isn't normal," he countered.

"You know what I mean," I said, throwing back the second shot. This had to be some expensive ass tequila, judging by the way it went down so smoothly. "Slim was up in here chillin' and watching a movie when we got here. Now y'all are watching the news like we weren't the cause of all that. How are y'all so calm?"

Jelani's expression sombered, his usual laid-back demeanor replaced with something darker. "This ain't new to us," he said. "It's kill or be killed—you learn to keep it pushing."

He paused, his gaze going distant like he was recalling a memory. "My mom tried to keep us out of my pop's shit, but after he got killed, it didn't matter. The streets came knocking, and Money had no choice but to answer. He wasn't about to let us go back to the hood."

He let out a dry, bitter chuckle. "I don't even think about it anymore. I can't. It's too much. I've just been lucky that it hasn't been me yet."

I stayed quiet. I knew Cash had his own demons when it came to his father's death, but Jelani never opened up like this to me before.

"Cash's mad at me," I blurted.

Jelani raised his eyebrows. "Mad? For what?"

I sighed, leaning against the counter. "I don't know. He's barely said anything to me since we got here, and brushed me off when I tried to help him."

Jelani hummed thoughtfully. "I don't think he's mad. Money… he's just got his own way of dealing with shit. Coming up here was no small play—it puts us at risk in a lot of ways."

"I didn't ask him to come," I retorted.

"Oh, so he should've just left you with your weirdo ex?" Jelani asked, pulling a bottle of water from the fridge.

"No…" I trailed off.

"Exactly. The nigga is just in his head right now. Trust me, he loves you."

"I—what?" I stammered.

He rolled his eyes. "You heard me. That man loves you, even if he hasn't admitted it to himself or you."

"Jasmine!" Cash's deep baritone voice called from the top of the stairs.

Jelani gave me a knowing smile. "Told you." He winked and headed down the hall to his room.

He loves you.

If he did, why was Cash acting all weird and distant? It didn't make sense.

Cash was waiting for me at the top of the stairs. I couldn't help but notice how, despite being bruised up, Cash was still so fucking sexy. My eyes trailed over his shirtless frame and down to the black basketball shorts that sat low on his hips. Even now, I couldn't stop my body from reacting to him. He'd gone ahead and bandaged the cut above his eyebrow, and the swelling on his lip had gone down.

I followed him into the bedroom, feeling all over the place. My body ached, my head was still reeling from everything that had gone down tonight, and on top of that, I wanted Cash, *real bad.*

He motioned for me to sit on the bed.

"Jelani was just—"

"I want you to stay in Atlanta."

"What?"

"With me," he said slowly. "I don't want you to move back to New York."

I reared back. "You—what? Cash, where's this coming from?"

His brows knitted together while he rubbed his jaw like he was still working out what he wanted to say. "When Marcus took you…" He trailed off. "That shit fucked me, Jas. Real talk. It felt like all the air was sucked out of the room. I kept thinking—what if I never saw you again? What if that was the last time I heard your voice?"

My chest tightened.

He paused. His gaze fixed on the floor before he looked up at me.

"You know I'm not the type of man to be on some wax poetic shit. That ain't never been me. I speak plainly, and my actions back up what I say. But you need to know… I'm always thinking 'bout you—and now anytime I think of the future, it includes you. Shit don't feel right unless you're around."

He exhaled sharply. "Then that nigga had the nerve to throw shit in my face—talkin' 'bout you regretted meeting me. And maybe after all this, you do. Maybe you wanna walk away from all this. From me." His voice dropped. "But I don't wanna lose you, Jasmine."

The air between us felt heavy. It was like everything over the past few days had stripped away his armor and cockiness, leaving nothing but his truth.

There was one more thing I needed to tell him. My heart twisted, not knowing how he'd take it.

"There's something you need to know," I said softly. "Marcus… he made videos of us. I didn't know he was recording—"

"I know."

I blinked. "How?"

"Fontaine found them when he hacked the cloud," he said calmly. "He deleted them and made sure there's nothing floating around."

My shoulders sagged in relief. "I was gonna tell you," I whispered.

"I know," he said. "But I handled it. I told you—I got you, baby."

I scooted off the bed, ignoring the ache in my muscles as I moved to him. I needed him to feel what I couldn't say.

My fingertips brushed the bandage on his forehead. I trailed my hand down his jawline and through his beard. Rising on my toes, I hesitated just for a second before pressing my lips to his.

He let out a low growl as his tongue slipped into my

mouth. His hands gripped my waist and pulled me close like he needed to remember how I felt against him. I tried to hold back, mindful of his injuries, but he just pulled me closer with a strained grunt, bruised ribs and all.

"Fuck, I missed you," he murmured against my mouth.

My hand slid into his shorts, and he cursed under his breath as my fingers wrapped around his dick.

"Jasmine," he groaned, resting his forehead against mine while I stroked him. My pussy thumped at the neediness in his voice. I wanted him inside me so bad, but I wanted to watch him fall apart first.

I tugged his shorts down as I dropped to my knees—my eyes locked on him the whole time. I licked my lips and started stroking him again, watching pre-cum glisten at the tip.

"Such a pretty dick," I murmured, running my tongue along the base. Cash's chest heaved as he watched me, his hands flexing at his sides as he fought to keep it together.

I started slow, gliding my hands over his length before taking him into my mouth.

"Shit, Jas," he hissed. His hands found my head, tangling in my hair as he pushed his hips forward. I moaned softly around him, and hollowed out my cheeks to take him deeper. His breathing turned ragged as I pulled back to swirl my tongue around the tip, then slid down again, taking him even deeper.

"Fuck," he grunted, his voice strained.

I gagged when he hit the back of my throat, but I didn't stop. Spit pooled at the corners of my lips and dripped down my chin. His grip in my hair tightened as he guided my pace with slow, deep strokes. My eyes watered, and I braced myself against his thighs.

"Baby, look at me," he said.

I blinked up at him through wet lashes. Sweat glistened on his chest. His lips parted as he watched me.

"Do you know how perfect you look right now?" he growled. "So fuckin' pretty with my dick in your mouth."

His words made my thighs clench, my pussy throbbing as I fought the urge to reach between my legs. I shoved his hands off and took control, using my hands and mouth until he couldn't take it.

"Shit… don't stop," he choked out, his body tensing as I bobbed faster.

"Fuck!" he grunted, holding me still as he spilled into my mouth. I swallowed every drop, licking him clean until he twitched and pushed my head back with a shaky hand.

I wiped my chin and stood, pride blooming in my chest as he leaned back against the dresser, breathless.

A small smirk tugged at my lips. "You alright?" I asked.

Cash let out a breathless laugh. "More than good now."

I giggled as he pulled me into a hug and held me there for a second before we headed into the bathroom. We brushed our teeth, moving in an easy silence, the weight of the night creeping back in as I crawled into bed.

Cash groaned slightly as he lowered himself beside me.

"You need a painkiller?" I asked him, ready to jump into nurse mode.

He waved me off. "This ain't the first time I been roughed up," he muttered. "Just lay with me."

I slid under the covers, cuddling up against him as he draped an arm over me, his fingers brushing softly against my arm.

"Goodnight, Cash," I muttered, my eyelids growing heavier.

He kissed my forehead. “Night, shorty,” he replied.

Just as I began to drift off, he shifted, his voice a low whisper.

“I love you.”

The words hung in the air as I finally slipped into the deepest sleep I’d had in days.

CHAPTER 30
CASH "MONEY" BANKS

THE SMELL OF BACON WOKE ME UP. JASMINE SNORED SOFTLY next to me, her leg tossed over mine. It was a habit she developed when she started staying over my house. I moved carefully, wincing as pain shot through my ribs. My face was also sore, but manageable. If I were home, Dr. Middleton would've patched me up, but I had to thug it out here.

We were only staying at CJ's safe house for three days. It would've been too hot to fly immediately after the gala. The police were probably reviewing flight records, and our quick trip in and out of New York would've raised a red flag.

Jasmine stirred, stretching before blinking up at me with sleepy eyes.

"Hi," she murmured.

I gently stroked her cheek. "Hey," I replied. This woman pulled a softness out of me that I didn't know existed. I'd been with plenty of women before and cared for a few deeply, but Jasmine had me ready to hand over my whole heart to her.

"Why you looking at me like that?" she asked with a furrow in her brow.

"I'm trying to figure out how you manage to look so pretty even though you got crust in your eye and your hair's all fucked up," I smirked.

"Oh, whatever," she laughed as she shoved me playfully.

My face twisted as pain shot through my side. "Shit," I muttered, closing my eyes until it passed.

"Oh my God!" She sat up. "Shit. I'm sorry! I forgot!"

I let out a low chuckle. "You tryna put me on the sick and shut-in list, huh?"

"Stop! I'm serious!" she fussed. "What do you need?"

I ran my fingers up the length of her thigh. I felt goosebumps rise on her skin. "I need you to sit that pussy on my face," I deadpanned, my fingers trailing between her legs.

"Cash!" she squeaked.

"You asked what I needed."

"But you're hurt," she argued.

I bit down on her shoulder hard enough to make her gasp. "I'm a grown ass man. You forget the first time you saw me, I'd been shot?"

She rolled her eyes and sat up with a huff. "You're ridiculous."

"I know," I grinned, adjusting myself on the pillows. "Now take them shorts off and feed me my breakfast."

She bit her lip. Slowly, she raised her hips, slid her shorts off, and tossed them off the side of the bed.

I took in every inch of her smooth brown skin. My dick bricked up painfully against my boxers. She hesitated, eyes scanning my face for any sign of discomfort.

I didn't care how needy I sounded. "Jas…" I pleaded.

She straddled me carefully, bracing her hands against the headboard as she lowered herself over my mouth.

"Good girl," I murmured, wrapping my arms around her

legs. I pressed soft kisses along her inner thighs and let my nose graze her clit, smirking when her breath hitched.

"Stop teasing me," she whispered, her body trembling slightly.

"You mean like this?" I asked, nipping at her again. She bucked against me and whimpered softly.

Her gasps filled the room as my tongue slid between her slick folds.

"Don't hold back, baby," I groaned against her. "Ride my face. Give me that shit."

She gripped the headboard tighter, her thick thighs quivering as she settled her weight on me. She rolled her hips slowly and dragged her pussy over my tongue, while I lapped up her essence. I swirled and flicked my tongue over her swollen bud before sucking it into my mouth.

"Money!" she cried out hoarsely. "Oh my… fuck!"

I held her steady and gripped her thighs to keep her right where I needed. She trembled above me, her breath coming out in shallow gasps.

"Come on, baby," I murmured. "I know you're close. "

Her head tipped back as she cried out, her body shaking uncontrollably as she came and coated my beard.

"That's how you start the damn morning," I said, my voice husky.

"You really are ridiculous," Jasmine laughed. She brushed her fingers along my jaw before kissing my cheek. A dreamy, satisfied smile spread across her face.

She wrinkled her nose. "Wait… is that bacon?"

On cue, her stomach rumbled loudly.

"Alright, I guess it's time to feed you for real," I teased.

She squealed happily and hopped out of bed.

I got up slowly, gritting my teeth as my body reminded

me just how banged up I was. A sharp huff escaped me before I could bite it back.

Jasmine's head snapped in my direction, concern etched across her face.

"Don't look at me like that," I muttered. I grabbed a clean shirt and made my way to the bathroom.

"You don't have to be hard all the time," she called after me.

I ignored her and started to brush my teeth. Jasmine came in a few moments later.

"I'm not acting like anything," I said, meeting her gaze in the mirror.

She sighed and grabbed her toothbrush, brushing her teeth in silence next to me.

When we finished, she reached over and wiped a stray drop of toothpaste from my chin.

I kissed her. "Your thoughts are written all over your face. Stop worrying."

I let her finish freshening up while I headed downstairs to the kitchen. The smell of eggs, bacon, and coffee hit me the moment I reached downstairs.

Jelani was at the stove, scooping crispy potatoes into a Pyrex dish while Slim scrolled through his phone.

Jelani glanced over his shoulder and smirked. "Y'all finish kissing and making up?"

"Shut the fuck up," I flipped him off and grabbed a glass from the cupboard. "Where's Fontaine and Nai?"

"They went to get Jasmine's stuff from Marcus's condo," Slim replied, loading food onto a plate.

"Wait a minute." Jasmine's voice cut in as she entered the kitchen. "Jelani cooks? Since when?"

"Don't let the handsome face fool you, nurse. I'm full of surprises." He winked and turned back to the stove.

"Does Monica know you can cook?" she asked, swiping a piece of bacon.

Jelani's smile faltered before he masked it with a smirk. He placed the home fries on the island. "She's still learning about me," he said lightly.

Jasmine frowned. "That's very vague, but okay."

I shot Lani a look, but he shrugged and went back to cooking.

"Aww shit!" Nairobi walked into the kitchen, rubbing her hands together. "Lani blessing us with breakfast?"

Fontaine followed behind with two suitcases in tow. He set them down, then looked at me. "Damn, Money, you look like shit."

I rolled my eyes and took a sip of juice. "I'm aware. Y'all ain't gotta keep telling me."

Nairobi walked over to Jasmine and handed her a phone.

Jasmine's face lit up."My phone! Thank you!" She threw her arms around Nairobi, who stiffened before awkwardly patting her back.

"The hospital probably fired me, but at least I can call Monica and Amber," she said.

Fontaine cut her enthusiasm short. "I'd hold off on calling your people until we get back to Atlanta. Your name was on the guest list, and you were Marcus's date. There's some chatter on the police lines about them wanting to bring you in for questioning."

Jasmine's smile faded. "What?" Her eyes darted anxiously between Fontaine and me.

"Can't you just scrub her from the system?" I asked Fontaine.

He grabbed a plate and sighed. "Theoretically, yeah. But I've been busy cleaning up the shit show from the Reapers. They had fucking rocket launchers, remember?"

"We'll rap about it after breakfast," I said, glancing at Jasmine. I still wasn't ready to talk business in front of her.

Thankfully, the mood lightened as we settled into our meal. Jasmine held her own—she was cracking jokes like she hadn't just been holed up with her psycho ex for nearly a week. Her bright energy was contagious, and even Nairobi's hard-ass demeanor seemed to soften around her.

After breakfast, Jasmine volunteered to clean up so I could talk with the others privately.

"Get a fucking room," Jelani grumbled as Jasmine went to kiss me. It was a quick peck, but since he wanted to talk shit, I reached around and grabbed her ass.

"Cash!" she fussed, swatting at my chest. Her brown cheeks flushed as she turned toward the sink.

In the office, Slim was already stretched out in one of the armchairs. He got straight to it. "Marcus's whole shit is a mess now that he's dead," he said. "CJ said the Reapers started hitting up his stash houses, and they're finna sell off his shit. They promised to keep it out of Atlanta, though."

I leaned back in my chair. "I feel like there's a 'but' coming."

Slim nodded. "But CJ wants the Reapers to be our only weapons supplier from now on."

I mulled it over. We'd always gotten our guns from the Cubans in Miami, but the Reapers had come through in a major way last night. If my pops trusted Big Creed in the past, that had to count for something.

"Whatchu think, Lani?" I asked.

"I don't see why not. If what they pulled out last night is any indication of what they're working with, we already up," he said.

"True," I nodded. "Talk to CJ and see what the prices look like. Let's make sure it's worth our while before we lock anything in." It was time my brother had more responsibility, and there was no better time than now.

Fontaine leaned forward. "We can probably get out of here in another day or two. There's a small private airport in White Plains we can fly out of. I'll change the names on the flight logs so everything's clean. West can meet us there."

"Good." I was itching to get back home and put this shit behind us. Jasmine still hadn't given me an answer about staying after her contract ended, but we'd cross that bridge eventually. After tying up a few more loose ends, we headed back to the living room. Jasmine was sitting on the couch, flipping through TV channels. Her face lit up when she spotted Nairobi.

"You look like you can handle guns," Jasmine said, throwing an arm around Nai's shoulder.

I snickered as Nai looked at Jas like she had three heads. "I can…"

Jasmine perked up. "Think you can teach me how to shoot when we get back to Atlanta?"

"I could teach you just fine," I offered.

Jasmine put a hand up. "Uh, no thanks," she shook her head. "You probably gonna be too extra with it and piss me off. I wanna learn from the Black Lara Croft."

I sucked my teeth. "You don't even know what she does forreal."

Nairobi glanced at Fontaine. He had an amused look as he waited for her response. She cleared her throat and chuckled nervously.

"We'll see," she said. "Depends on my next contract."

Jasmine was oblivious to the shift in energy and handed Nai her phone. "Here, give me your number so we can keep in touch."

Nai quickly entered it and passed the phone back. Jasmine

turned her attention to Jelani and smacked him upside the head as he plopped down next to her.

"You think Monica knows how to use a gun?" she asked.

"Fuck if I know. Ain't that your friend?"

She raised an eyebrow. "Ain't that your girl?"

Nairobi used their bickering as an opportunity to slip out of the room. Fontaine's eyes tracked her, and after a beat, he pushed off the wall and followed.

Slim nodded toward the hallway. "So that's a thing, huh?"

"Been a thing, but I guess they're done hiding it," I mused.

Slim snorted. "Well, good luck to that man. Nairobi is a runner."

I cut my eyes at him. "How you know so much about her?"

Slim shrugged. "You work with someone long enough, you figure out their habits. That woman's all about her bag and nothing else. Fontaine might complicate things, but shorty finna hit the bricks on that nigga."

He had a point. Nai's ability to slip in and out of lives made her an asset, but a liability for someone like Fontaine.

"They're grown, they'll sort it out. Ain't got shit to do with us unless it affects business," I said.

"True," Slim replied. "But you already know that nigga's in for a rude awakening if he hasn't prepped himself."

He was right. But at the end of the day, it wasn't our business, and it was another reason why I never mixed business with pleasure. There was too much potential for mess.

"Ay, Money!" Jelani called from the couch. "Get your girl, she doing too much!"

CHAPTER 31
JASMINE MILLER

THE DAY WE WERE SET TO LEAVE, A DETECTIVE NAMED Murdock finally called.

"Ms. Miller," he started. "I'd like you to come in for questioning regarding Councilman Dorsey's gala and anything you may know about the murder of Marcus Stokes."

"I'd be happy to answer any questions you have—with a lawyer present," I replied evenly. I didn't have a lawyer, but I'd watched enough true crime documentaries to know the first rule: keep your mouth shut when talking to the police.

"You're not a suspect," Detective Murdock said. He was polite, but his irritation was evident. "We're just gathering information. Surely you can help with that."

"Not without my lawyer."

He sighed, clearly frustrated. "Fine," he said curtly before hanging up.

I tossed the phone on the bed. "I can't afford a fucking lawyer," I groaned.

Cash zipped up his bag. "I got you," he said.

I hesitated. I loved how quick he was to step in, but I

didn't want to rely on him for everything. "It's fine. I'll figure it out, I still have some money in my savings."

He turned, his deep brown eyes boring into mine. "Jasmine, do you trust me?"

"With my life." The past few days had proved that much. Cash was willing to risk it all for me, no questions asked.

"Then trust me to handle this. Let me be your man and take care of it," he said firmly.

I nodded, swallowing my pride. "Okay."

He came closer, kissing me softly. "I told you—we're locked in. I'm always going to protect you."

A few hours later, we piled into an SUV and headed to the airport. Slim drove with Jelani in the passenger seat, Fontaine, Cash, and myself were in the back two rows.

I glanced around as Slim reversed out of the driveway. "Where's Nairobi?"

"She's dumping one of the cars we used," Fontaine replied.

The ride to the airport was quieter than I expected. I'd started to feel comfortable with Cash and his crew over the past few days. Despite the mess, there were moments where shit felt… normal. I thought the drive would be the same, but even Jelani—who never shut up—kept his mouth closed.

At the private hangar, the small flight crew moved quickly to load our bags onto the jet. Fontaine stayed near the SUV, phone to his ear, scanning the lot.

"She should've been here by now," he muttered. I lingered near the steps of the plane, watching him as the others boarded. Fontaine stood, staring down at his phone.

"Go 'head," Cash said, nudging me up the steps.

I boarded reluctantly and chose a window seat where I could still see him. Outside, I watched as he approached Fontaine, who showed him something on his phone.

Fontaine's shoulders slumped while Cash read whatever was on the screen. He shook his head and placed a hand on Fontaine's shoulder as they both turned to board the jet.

"Is she—" I started, but Cash shook his head sharply as he slid into the seat next to me.

Fontaine dropped into an empty seat across from us, still gripping his phone. He stared blankly out the window, ignoring the flight attendant when she came around to offer him a drink. An uncomfortable silence settled over the cabin as the plane began to taxi, everyone pretending they didn't notice Nairobi's absence.

I jumped as the pilot's voice came over the speakers. Cash squeezed my thigh gently in an attempt to reassure me, but it did nothing to settle the unease I felt.

This wasn't a mistake. Nairobi had made a quiet and deliberate move. I thought back to the hesitation when I asked for her info, the way she dodged certain conversations. I'd hoped we could be friends, but truthfully, I didn't know shit about her. I was still learning how Cash's world worked. Everything was complicated.

Cash never mentioned her and Fontaine being together, but judging by the look on Fontaine's face, this was more than a little situationship. It wasn't casual. That was a heartbroken man.

CHAPTER 32
FONTAINE JACKSON

Unknown: I'm sorry.

CHAPTER 33
CASH "MONEY" BANKS

THREE WEEKS LATER...

JELANI RUBBED THE BACK OF HIS NECK AND LOOKED AROUND the room at our top lieutenants. The vibe was more relaxed than the last time I called them to meet at the farmhouse.

He turned his back on the others who were talking amongst themselves. "You're sure about this?" he asked.

I clapped his back. "Yeah. I told you, this shit is all you. I'm done running point—it's your time to shine, bruh."

It was official. I was stepping down as head of the crew to focus on our commercial real estate business that we'd built to clean our money.

This wasn't a random decision; I'd been thinking about this move for over a year. Before Jasmine came into the picture, I'd been ready to lean into the legit side of things. She'd just made the choice easier. And I wasn't leaving the game entirely—washing money was still illegal. Slim and Fontaine would help Jelani run things, and if shit went left, I would be right there.

"This nigga really about to play house," Slim chuckled.

I shrugged. "A nigga not trying to be forty and still knocking heads together. Gotta work smarter, not harder," I looked at my brother again. "Plus, Lani loves this shit—he'll be good."

Fontaine stayed quiet, which had become his new normal since Nairobi ghosted us in New York. He'd never said outright that they were dealing with each other, so no one was sure how to approach it. I was sure he was using his free time to track her down, but the question was, would he go after her when he found her?

"Just don't act brand new when we need to get shit poppin'," Jelani said.

"Never that," I dapped him up.

The room cleared out, and I stayed back, lost in thought. Some of the local crews might try to test Jelani now that I was stepping down, but I wasn't too worried. My brother was a menace, and he'd show them real quick that he could hold his own.

I welcomed the cool breeze as I walked to my car. I pulled out my phone and dialed Jasmine.

"Hey," she answered.

"What's your sexy ass doing?"

She laughed. "I just got in from work. About to take a shower, why?"

"I'm picking you up. I should be there in thirty minutes," I said, unlocking my door.

"Is this like a dressy thing, or…?"

"Be comfortable."

"Okay…" she dragged the word out clearly, waiting for me to explain.

"I'll see you soon." I hung up before she could press me further.

Traffic was light, so I made the thirty-minute drive in

about twenty. I tapped the wheel, glancing at the entrance as a small wave of nervousness hit me.

Outside.

Five minutes later, she was stepping out in a pair of jeans and an oversized sweatshirt.

“Is that mine?” I asked as she got in.

“Maybe,” she gave me a quick kiss before putting on her seatbelt.

“Oh? So we stealing clothes now?” I joked as I started the car.

“They look good on me!”

”Everything looks good on you,” I said, glancing at her.

She rolled her eyes, but I caught the smile she fought back.

“Alright, so where are we going?” she asked, shifting in her seat.

“You’ll see.”

“Cash…”

“Baby, just relax.” I turned up the volume on the radio.

She sighed and leaned back in the seat.

The drive was quiet, save for the R&B music playing softly, filling the car. It wasn’t long before I pulled into an underground parking garage beneath a high-rise building. Jasmine sat up, looking around.

“Where are we?” she asked curiously.

I parked in the assigned parking spot and cut the engine. “I’ll show you.”

She followed me toward a private elevator—I could feel her curiosity growing with each step. I tapped the fob to call it, sliding my arm around her waist once we were inside.

Silence stretched as the elevator climbed. Not awkward,

but expectant. I cleared my throat and adjusted my stance, trying to shake off the nerves. This was a big step. Bigger than anything I'd ever done before.

When the elevator dinged, I placed my hand on the small of her back and guided her forward. Jasmine glanced at me, her brows raised, before turning her attention to the sleek hallway in front of us. The walls were lined with art, leading to a single door at the end of the hall. I swallowed the lump in my throat as I stepped ahead of her and tapped the fob against the lock. The door clicked, and I pushed it open wide.

The penthouse stretched out in front of us. Recessed lights cast a soft glow over the hardwood floors and bounced off the tall windows that stretched along the living room. From the thirtieth floor, we had the perfect view of the Atlanta skyline. The faint scent of fresh paint and cleaning products still lingered in the air.

Jasmine walked in, her mouth slightly open as she took it in. "Baby, what is this?"

"It's ours."

She spun around to face me. "Ours?"

I nodded. "I bought it for us. I want you to move in with me."

She pressed her palms against one of the floor-to-ceiling windows. "This view is… wow," she said quietly.

I watched her. I knew this was a lot and hoped she wasn't overwhelmed.

"It's a big step. But your stubborn ass not quitting the hospital any time soon, and my house is too far. So… this is home if you want it to be."

She turned around, her eyes shimmering with tears.

Work was the only thing that would send her back to New York—whether we were together or not. She knew I'd take care of her, but she loved being a nurse. So I made a few calls, lined a few pockets, and made sure Southside General gave her a full-time position. It was less chaotic than Peachtree, and she'd be working with Monica again.

"You really not trying to sleep in my queen-sized bed, huh?" she teased.

I smiled wickedly. "Nah. I want you bringing yo' ass home to me, so I can wear you out on the California king, or up against the window."

Her mouth dropped open as she smacked my arm. "I can't stand you." She shook her head. "I guess since I got that new position, I can hang down here with you a little longer."

"Forever," I corrected her. "I wanna show you something."

I took her hand and led her down the hallway to the master bedroom. The penthouse had three bedrooms and two full bathrooms, spacious enough for us to start this new chapter. What she didn't know was that I hadn't just bought the penthouse—I'd also purchased a stake in the building. I wasn't just thinking about right now. I was laying the foundation for our future.

I pointed to a door on the far side of the room. "Go look in the closet."

She let go of my hand and walked over. "Baby, what the fuck?" she exclaimed as she stepped inside.

The walk-in closet was massive, easily the size of her living room. It had custom-built shelves and recessed lighting. Half of it was empty, but I'd gone ahead and filled the other half with brand new clothes, shoes, and bags—all things I knew she'd love.

"I wanted to make sure you'd feel at home here. I know you've got your own spot, but this is really for us."

She glanced between me and the closet a few times. Before I could say anything else, she grinned, ran over to me, and jumped into my arms. The impact sent me to the floor with a grunt. Her laughter rang in my ears.

"I guess you like it?" I asked. She straddled me and wrapped her arms around my neck.

"I love it!" She covered my face in kisses. "But Cash, who does this? That closet is damn near bigger than my apartment!"

I chuckled. "You know my audio gotta match my visual, shorty. I told you from the jump I wasn't coming off you. It wasn't enough for you to hear it—I needed you to see it."

"I don't even know what to say," she said.

I slid my hands up to rest on her thighs."There's one more thing," I said. "I made it official—I'm stepping down from heading the crew. Jelani's gonna run everything now."

Her eyebrows shot up. "So you're retired?"

"Not quite," I laughed. "I'm getting more involved with our commercial real estate company. It's not completely legal, but it's more about making deals and less about running up on niggas."

A thoughtful look crossed her face. "Are you sure this is what you want to do? And not just because of me? I don't want you stepping away from something you built and then regretting it later."

"What happened to 'I don't date dope boys'?" I teased.

"I recall someone swearing up and down they were a businessman," she shot back playfully.

"Mhm," I grinned, brushing my thumb along her leg. "But to answer your questions, this ain't only about you. I've been thinking about it for a minute—way before we met. The shit in New York just made me move up the deadline, but this was always the plan."

She studied me for a moment, her hand drifting up to stroke my beard. "I love you," she said softly.

"What?" I'd whispered those words to her when I thought she was sleeping back at the safe house, but hearing her say them now?

She leaned down to kiss me. "I love you, Cash Maurice Banks," she repeated. When she sat back up, a coy smile tugged at her lips. "And I know you're unhinged ass loves me too."

"Yeah, I love you, sweetheart. Real bad."

I pulled her down into another kiss, this time it was slow and deep. She moaned softly, her body pressing into mine.

She pulled back and licked her lips. "Mm. Let me show you how much I appreciate this penthouse you just bought us," she giggled, sliding back so she could unbutton my jeans.

CHAPTER 34
JASMINE MILLER

"So, when are we meeting him?" Mama asked, resting her hand on her chin. "The condo is beautiful, but I'm ready to meet the man who swept my Jazzy Bear off her feet."

Telling my parents I was moving in with Cash hadn't been easy, but at the end of the day, I was a grown-ass woman. Six months might not seem like a long time to know someone, but with everything we'd been through, it felt like we'd lived a lifetime already.

When I finally told them, my parents, understandably, had their reservations. But I reminded them that despite Cash's wealth, I was still working and making my own money. I wasn't dependent on him—even though he'd started making those "just cause" deposits. I never asked for them, but wasn't about to tell him to stop.

Honestly, I didn't *need* the money. Since Marcus and I were technically married, a portion of his assets came to me after he died. The rest went to his family—people I never contacted and thankfully hadn't heard from. As much hell as he put me through, that might've been the kindest thing he ever did. Cash made sure everything else was handled.

His lawyers stepped in and tied up the rest of the loose ends.

"Soon," I said, settling onto a stool at the kitchen island. "He has some work things to wrap up, and then we'll figure out time to come up there. I promise you'll love him."

Her tone softened. "Well, you look happy, and that makes me happy. I just want to make sure you're maintaining your independence. You know we raised you to stand on your own."

"Yes, ma'am."

"Is that my Jazzy Bear?" Daddy's voice boomed in the background.

Mama rolled her eyes and leaned closer to the screen. "I don't know why he's asking when he can clearly hear you," she whispered. "Yes, Reg, it's your daughter!" she hollered back at him.

Daddy's face appeared next to hers, crowding the frame. "When are we gonna meet this friend of yours?" he asked, raising his thick eyebrows.

"Daddy, please," I laughed. "Like I told Mama, soon."

"And what you said he does again?"

"Commercial real estate. Daddy, just Google 'Banks Enterprises Atlanta'."

"Reg, stop harassing the child before she doesn't come at all," Mama fussed as she playfully elbowed him out of the camera's frame.

It was time to wrap it up before they started doing the most. "Alright, I gotta go. Love you both!"

"Love you, Jas," Mama said, blowing a kiss at the camera before I ended the call.

I set my phone down as Cash walked into the kitchen. "Your parents?" he asked.

I nodded. "They are so pressed to meet you."

I thought it'd take weeks to get everything in order, but three days after he showed me the place, my apartment was packed up, and the remainder of my lease was paid off. Cash bought a few pieces of furniture to get us started, then handed me his black card and told me to buy whatever I needed to make the penthouse feel like home. Of course, I let him pick out the art since that was his thing.

"We can go next week," he said, loosening his tie.

"Just like that?" I asked skeptically.

"Just like that," he replied and closed the distance between us. He wrapped his arms around me, pulling me into a tight hug as he buried his face in my neck. "I never get tired of walking through that door and seeing you here."

He kissed me softly as I ran my fingers over the back of his head. "Aw, what would your boys think if they saw you being a big softy right now?"

"Fuck them niggas," he said with a low laugh. "They wish they had somebody like you to simp over."

I leaned into his chest and smiled. Never in a million years did I think taking a nursing contract in Atlanta on a whim would lead me here—wrapped up in the arms of one of the most powerful men in the game.

Cash ruled everything—including my heart.

EPILOGUE

CASH "MONEY" BANKS

JASMINE WANTED THIS TO BE A QUICK TRIP SO HER PARENTS would stop bugging her about me. I couldn't blame them for being cautious. Things had moved fast between us, and she was their only child. But there were no rules to this love shit. To take some of the pressure off, I suggested we turn it into a group trip. I roped Jelani and Monica in since they were giving an exclusive relationship a go. Slim invited himself as soon as he heard—he claimed he was bored—but we knew it was an excuse to see his shorty in Brooklyn.

Fontaine had left for Miami a few days earlier after getting a lead on where Nairobi might be.

"You bringing her home?" I asked when we linked up before he left.

"I don't think she knows where home is," he said. There was a heaviness in his voice I'd never heard before. I wasn't sure how their story would end, but I hoped my boy wasn't getting caught up chasing a ghost. We all loved Nairobi, but she was hardheaded, and Fontaine might be wasting his time trying to get her to come to her senses.

We settled into our seats on the plane. Two flight attendants were working the flight, and the pretty brown-skinned one immediately set her eyes on Jelani. She was gonna be a problem. Her hair was pulled back into a sleek, low bun. Her uniform was about a half size too small and clung to her curvy body. Every time she passed Jelani, she showed all thirty-two of her teeth and lingered a little too long.

"The fuck she keep smiling in your face like that?" Monica muttered under her breath, side-eyeing the woman.

Jelani brought her hand to his lips for a kiss. "Chill, Baby Doll," he said. "She's just doing her job."

The captain's voice announced we'd be taking off soon as the attendants did their final sweep, and of course, that same flight attendant made her way back to Jelani's seat, this time with an extra button on her blouse undone.

She leaned over him and batted her eyelashes. "Can I get you anything else?" she asked sweetly.

"You can get the fuck out his face," Monica snapped. "He don't need shit else."

"Here we go," Jasmine muttered next to me, shaking her head.

The attendant quickly stepped back, mumbling something about preparing for takeoff.

Jelani snorted, trying to stifle a laugh. "You ain't have to do all that."

"Don't fucking play with me, Jelani," Monica said as she jabbed a finger into his chest. "Bitch had her titties in your face like she don't see me sitting right here." She turned to me. "Money, these people work for you? Can you fire folks? Cause I don't like that shit." She spoke loud enough for the flight attendant to hear.

"Monica!" Jasmine burst into laughter, covering her face with her hand.

Slim pulled his headphones down. "Y'all cutting up, and we haven't even taken off. This about to be a long ass flight."

I glanced over at Jasmine once we were in the air. She was staring out the window, deep in thought.

"What you over there thinking about?" I nudged her gently.

She smiled softly. "I'm just a little nervous."

"You think Sydney Banks didn't raise a gentleman?" I teased. "Stop worrying, it'll be fine." I kissed the top of her head.

When we landed in New York, her anxiety seemed to have gone up a notch, even though we weren't heading to Queens until the next day.

"Jas, what's the real issue? You barely said two words at dinner, and you were quiet the whole ride back," I said, watching her take out her pajamas.

She huffed, tugging her tank top over her head. "Maybe we should've waited. I don't know that I should've told them so soon."

I scrunched up my face. I wasn't used to seeing her like this. "You scared of your parents or something? I need to bring my gun?"

"Cash, please be fucking for real." She glared at me. "And don't bring your gun tomorrow."

"Uh-huh," I replied. My gun was definitely coming to dinner.

She let out a deep sigh and climbed into bed, getting under the covers next to me. "I'm not scared of my parents. It's just… a lot. I'm overwhelmed."

I pulled her into my chest. "Where's this coming from? Aren't y'all close?" From everything she told me, her folks were everyday, God-fearing, upper-middle-class people who doted on their daughter. Nothing about them suggested they were difficult.

She intertwined her fingers with mine. "We are, but I've never really brought anyone around for them to meet. Not even…" she trailed off.

"They never met Marcus?" I asked, surprised, given their history.

"Nothing more than a brief hi," she admitted. "He'd pick me up sometimes, but I mostly just met up with him. You know… the whole dating a dope boy thing."

"Damn," I said. "I definitely got it better than that bitch nigga in more ways than one."

Jasmine groaned, burying her face in my chest. "Can you not?"

I chuckled. "Facts are facts, shorty. But seriously, any trouble I've gotten into has been scrubbed. And you already know I can handle myself."

She tilted her head to look up at me. "I just want them to like you."

"Jas, I'm not even gon' hold you—it'd be great if your parents like me, but I don't really care. That's not gonna stop us from being together. If they don't see how much I love you, then that's on them, ain't got shit to do with me."

She let out a soft laugh. "You really don't be giving a fuck, do you?"

"Nope," I said, leaning down to kiss her. "Not too concerned with the opinions of other people. I give a fuck about you, my family, and this money. That's it."

She rolled her eyes, but I could feel the tension in her body finally ease. "Mhm. Love you too, nutty ass man."

"You wanna show me how much you love me?" I said, kissing her deeper. My hand went to her neck, tightening around it slightly. Jasmine moaned low against my mouth before pushing away.

"We need to sleep," she said breathlessly, biting her lip.

I could see the internal tug of war in her eyes, so I just laughed and turned off the lamp.

$

Jasmine's parents lived in a nice-sized stone home in a quiet Queens suburb. They had a small but well-kept lawn with trimmed rose bushes out front. I'd kept my outfit simple—a black V-neck sweater and ash colored slacks. Jasmine wore a fitted burgundy sweater dress, and her freshly braided hair was up in a bun.

Jasmine used her key to let us in. The second we stepped inside, the smell of dinner hit us— her mother was clearly throwing down in the kitchen. Oldies R&B drifted from deeper in the house.

"Mama!" Jas called as she kicked off her boots. I lingered in the entryway, glancing around the cozy space. The walls were lined with family photos, childhood pictures of Jasmine, and colorful art prints. Two antique-style sofas faced each other, with an ornate glass coffee table in the center.

A loud clatter followed by a squeal of laughter came from down the hall. A moment later, Jasmine reappeared with a petite woman a few shades darker than her—the same woman I'd seen in photos and on FaceTime calls. She had Jasmine's high cheekbones, and her salt-and-pepper curly hair was cut low.

"Mommy, this is Cash," Jasmine said, glancing nervously between us. "Cash, my mom."

"It's so nice to meet you in person, finally, Mrs. Miller," I said. I stepped forward and offered her my hand.

"Boy!" Mrs. Miller swatted my hand away and pulled me into a warm hug instead. "And please, call me Vera."

I handed her a gift bag. "Yes, ma'am," I smiled.

"Oh, and he's a real southern gentleman," Vera teased as she peeked inside.

"Georgia born and raised," I replied. "My mama would've cussed me out if I showed up empty-handed."

Vera's eyebrows shot up as she pulled out the bottle. "Dom Perignon?" She looked at Jasmine and started toward the kitchen. "I think I like this one, Jazzy Bear."

Jasmine's head whipped toward me. "You got a bottle of Dom?" she hissed under her breath.

I shrugged. "You wanted them to like me, right?" I might be a little rough around the edges, but Sydney didn't raise no damn heathen.

All the counter space in the kitchen was full of food. There was roast chicken, a pot roast, mashed potatoes, green beans, and macaroni and cheese.

"Mama, why'd you cook all this food?" Jasmine asked. "It's just the four of us."

"The spirit of cooking took over this morning," Vera said. "Besides, leftovers mean I don't have to cook for at least two days." She picked up the serving dish with mashed potatoes. "Your father's having a cigar in the basement. I told him not to come up here smelling like smoke, but you know how he is."

"You want me to get him?" Jasmine asked.

"He'll come up when he's ready." Vera pulled out a chair. "Come sit, I want to hear all about how y'all got together."

Jasmine and I exchanged a glance. We'd already figured out the family-friendly version of our story to give to her parents that left out the kidnapping and all the shit with Marcus. We sat and joked about how we first met. Jasmine told Vera the story of me showing up on her date with Ahmad —or whatever that nigga's name was—conveniently skipping the part where I pistol-whipped him.

A throat cleared in the doorway. I looked up to see a tall, broad-shouldered man with gray streaks in his tapered fade. His tawny complexion matched Jasmine's, and his solid build made it clear he could handle himself if needed.

"Daddy!" Jasmine shot out of her seat and wrapped him in a hug. It was clear my woman was a daddy's girl, and there was no mistaking the love in his eyes for his daughter.

"Hey, Jazzy Bear," he said with a soft smile.

Jasmine pulled back, still smiling, and turned to me. "Daddy, this is Cash. Cash, my dad."

I stood and met his gaze head-on as I extended my hand. "Nice to meet you, Mr. Miller."

"Reg, " he said. He gripped my hand with enough pressure to make a point. It was a challenge, but I didn't flinch, keeping the polite smile plastered on my face.

Vera stood from her seat. "Alright, now that everyone's here, let's eat. Reg, grab that bottle of wine out the fridge."

Reg gave me one last look before he headed toward the kitchen. Jasmine's hand grazed mine under the table.

"This isn't so bad, is it?" I leaned in slightly.

She squeezed my fingers. "You're doing fine."

Reg came back with an open bottle of red wine in hand and took his seat at the head of the table. Vera followed behind him, setting a big bowl of salad beside the other dishes. After Reg gave a short blessing over the food, we started passing everything around and filling our plates.

"So, Cash," Reg said, swirling his wine. "What exactly do you do?"

Jasmine groaned. "Daddy…"

"It's fine, baby," I reassured her. I wiped my mouth with my napkin and met Reg's gaze.

"Well, sir, I run a commercial real estate business with my younger brother. We acquire, manage, and lease everything from retail spaces to office buildings. I also oversee a few residential rental properties."

Reg nodded. "That's not an easy market to break into. And you're how old again?"

"Thirty-eight."

"Hm. Still young. How'd you get into it?"

"Family business. My father started it when I was in college, but he was killed," I paused. "I dropped out of Duke to help settle his affairs and fell into it." It wasn't a total lie.

Vera's hand flew to her mouth, her face softening with sympathy. "Oh, honey. That's awful about your father. I'm so sorry."

"Thank you," I nodded solemnly. "He was a good man. Taught me a lot of what I know. When it happened, I felt like I had to step in and make sure my mom and brother were taken care of. I didn't finish my degree, but I made sure my brother did."

Reg's expression shifted—a look of respect flickered across his face. He leaned forward. "Stepping up for your family like that is admirable."

"It wasn't easy, but it was worth it for them. My brother's now my business partner, and my mom's comfortable. That's all I can ask for."

"Well, I'd say you've done a great job, Cash. How about dessert?" Vera smiled, patting my hand as the doorbell rang.

"You guys expecting anyone?" Jasmine asked.

Reg pushed back from the table. "No, probably a delivery package for your mother."

He disappeared down the hall, and Vera excused herself to get dessert from the kitchen.

"Jasmine!" Reg called from the front room. "It's for you."

Jasmine frowned as she headed into the living room. I followed, catching the familiar voices drifting from the doorway.

"What the—?" Jasmine stopped in her tracks. Her mouth fell open as she saw Amber, Monica, Jelani, and Slim step inside. "What are y'all doing here?"

I coughed to catch her attention. When she turned, I dropped to one knee and pulled a small velvet box from my pocket. Her hand flew to her mouth, eyes wide.

The room stilled, the weight of the moment settling over everyone.

"Jasmine," I began. My voice was steady despite my heart beating wildly. "My first thought when I saw you at Palladium was —'That's my wife'," I chuckled at the memory. "Sounds crazy, but I swear I just knew. There was this light about you, something that pulled me in. And I was gonna do whatever it took to get in your orbit."

Her hand trembled slightly, her brown eyes glistening.

I took a deep breath. "It was like the universe was working overtime to make sure our paths crossed. And since then, we've turned each other's lives completely upside down in the best way. You've shown me what love looks like—the kind of love my parents had, your parents have." I stole a glance at them.

I opened the box to reveal the 3.5-carat solitaire, pear-shaped diamond in a platinum setting.

"Baby, you're my everything. My peace. My love. And I want to spend the rest of my life making you happy. Will you marry me?"

Jasmine's lip trembled. She looked at the ring, then at our friends and her parents.

I'd been planning this since the day we got back from New York. The ring was the first thing I bought. A week after she moved in, I flew back to New York to meet her father and asked for his blessing. Reginald Miller wasn't the kind of man who played when it came to his daughter. And I wasn't the kind of man who played about Jasmine.

The conversation had to be man-to-man. Over lunch, I told him my intentions—my plans to build a life with her, to make sure she never had a want for anything. There was no pressure for her to quit nursing, but if she wanted to, it was always an option. I wasn't asking for permission, but I wanted him to know exactly the type of nigga I was.

"Everything I have is already hers," I told him. I'd made Jasmine a beneficiary on my life insurance. Jelani and my mom were more than financially secure. If something happened to me, there wouldn't be any drama.

"Yes," Jasmine whispered shakily, before she repeated it louder. "Yes!"

"Period!" Monica yelled as cheers erupted around us. I slid the ring on her finger and stood as she threw herself into my arms.

"I love you," she murmured against my chest.

"I love you too, baby girl," I said, kissing her. Amber and Monica pulled her away to gawk at the ring, while Jelani came over to dap me up.

"Good shit, bruh. Sis is a good look for the family," he smiled.

Vera and Reg looked on, their faces warm with approval. Vera ushered everyone into the dining room to eat and celebrate.

"Is this why she made all that food?" Jasmine asked as we hung back in the living room.

"Maybe," I chuckled.

She stared at the ring. "I can't believe you did all this."

"You know I had to make it special for you," I said softly, and I brushed a tear from her cheek.

"You did real good," she whispered.

Her smile shone as bright as the diamond on her finger. Our forever was just beginning.

ACKNOWLEDGMENTS

Firstly, shout out to Big Sandals, big God, Olodumare, the Supreme Creator, for giving me the strength and fortitude always to do what I say I'm going to do. There were many times, up until the final moments of writing this book, when I said, *"I don't know if I should be doing this."* But God!

Big thank you to Dana V. and Sheryll for being the earliest believers in this book and these characters. Thank you for reading every draft, every screenshot, and for listening to every voice note. Y'all are stuck with me for life.

Thank you to my sister, Tanya, for your words of encouragement and love, and for helping me flesh out those pesky bits of my plot. You next!

To my husband, Chizzy, thank you for supporting every dream and goal I've ever had, even if it goes against your Virgo sensibilities lol. You make it easier for me just to be. Wouldn't ever want to do life with anybody else. Love you.

To my friends and family who end up reading this. Thank y'all for always showing up and loving every version of me.

And thank you, dear reader! Thanks for taking a chance on lil' ol' me. There are 50-11 books out there, and you took a chance on mine. Appreciate, y'all!

If you've made it this far and are wondering if Fontaine and Nairobi are getting their own story, the answer is yes.

Follow me on Instagram and Threads for updates on those two.

ABOUT THE AUTHOR

Roxanne Taylor is a Black romance author. This is her first book.

Born and raised in New York, she currently resides in Baltimore with her husband and her shady-ass cat.

www.ingramcontent.com/pod-product-compliance
Lightning Source LLC
LaVergne TN
LVHW090553110826
845146LV00001B/113

* 9 7 9 8 9 9 3 8 2 3 8 1 2 *